THE CHILD WHO NEVER WAS

JANE RENSHAW

INKUBATOR
BOOKS

PROLOGUE

The biggest risk, of course, was that some busybody would see the smoke and in due course mention it to the police. In fact, she wouldn't put it past the village busybody-in-chief, Mrs Bowles across the lane at The Laurels, to come and see what was burning, to 'pop over just to check everything was okay' – because autumn or winter was the proper time for a bonfire, not the middle of June. Not the middle of the breeding season. Only a barbarian would cut back and burn vegetation while birds might still be nesting in it.

But it had to be a bonfire.

She could hardly dump a binbag of blood-soaked clothing in the charity recycling bank at the village hall. Or in their own or a neighbour's wheelie bin. The police were unlikely to devote much in the way of resources to the investigation, but she couldn't count on them being slack enough to neglect the basics.

If she'd had a bit more time, she could have jumped in the car and driven thirty miles and left the bag in a random bin no one was going to search.

But she had no time.

And complete incineration was the safest option.

She wanted to know that it was gone. That all trace of what she had done was gone. Maybe then she could get into the mindset of the person she needed to be when the police got here, like an actor, a method actor inhabiting her role so completely that she almost believed it herself, almost believed that she was just a poor traumatised soul who was as bewildered by the whole thing as anyone else.

The traumatised bit was going to be easy enough.

Her hands were shaking so much that she dropped the matchbox into the tangle of sticks and logs that she'd built up and had to rootle around in them to retrieve it. Striking a match was the next challenge, but she managed it; she managed to hold the wavering flame to the scrunched-up newspaper until it caught and flared.

Only when the fire was roaring away, the centre glowing orange with a heat so fierce that she had to stand back from it, did she throw on the first of the garments.

The saturated T-shirt.

It smouldered for a while, damping down the flames under it, sending streams of billowy white smoke up over the yew hedge that screened this workaday part of the garden from the lawns and the house. Then, when the moisture had evaporated off, the material caught and started to char, permeating the air with the aroma –

She staggered away from the fire, bile rising as, in a vain attempt to dislodge the smoke trapped there, she forced a long breath out through her nose.

But then she had to breathe in again and *oh God*.

Yes. What she was breathing, what she was tasting at the back of her throat, was the savoury aroma of a summer barbeque.

She couldn't do this. She just couldn't.

She had to get away from the smoke so she ran, she ran down the shadowed path between the woodshed and the hedge, feet pounding on the damp, moss-slick packed earth –

And straight into the person standing there, quite still, in the gloom.

The person standing there, silent and wide-eyed.

1

liver Oliver Oliver.

Her feet seemed to beat out his name on the road as a sort of invocation, a prayer, an entreaty to whatever gods there may be, whatever forces for good there may be, that had the power to keep him safe.

Oliver Oliver Oliver as she ran through the dark, through the funnels of light under the streetlamps that illuminated, briefly, the rain that stung her face and hands, as she ran through the foaming sea that crashed onto the road, flung against her by a wind so strong it was like a solid thing, a thing she had to push through, breathe against, somehow.

Let him be safe.

Let him be there.

Let him be safe as she ran past all the empty blank windows of the empty cottages to the one she needed, the one where he must be.

Oh please.

Oliver.

The pend, the lane between the fisherfolk's cottages, was so narrow that she could almost have reached out and touched the wall of Evie's house and the wall of the house opposite at the same time. In the shelter of the buildings, in this shelter from the storm – *please let this be his shelter from the storm* – it was possible, finally, to breathe.

She filled her lungs and shouted:

'*Evie!*'

She tried to put her finger on the doorbell but her hand was shaking so much it slipped off the little plastic nub and she had to hold that hand with the other one, she had to *focus focus* on pressing that white plastic nub and she was still shouting and why was it so dark in there? And *please please Oliver*.

Why weren't there any lights in the windows?

She banged on the door and she kept shouting her sister's name.

'*Evieeeee!*'

Where was Evie? Why would she have taken Oliver? Without even *telling her*?

A widening triangle of yellow light shone on the rain as a door opened but not Evie's, it was the door of the next cottage and it wasn't her own face looking back at her, it wasn't her own twin's face, it was an old woman, it was Margaret who lived next door and

'*Where's Evie?*' Sarah shouted into her saggy face and Margaret just stared at her, she stared and then she shook her head and said something, but Sarah didn't know what she was saying, there was too much noise from the wind and the crashing sea and Margaret was standing back inside her house and

'*Oliver!*' she shouted and '*Oliver's missing!*' and

'Who?' said Margaret with a funny pursed-up face and

'*Oliver!*' and

'Who's Oliver?' said Margaret and

Oh God and 'My son, my *son!*' and please let Margaret not have dementia, surely Evie would have said if she had, but

Sarah hadn't seen Margaret for months – no, *years* – so this was possible, this could be, because sometimes Evie didn't tell her things she thought might upset her but

The stupid old bitch!

It wasn't her fault, she knew it wasn't poor Margaret's fault, with her staring eyes, her frightened eyes but

'My son!' She pushed the words out. 'You know – my son – you know – *Oliver*! He's *missing*! I just – checked. His cot. *He's gone* – someone's *taken* –' She dived at the closing door but she was too late, the old woman had slammed it and when Sarah tried the door handle and pushed she met the resistance of a lock, the bitch, didn't she *care*, didn't she *care* that *a little boy was missing*? That Oliver was *gone*? He was out here somewhere –

And suddenly she couldn't move, she couldn't do anything but stare at the locked door. There was a tightness in her chest, as if her lungs were shrinking and shrinking and every time she breathed out they shrank a little bit more. Soon she could only get sips of air, tiny sips, before her tiny shrunken lungs pushed it back out again.

Oliver.

She shut her eyes and made herself *not* breathe. Made her lungs be still, as Evie had taught her.

Oliver loved being outside.

He wasn't afraid. It wouldn't even occur to him to be afraid.

She heaved in a breath.

The sun is coming out to play...

When he was born, when Evie had seen him for the first time, she'd whispered, 'Rah-Bee!' – the twins' childhood code-name for Sarah, Sarah Booth, Sarah B., Rah-Bee – 'Rah-Bee, he looks exactly like the sun in Teletubbies! You know, the sun with the baby's face in it!' Evie had started watching children's TV, even before Oliver was born, to select the programmes she thought would be suitable for a child prodigy, which of course he was going to be. Oliver's red little newborn scrunched-up face didn't really look like that Teletubbies baby, or, indeed, any kind of prodigy, but that was where it had started, with Evie saying that.

'The sun is coming out to play,' Sarah would warble at him whenever they were going outside to the garden. '*Hello* Mr Sun, how are you *today!*' And she'd pop a sunhat on Ollie's head, or, in cold weather, bundle him up in lots of cosy layers and a woolly hat and a hood until he looked like an adorable little maggot.

And as he'd got bigger, as soon as she started to hum it, Oliver would stop whatever he was doing and start squirming in time, his head rocking comically from side to side, his arms held out with his little palms turned upwards as if he were holding a giant invisible ball. Sometimes he would smile like the Teletubby baby, but mostly it was a serious business, his sun dance. Lately, he'd begun trying to sing along –

Oliver.

Where are you?

He couldn't have somehow wandered off himself, could he? She couldn't have somehow left the doors unlocked and he'd managed to get out of his cot and stomped down the corridor and into the hall and through the atrium and out on his little sturdy legs, out into the dark and the storm, his high voice happily burbling:

'Sun as cowin *ow* an pay!'

His tiny chubby palms lifted to the storm –

No no no, she had locked both doors, of course she had, she always locked them, she'd had to *un*lock them to leave the house –

And she could feel herself, now, slipping inside her head, slipping down, like she hadn't since the night Oliver had been conceived. And she wanted to squat there on the streaming wet concrete where a brave winter weed was peeping from a crack, and she wanted to put her arms over her soaking hair and push her face into her knees –

No.

She had to find him. She had to be stronger for him now than she'd ever been.

Oh, *Evie!* She needed *Evie*, or *someone* at least, but in the winter there was no one here, all the holiday people had gone and there was only Evie and stupid old bitch Margaret and

Lewis!

There was *Lewis*, he was a *doctor* and he was kind, he'd know what to do, he'd know how to find Oliver!

Sarah ran.

She ran back down the pend to the road and the harbour, and she remembered that Lewis's house was the last one of all, the one right at the end of the road where it stopped because there was just the long line of the rocky shore and the sea after that.

'*I'm coming!*' she sobbed aloud. '*Mummin's coming!*'

She ran into the wind, into the storm.

Lewis. Lewis would help her.

The little harbour was invisible in the dark beyond the streetlamps, but she could hear the sea sucking and crashing, she could taste it on her lips, she could feel it on her head, like a big cold wet blanket someone kept throwing over her, pressing down her hair, pressing her soaked sweatshirt down onto her shoulders and her back.

'*Lewis!*' she shouted, stupidly, because how could he hear her, inside his house?

Lewis's cottage faced the sea, not like the others, the others that had their shoulders to the weather, as Evie put it. Lewis's house had its garden in front of it – sea, road, garden, house – and Sarah had to open the little gate, hands stupid and fumbling, to get in.

There were lights on inside, the windows a welcoming orange glow.

Lewis must be here!

She banged on the door, she banged the iron knocker until the door opened and Lewis was standing there saying, 'My God! Sarah!' and 'Come in, come in!' and she was shaking so much she couldn't speak, she could hardly move, she moved like an old woman into his narrow hallway and then she was able to say it:

'Oliver is missing.'

'You're soaked to the skin!' He led her down the hall, guiding her into his sitting room, where the wood-burning stove was roaring and big round copper table lamps glowed.

The warmth enveloped her, but she couldn't sink down into it, she had to tell him:

'I think – Evie's – taken him. But I can't – find her either. Not answering her phone.' She felt so tired she could hardly think, she could hardly get the words from her brain to her lips. 'We need to call the police.'

He was very tall, Lewis. Very good-looking, very alpha. She remembered boys like him at school who had had everything, who were handsome and funny and nice and clever, who were destined for careers in medicine or law, who were almost like a different species from the rest of them –

'Police,' she managed.

'Okay. I'll call the police. You get warm. I'll get you a towel and some dry clothes –'

'No, *now*. Call them! *Please!* He's... He's not even two years old!' Her jaw spasmed. 'Evie... Maybe it's not – Evie... Why would she take him without telling me? He was in his cot. Sleeping. When – I went to check – after supper – *he wasn't there!*'

Lewis frowned. 'I'm sure there's a simple explanation, but

yes, okay, I'll call the police right now.' He shook his head at her, his handsome face full of concern. 'Come here.'

He folded her into his arms, rubbing her back, murmuring, 'It'll be all right.' His voice was a little bit nasal, like he permanently had a cold. 'We'll sort this out. Don't worry, Sarah. Don't worry.'

As she slumped against him, against the solid warmth of him, she felt the spinning in her brain slow, the feeling of vertigo, of falling down and down to a place she couldn't get back up from for anything, not even her own child... she felt it all recede until she was able to take a deep breath, and pull away, and thank him quietly.

And then he was gone, and Sarah stood in front of the stove, mesmerised by the dancing flames and dripping onto the colourful ethnic rug, all oranges and browns and greens and yellows, that he'd probably bought in Kathmandu on a trip that was more like an ordeal than a holiday.

He was back more quickly than seemed possible.

'Did you call them?'

'Yes. They'll be here soon.' He dropped a large towel and a bundle of clothes onto the sofa. 'A bit big for you, but you can roll up the sleeves and the legs.'

'Thank you,' was all she could say.

He left the room while she dried herself off and changed into the soft grey joggers, black T-shirt and multicoloured, slightly oily-smelling woolly jumper, which had probably been knitted from yak wool in a hill village in Mongolia. They were all much too big.

And suddenly she wanted to pull off these warm dry clothes and wriggle back into her cold wet ones, because how could she be nice and safe and warm while Oliver –

Oliver was out there –

Maybe alone –

Maybe freezing cold and wet and terrified –

And not understanding why Mummin didn't come.

'Are you decent?' said Lewis from behind the door.

'Yes.'

He came in and made her sit down on the sofa with him, and he put his arm round her and rubbed her shoulder.

'The police –' she got out.

'On their way.'

They would search for him, wouldn't they? A little boy missing would be their very top priority.

They could probably use Evie's phone to find her. They could track people's locations using their phones, couldn't they? Maybe Lewis was right and there was a simple explanation – maybe Evie had taken him for some reason and left Sarah a note, but Sarah had been too panicked to see it –

But why would Evie do that? Why leave a note, when she knew that Sarah was *right there in the house*?

'Someone – I've been thinking... Someone could have got a la-ladder...' She stuttered on the word – 'They could have used a *ladder* to get onto the roof, and pulled it up, and lowered it down into one of the courtyards, and climbed down and got in that way – I often don't lock the sliding glass doors into the courtyards, which is so stupid, I know, but they're secure, they're safe, that's what I thought. The house is *safe*...'

It had always felt safe, with its blank outer walls and its internal courtyard gardens, onto which all the rooms faced. A modern take on a Roman villa; that had been her 'vision', as Evie called it.

'I think that's pretty unlikely, don't you?' said Lewis gently.

He was rubbing comforting circles on her shoulder with his thumb, and it felt so nice, but she didn't want to be comforted. She pulled away from him, and in the same moment the doorbell jangled.

Lewis stood. 'They've made good time. You wait here in the

warm, Sarah, and I'll bring them through.' He left the room and closed the door behind him.

She sat on the sofa for three seconds.

She couldn't sit.

She went to the door and opened it and she could hear their voices and smell the drift of wet salty air, and she could hear Lewis saying, '... remitting/relapsing delusional disorder. She's also severely agoraphobic. She's very confused.'

'You're her GP, sir, is that right?' It was a woman's brisk voice.

'Yes. Dr Lewis Gibson – here's my photocard ID. I'm going to have to authorise an emergency detention, I'm afraid, under Section Two of the Mental Health Act. I'll come with you to the hospital – to Marnoch Brae. We can do the paperwork there.'

'And social services?' This was a man's voice, deep and calm.

'Yes, I've called them. An AMHP – an approved mental health professional – will meet us there.'

'Will she require restraint?'

Sarah barrelled into the hall, she barrelled past Lewis, she grabbed the woman in her bulky black uniform and she screamed at her: 'My eighteen-month-old son is *missing*! I don't need you to take me to a *hospital*! I need you to *find my son*! My *child* who's *missing*! Who's been *taken*!'

From behind her: 'She doesn't have a child,' said Lewis.

Sarah stared into the policewoman's carefully blank face. Had she heard that right? Or had she imagined it?

When she turned, when she rounded on him, when she said 'What?' he repeated it, over her head:

'She doesn't have a child.'

And now he looked down at her, his handsome face full of sympathy and understanding and pity.

Why was he saying that?

'Of course I have a child! Lewis! What –'

'Sarah.' He reached for her arm but she pulled away, she backed away, she turned to the policewoman.

'I have an eighteen-month-old son and his name's Oliver, Oliver Booth, and he's disappeared! I don't know why he would say –'

'All right, Sarah,' said the woman, finally, looking at Lewis. 'Does she have shoes?'

Sarah ran.

She ran the other way, into the kitchen, making for the back door, but she could hear them behind her, the policeman saying, 'This isn't helping anyone, is it?' and she felt herself grabbed from behind and then she was *smack* down on the floor, her face pressed to the wood-effect vinyl, her arms yanked up behind her back, cold metal handcuffs snapping on her wrists.

2

Sarah woke from a muzzy, headachy doze to find a large, doughy, thin-lipped face looming over her, unblinking, unsmiling. It was the face of the fat blonde nurse she vaguely remembered trying to punch last night.

But had that actually happened, or had it been one of the nightmares that had spooled through her head, one after the other, all night? Nightmares in which Oliver was washed out to sea and she was left helpless on the shore, unable to move, unable even to call out; nightmares in which she ran through abandoned warehouses looking for him as fat nurses pounded after her, clawing at her clothes, her hair, pulling her back –

So real. It had all seemed so real.

'I thought you wanted to see the doctor,' said the nurse. Her name was Carol, according to the badge on the dark blue uniform.

'What doctor?'

The nurse gave a huge sigh, as if she could hardly bear the tedium of this exchange a moment longer. 'Dr Laghari.'

Dr Laghari. Yes. She needed to see Dr Laghari. He was the one she had to convince. It was no good screaming and shouting at the nurses, shouting that Lewis should be locked up, not her. No good punching their lights out. No good throwing her breakfast at the wall, as she was pretty sure she had done this morning. She remembered this nurse, Carol, snapping at her as she'd cleaned up the mess: 'You can see Dr Laghari when you're calm.' She remembered that now. She remembered everything. She remembered why she had to see the doctor.

It was because he was the one with the power.

He was the one who could call the police and make them listen.

He was the first step to finding Oliver.

And so she must be calm. Yes. She was calm now, wasn't she? That was why Carol was saying she could see the doctor. Because Sarah was nice and calm.

The medication was helping, of course. They presumably had her on antipsychotics and a high dose of sedatives – she recognised the flat feeling, the cotton-wool fuzziness that was making it hard to control her thoughts, to stop them butterflying away from her. Not that the nurses had specified what the pills actually were – they arrived in a little plastic beaker, unlabelled, and seemed to be none of Sarah's business.

'Yes,' she said. 'Yes, please. Dr Laghari.'

She sat and put a hand through her hair and looked down at herself. She was wearing busily patterned pyjamas in blue and red and white and yellow.

'Robe and slippers,' ordered Carol, but didn't move to help.

There were white, foam-soled slippers lined up neatly under the bedside cabinet. Sarah slipped her feet into them and stood, but had to put a hand behind her to the bed to steady herself. Sighing again, Carol twitched the pale blue waffle robe from the back of the door and handed it to her.

Was it a deliberate policy, to make psych patients wear nightclothes during the day? It immediately put you at a disadvantage; underlined the inequality of the relationship between patients and staff.

Calmly, she put on the robe and tied the belt. Calmly, she walked after Carol into the corridor, when what she wanted to do was slam the bitch against the wall and make a break for the exit.

Oh, my darling! Where are you?

Why had Lewis told the police she didn't have a child? How was she going to make them believe her, when Dr Lewis Gibson, respected local GP, had told them Oliver didn't even exist?

There was a woman shuffling along, pulling what looked like a charger behind her on the polished grey vinyl floor, the cable between it and the plug she was holding alternately slackening and extending as she tugged it after her. One of her eyes was slightly higher than the other.

Carol ignored her, but Sarah found herself stopping and staring, sinking into a medicated fug as a random image popped into her head: Oliver's wooden dog, whose tail wagged when you pulled it along. He loved it. It had been a present from Evie, a sort of joke, a commemoration of their own child-hood 'pets'.

When they'd been about nine, the twins had spent a giggly afternoon in the woods selecting the perfect logs to transform into the perfect pets – Evie's long and elegant with a sticky-out bit at one end that looked like a head, and Sarah's squat and cute and amorphous.

After they'd smuggled them into their room, Evie had begun painting eyes on hers.

'He's a dachshund,' she had announced. 'What's yours?'

Sarah had been drowsing in bed. 'A woodadoodlum.'

And there had followed five minutes of the two of them laughing so hard that Evie had had to smother her face in her pillow. 'A woodadoodlum!' she'd kept repeating. 'A wooda*doodlum!*'

The next day, they had selected Kennel Club names for the log dogs. They'd looked up the German dictionary in the vicarage library and found that 'tree' was 'baum' in German, and Evie had decided that her dachshund was Baron Fritzl von Baum-Baum. After a lot of thought, she had suggested La Belle Dame Sans Merci for Sarah's dog, familiarly known as Belle. The Baron was in love with Belle, but she would have none of it. Evie had recruited Jacob, who did the garden and odd jobs around the vicarage, to help her attach a toy car to each corner of the Baron so that he could roll along smoothly, as befitting his status, when out for a walk on his lead – a length of bright blue nylon string – while the distinctly unaristocratic Belle bounced along, head over heels, on her scruffy old bit of rope. What fun they'd had, stopping at lamp posts and waiting, hands on hips, as the log dogs did their 'business'.

They had drawn up elaborate breed standards. At Crufts, they decided, in the woodadoodlum class the judges would be looking mainly for cuteness, but also for well-defined grain, no cracks – or as few as possible – and the bark still to be in place. When Belle, without warning, had shed her bark one day outside the butcher's, they had howled in mock dismay and collapsed against the wall in hysterics, much to the bemusement of passers-by.

People in the village must have thought the vicar's twins had a screw loose.

'Sarah!' snapped a voice, yanking her back to the overheated corridor, to Carol's hostile glare, to Oliver who was missing, who was missing, who was *missing* –

And Sarah couldn't do anything about it, she couldn't even think properly about it because her head was all over the place, because these bitches had pumped her full of drugs because

Lewis had told them she was delusional and didn't have a child because –

Because what?

'We haven't got all day,' said Carol. 'If you're not bothered about the doctor, there's other folk he can be seeing.'

Sarah shook her head. 'Sorry. Yes, sorry.'

Where was he? Where was Oliver?

Please let him be with Evie.

But that made no sense. Evie would never just take him without telling her.

Oh Evie! I need you!

'SARAH.' The doctor smiled. 'Hello – it's nice to see you looking better. Come on in.'

As if it were some sort of social occasion. She almost expected him to attempt an air kiss.

The room was too bright, winter sun streaming in at the windows, making her want to cover her eyes with her hands and crouch down on the floor and sink back into the fug. But she managed to smile back at the doctor and follow him across the bright expanse to the chairs, Carol lumbering behind. The room was trying hard not to be institutional, with tub chairs arranged around a coffee table and framed photographs of serene misty lochs and mountains on the walls. But the tub chairs were covered in maroon wipe-clean faux leather stuff, and there was nothing on the coffee table except a box of tissues. Like every room in the place, it was boiling hot.

And now, even through the meds, she could feel the white mist, as Evie called Sarah's panic attacks, gathering, trying to claim her, making her pulse race and her chest tighten. Grey splodges threatened her vision, but she looked straight through them. She fought them. She needed to keep it together if this man was ever going to believe her.

Carol escorted her to one of the chairs and waited until she'd sat down before leaving.

The doctor sat in the chair opposite, hitching up the knees of his suit trousers. There was a blue folder on his lap with her name on it, *Sarah Booth*, but he didn't open it. He didn't even look at it. 'My name's Jagan Laghari.' He was in his fifties, she guessed, with clever black eyes in a fleshy face. 'I'm going to be your psychiatrist while you're here.'

She wanted to take Jagan Laghari by his sharp lapels, by his already tightly knotted navy polka-dot tie, and shake him, scream at him that this was just wasting time! He had to call the police and *make them find Oliver*!

Into her head flashed Oliver's face, his trusting little face, his cherub mouth slightly open in a little 'Oh', the way he looked at you when he was worried, concerned, but quite ready to be reassured –

'Okay,' she said, and smiled what she hoped was a pleasant, normal smile.

Which was all wrong. Why would she be smiling, with Oliver gone?

Oliver! It was so terrible that it almost didn't seem real; it didn't seem possible that it had happened, that Oliver had just suddenly *gone*. It *had* happened, though, hadn't it?

Her heart lurched. A pit threatened. A pit she could so easily fall into –

Dr Laghari opened the folder. 'You've been having a bit of a bad time, haven't you?'

She heaved a breath. 'You could say that, yes.'

'Do you remember what happened yesterday?'

Another breath. 'I'm hardly going to forget that my son is missing.'

He looked at her, but said nothing.

'And so is my sister Evie. Lewis Gibson, my GP... for some reason he told the police that I don't have a child, but I can easily prove that I do. *Easily*. It's Lewis who needs to be in here, not me. The only explanation I can come up with is that he's had some sort of... mental breakdown. Why else would he say that Oliver doesn't exist and – and section me when all I'm trying to do is find him?'

'As far as I know, Dr Gibson doesn't have any issues of that nature.'

'But –'

But what? Her stupid fuzzy brain was too slow. Thoughts kept coming and then dancing away from her, and her stupid fuzzy brain was too slow to catch them.

Oliver. The one certainty she had in all this. *Oliver is missing*.

'The police,' she said, 'need to start *looking for Oliver*. My hope is that Evie has him.' She clamped her trembling jaw shut. She took a moment. He was looking at her with such kindness in his eyes, such patience, that she was able to continue, sooner than she had thought possible: 'Can I call her? Or can you?'

He nodded. 'We're trying to contact your sister.'

'Oliver goes missing and Evie does too – that can't be a coincidence.'

'So what do you think has happened?'

She could only stare at him. She didn't know. She didn't know what had happened, but she had to say something. She had to think.

Think think think!

'Maybe someone – maybe even Lewis himself – snatched Oliver and... and Evie tried to stop him.'

He just sat there watching her with his kind eyes.

'Every minute could be *crucial*.' She couldn't stop the tears coming. 'Oliver... is only eighteen months old.' She could hardly get the words out.

She got to her feet. She couldn't just sit here while Oliver could be *anywhere*, with *anyone* –

And *Evie* –

'All right, Sarah.' He didn't get up. 'Please sit down, and we'll see what we're going to do about all this. All right?'

'No, actually, it's not *all right*! Do you have children?'

He inclined his head. 'I have two.'

'How would you feel if they went missing, and then, instead of searching for them, the police *handcuffed you* and chucked you in the loony bin and stopped you doing *anything to find them*?'

He said nothing, just waited.

Sarah gulped air.

And suddenly it came to her! An explanation!

'George might be involved. Evie's ex-husband. George Benson. He's always hated me. And he hated Evie too, in the end. He might have taken Oliver.'

'Okay –'

'He's capable of it. He definitely is.'

'Does he have a history of criminal behaviour?'

A history of criminal behaviour. George, with his conventional suits and conventional opinions; his desperation to conform. She and Evie had laughed their heads off when a parking ticket had precipitated one of his existential crises. The ticket was a mistake, he had tried to explain to them, over and over. And it had been – there'd been something wrong with the parking meter, and his appeal against the ticket had been upheld. Sarah used to wind him up about it, saying he'd got off on a technicality, and he'd go red in the face and start, yet again, on a long explanation about the defective meter.

'Sarah?'

She blinked. 'Yes.'

'Does your sister's ex-husband George have a history of criminal behaviour?'

'Yes. Maybe. Evie probably wouldn't have told me if he had. She often doesn't tell me things...' ... *if she thought they would upset Sarah*. But she couldn't say that. It would make her sound fragile and pathetic. 'But what I do know is that George is self-ish, and he can be cruel.'

She used to hear them through her bedroom wall in the London flat. Arguing, for hours at a time; George accusing Evie of *facilitating* Sarah's problems, as if he knew the first thing about them.

'He hates me,' she repeated, walking to the window, staring out at the view of the lawn stretching to the road, staring out at the brightness even though it seared through her eyeballs and into her aching head, staring out at the light in the hope that it would cut through the fuzz and let her *think*. 'He probably believes I stole Evie away from him, so now *he's* stolen Oliver from *me*.'

'And where would your GP fit into this?'

She turned away from the window.

'I don't know,' she heard herself say, but way back in her head, as if her mouth were on the other side of her skull. 'George probably paid him to have me sectioned.'

Silence. Then: 'Sarah. Please, come and sit down.'

She knew that what she was saying about George sounded mad. Bizarre. Hugely unlikely, at the very least. It *was* hugely unlikely. He was expecting her to explain something she had no way of explaining, because she had no idea what had happened.

And then, through the pain, through the fug of the meds, a thought slammed to the front of her consciousness as if it had been catapulted into her head from outside. It was like when she couldn't think of an answer in class, and she used to look over at Evie, and suddenly it was there in her head, the answer, like Evie had telepathically put it there –

I don't have to explain it.

Of course she didn't! All she needed to do was prove that Oliver existed. Which would be simple enough. She just needed Dr Laghari to do some basic checks.

She walked back to her chair and sat, interlocking her fingers in front of her stomach.

She took a long breath, but before she could say anything, Dr Laghari got in with: 'Can you remember what happened when you were admitted here?'

Okay. Play along. She had to come across as rational and cooperative. 'I remember... being confused. And upset, naturally, about Oliver.'

'Do you remember being very agitated?'

'Of course I was *agitated*. My son had just *disappeared*.'

'That wasn't the only thing that was troubling you, though, was it?'

'Isn't it enough?'

'You were shouting at the nurses to leave you alone.'

And now she remembered.

'Yes. Because I thought –'

He nodded encouragingly. 'What did you think?'

She shook her head.

'What did you think they were trying to do?'

'My kidneys,' she whispered.

Another gentle nod.

'I thought they were trying to... to... take them.'

'And why would the nurses want to take your kidneys?'

'I thought they were trying to harvest them.'

'Harvest them,' he repeated neutrally. He obviously knew all this already, so why was he making her say it?

She rapped out: 'I thought they were trying to harvest my organs and sell them to China. Which is nonsense, of course. I realise that. Obviously I was confused. I'm not any more. I'm not confused about Oliver.'

He nodded yet again. 'I see from your notes that you've had a delusional episode before –'

'That wasn't my fault. It was the antidepressants.'

'Sarah, no one is saying that any of this is your *fault*.'

Really?

But she needed to be calm. 'You probably know I have agoraphobia and anxiety problems, and I get panic attacks. They'd put me on antidepressants in the hope they would help. This was about two years ago. But it was a disaster. The antidepressants caused – all sorts of issues. Apparently, in rare cases they can trigger delusional episodes, and that happened to me.'

'That must have been very frightening.'

'Yes.'

'You're not taking antidepressants now?'

'No, of course not.'

And then it struck her, what he was implying.

'Are you saying I've had another – another delusional episode? Because of the organ-harvesting thing? Okay, maybe I've been confused...' She stared at him, trying to make her fuzzy brain think this through. If they thought she was delusional, no wonder they didn't believe her about Oliver. 'If I have had another delusional episode,' she said, slowly and clearly, 'it must have been triggered by the stress of Oliver being missing.' She swallowed. Her mouth was so dry, but there didn't seem to be any water on offer. Presumably a glass, or even a plastic cup of water, was a potential projectile.

'Agoraphobia, anxiety and panic attacks,' Dr Laghari said, looking down at the file, ignoring, once again, the mention of Oliver. 'Your agoraphobia is very severe, isn't it?'

'It's quite bad, yes.'

'It's so bad that you're unable to attend outpatient appointments or go to the hairdresser or the shops. You're virtually unable to leave your house. That must be making it very difficult to be here.'

'That's not true. I can leave my house.' Tears were prickling at the back of her throat. 'I – there's a walk along the coastal path, to a ruined castle. I've done that walk a lot.' Although not for weeks. Not for months. Not, in fact, since Oliver was born.

'When was the last time you left your house?'

'*Yesterday!*' she sobbed. 'I left my house *yesterday*, when Oliver disappeared and I had to... I had to...'

'All right, Sarah. I'm sorry.' He held out the box of tissues, and she grabbed a handful. 'So you've been dealing with quite a range of mental health issues.'

She wiped her face. Took a long breath.

Calm.

She had to be calm, but she also had to take control of this conversation.

'That's not my fault either. I know you're going to say mental health issues are never the person's fault – What I mean is that there's not something *inherently* wrong with me. I never used to be like this. It all started after a trauma I experienced nine years ago.' On the rare occasions on which they referred to it, she and Evie called it *What Happened to Mum and Dad*, as if it had been outside anyone's control, as if their parents had been struck by lightning or crushed by falling masonry. She gulped a breath. 'Yes, I have some problems, and yes, I've had a delusional episode before, as a side effect of medication – but *Oliver* isn't a delusion. There's plenty of proof that my son exists. I've got all his paperwork, and he'll be in any number of databases. The NHS database, for a start.'

'Okay. So tell me about "Oliver".'

Finally!

Oliver leapt into her head, his mouth open wide in a tantrum. He didn't often have one – he was such a good little boy, usually – but when he did, he gave it his all. And the funniest things would precipitate it. On the last occasion, he'd been devastated and enraged by a new bottle of shampoo, and Sarah had had to search through the recycling until she found the old bottle, and decant the new shampoo into it.

'Sarah?' he prompted.

He didn't believe Oliver existed, but he was humouring her,

he was 'exploring the content of her delusion' and hoping to get her to see sense. She remembered the process from last time. But this was her chance to convince him.

'He was born eighteen months ago. In my house near Achnaclach. I have his birth certificate, at home. And all his other paperwork, his immunisation records and... and there are lots of photos of him, and all his stuff is there. But the documents are the important thing. They're in the top drawer of the desk in my study – it's locked – the key's hidden under a little wooden car with... with pigs in it, on top of the filing cabinet. I think I left the front door unlocked. Someone could go now and check all this. Although maybe it would be quicker if you just checked the NHS database – you presumably have access to that – Oliver will be on there. Oliver Booth. Date of birth 10th of July 2017.'

He looked down at his notes and wrote something. Did that mean he was at least considering that what she was saying was worth checking?

But then he looked up and said, 'And can you tell me what happened last time you had to be admitted to hospital? After the reaction to the antidepressants? That was just over two years ago, wasn't it?'

She shut her eyes. 'Yes.'

'Can you tell me about it?'

'I can try.'

Her memories of that night were fragmented and strange, as if they belonged to someone else entirely. That hadn't been her, that hadn't been Sarah Booth who had had drunken, frantic sex with a man in a pub toilet in Inverness. But she remembered the cheap melamine counter into which the sinks were set, splattered with gobs of bright pink liquid soap; the corroded faux-chrome hand dryer she'd grabbed at one point; his body odour, musky and animal.

And she remembered the sense of panic afterwards, sitting

on the sticky moquette in the gloom of the lounge bar, in a shirt she couldn't do up properly because two of the buttons had popped off when he tore at it; sitting and waiting for him, her partner, as she had thought him, to come back from the bar with their drinks; the sense of mounting panic when she'd realised he had gone.

She didn't remember accosting the other customers, demanding to know where he was; she didn't remember screaming at them, cursing them, calling them liars; she didn't remember hurling glasses about, or picking up a chair and smashing the optics behind the bar; smashing the windows...

But all that had been detailed in the police report.

She remembered being groped by one of the men in the bar as he sat on her back, ostensibly to restrain her as they waited for the police to arrive. But she wasn't sure if that had actually happened. She wasn't sure, now, what had been real and what had been part of the delusion.

But the sex must have happened, because she knew she wasn't imagining the child who had resulted from it. Oliver.

It was a never-ceasing source of wonder to her that the dearest, most innocent, most precious little being could have come from such complete degradation and squalor and shame.

But he had.

And he had changed her life.

When he was born, it was like someone had reached inside her and ripped out her soul, like some awful science-fiction scenario in which, when you became a mother, your soul wasn't contained inside you any more – it was this tiny helpless thing that had to exist independently out there in the big bad world.

Out there, somewhere.

'So,' said Dr Laghari, when she'd finished her halting recitation. 'You now accept that this man in the Crown and Thistle pub was *not* your long-term partner?'

'Yes. Of course I *accept* it. But we really did have sex. I became pregnant as a result. *With Oliver.*'

'At the time, you thought your "partner" had abandoned you in the pub?'

She nodded.

He blinked at her, his mouth quirking sympathetically. 'A recurrent feature of your concerns seems to be people going missing?'

3

S arah's room looked out onto a wall and concrete slabs interspersed with ground-cover planting – heathers and cotoneaster and that low, spreading thing like a conifer gone wrong that always made her think of sheltered housing complexes. Last time she'd been sectioned here, after smashing up the Crown and Thistle, she'd been at the other side of the building with a view across the lawn to the street.

This was better, in terms of keeping the white mist at bay. In that other room, it had been a constant battle with the nurses to have the curtains tightly closed. The last thing she needed was to see traffic and people whizzing past.

It was so much better when there were no people.

She sat in the wing chair by the window, a Parker Knoll-type chair covered in the same maroon leather-look stuff as the tub chairs in the consulting room. She was so tired. She felt as if her whole body was shutting down, like someone had pressed the power-off button and it was useless trying to fight it. She just wanted to lie down on the bed and close her eyes, but if she did that, she knew she would sink back down into the fug, and she needed to think.

She needed to think about how she could get in touch with Evie.

Last time she'd been sectioned, she had tried, over and over, to tell them that it was a waste of time keeping her locked up here. That all she needed was Evie. Her twin. Even after What Happened to Mum and Dad, Sarah had refused to see a therapist – what was the point? No one knew her better than Evie. They had talked and talked, cried and cried, hugged and hugged for hours, days, weeks. They had got through it together, like they always did.

What therapist in the world could do that?

They were twin-sufficient, as Evie said. All Sarah needed was Evie.

Borrowed light.

For her kitchen in the Roman House, Sarah had chosen a Farrow and Ball colour called 'Borrowed Light', a soft, light blue that was described as 'evoking the colour of summer skies.' She had been drawn not so much to the colour, although it was completely right for that simple, sleek kitchen space, but to the name itself.

Borrowed light.

After What Happened to Mum and Dad, after her retreat from it all, she had begun to live a sort of borrowed life, borrowed from her twin, her wonderful sister Evie whose love had saved her. In those early years of Sarah's isolation in the London flat, Evie used to take hundreds of photos a day on her phone, and then in the evening she'd load them onto Sarah's laptop and they'd sit on the big couch and scroll through them while Evie told Sarah all about her day, and Sarah imagined herself there, sitting at Evie's desk in the office eating that pink-iced donut, or walking through the leafy summer-smelling park, or meeting Erica and Yvonne and Debs in the beer garden of their favourite pub by the river – 'Look at Debs's sunburn! And oh my God, we've only been there five minutes and this random guy's buying Erica a drink – I managed to get a candid shot of him – see? The one with the hair?'

Evie had had a professional video taken of her wedding, although Evie hated wedding videos, just so Sarah could feel she was there. Watching it in the flat with Evie, George, and George's parents, she had almost felt as if she were watching herself. As if that were her life as well as Evie's. When they'd got to the vows, when the vicar on the screen had done his 'Do you, Eve Frances Elizabeth, take this man' bit, Sarah had interrupted him with a resounding 'No!', and Evie had had to pretend that Sarah had wanted the vicar to call her 'Evie' not 'Eve'. George's parents had seemed to accept this, but George had rolled his eyes.

As the video had gone on, though, as she'd spotted Erica and the guy with the hair, as Evie had smiled and laughed her way through it all, so obviously ecstatically happy, Sarah had found herself smiling too, feeling what she was feeling, living it with her. Borrowing the happiness of Evie's special day for herself.

Oh Evie.

Evie.

She looked out at the plants, at the rain just starting to spatter against the window.

She had to think, to catch the butterflies.

She needed to persuade Dr Laghari to check out what she'd told him. To look up Oliver Booth in the database and see that yes, he really did exist: Sarah Booth's eighteen-month-old son Oliver, who'd last attended Golspie Health Centre for earache on the 15th of December last year.

She remembered that day vividly – Oliver's hot, angry little face, his uncomprehending distress as he'd writhed in her arms, the solid, surprisingly strong little limbs thrashing as he refused her efforts at comfort. He hadn't been able to understand why Mummin couldn't make it better, or why it had to be

Evie who took him to the nice lady who was going to look at his ear and give him medicine to make it go away.

But Dr Laghari wasn't going to check her story. He didn't believe a word that came out of her mouth – and why should he, when she'd arrived at Marnoch Brae raving about organ harvesting? She was asking him to believe a woman with a history of mental illness over that pillar of the community, Dr Lewis Gibson.

How was Lewis involved in this?

She'd read about cases where dentists and doctors took advantage of children in their care...

But her brain skittered away from the thought.

She needed Evie. She *needed Evie*. She had to get to a phone.

'Evie,' she said, out loud.

'No,' said an amused voice. 'It's Julia, actually.'

Sarah jumped up out of the chair.

A skeletally thin girl was sitting on the bed, her face gaunt, her skin so translucent you could almost see the jutting cheekbones and jaw through it. She was so insubstantial that it was easy to believe that she'd drifted into the room, soundlessly, on a current of air.

'Julia,' the girl repeated. 'So you're in here for what?'

Sarah gave her a smile, putting all the warmth she could muster into it. 'I'm Sarah. It's good to meet you, Julia. This is going to sound kind of rude, but can I ask you...'

'Yeah, they say I've got anorexia.'

Ordinarily, she'd have been sympathetic. Ordinarily, she'd have let Julia talk about herself and tried to help; tried to give her the benefit of her own, if brief, experience of an eating disorder. But not today.

'No. Sorry, I mean, I'm sorry about that, but – I've got a bit of an emergency here. I need to call my sister, but they're not allowing me near a phone. Do you have one, or do you have access to one?'

'Nope. Ditto. They don't let me have access to phones in case I contact my mates on the forum.'

'Oh.' A forum for anorexics, presumably – not that they'd call themselves that, unless ironically.

Sarah was about to ask her something else, something else important, when the girl fractured her thoughts by saying: 'Okay, I'm guessing you're bipolar?'

'No.' What was it she had to ask? It was there, the question, just out of reach. 'I've got what they call a "suite" of conditions which they lump together under the umbrella of post-traumatic stress disorder. But –'

Julia grimaced, her lips pulling back from teeth that, in her skeletal face, seemed huge and horse-like. 'Were you, like, in the military?'

Sarah had to laugh, but the sound that came out of her mouth was more like a yelp of pain. 'No. I'm an architect. The trauma was – a family thing.' And then, as was often the way, as soon as she'd stopped trying to recapture the thought, it came back to her. 'Are you having any visitors today?' She tried to keep her tone light.

'Nope. But my mum's coming in tomorrow.'

'Could I ask you a *huge* favour? I need to contact my sister urgently. Do you think your mum would get in touch with her for me, and tell her where I am and that Oliver's missing? I'll give you her phone number, and she could try Facebook and Instagram. Evie Booth is her name. Could you ask your mum to do that?'

Julia made a face. 'I can ask, but Mum's kind of got a one-track mind, you know? All topics of conversation end up at Food Issues Central.'

Sarah couldn't deal with this now. 'Well, don't you think she might have a point?'

'Okay I don't eat much, but that's because I have a slow metabolism. I just have to look at food and it goes straight to my belly.' She prodded at her sweatshirt top.

'That's not belly fat, that's kwashiorkor,' said Sarah briskly. 'As I'm sure they've told you. A swollen gut caused by malnutrition. Been there, done that. After – the trauma thing, I virtually stopped eating for two months. They had to put me on a drip in the end. I didn't think I had a problem either, and it almost killed me. You're never going to get on top of it unless you face up to the fact that it's your problem, not anyone else's.'

Julia stared at her.

'They're probably pussyfooting around you, are they, listening to your crap about a slow metabolism? When what you need to hear is simply this – you're wrong and they're right. Take it from someone who's been there and got the T-shirt.'

Julia stood.

'I've got a *real* problem here to deal with,' said Sarah.

'Oh right. So your problem's real and mine isn't?'

'My problem is that my little boy's missing and no one believes me. So yeah. I think a *possibly abducted toddler* kind of trumps someone in denial about their eating disorder.'

'Okaay.' Julia floated to the door. 'I thought I had issues, but you are *really* nuts. That's one good thing about this place. Makes you realise you're not as bad as you thought.'

Damn. Sarah had handled that all wrong. 'I'm sorry – Julia, can I just give you my sister's number –'

Julia, without looking round, gave her the finger.

And the energy Sarah had got from somewhere, the energy she'd been using to try to bend the girl to her will, suddenly drained away, leaving her weak, leaving her so woozy she could hardly stagger across the room to the bed and flop down onto it and let herself sink down, down and down and –

Evie!

Evie was here! She could hear her, she could hear her saying her name.

'Sarah. *Sarah.* Hey. Hey there.'

Sarah opened her eyes.

Not Evie. A stranger, a middle-aged woman with hair so thin you could see scalp, was standing over the bed, smiling and nodding at her. A woman in a fluffy white onesie and fluffy pink earmuffs.

'Hey there,' she repeated.

'Hi.'

'Got something here you might be interested in!' And, from behind her back, she produced a small box of chocolates. Peppermint cremes.

Sarah stared dully at the illustration on the front of the box, of three unfeasibly large dark chocolate peppermint cremes, one cut open to reveal the fondant centre, nestled beside a sprig of mint.

'Oh,' said Sarah. 'Thanks. But I'm not hungry.'

The woman laughed. She opened the box to reveal that half the chocolates had been eaten. Setting it down on the waffle blanket covering the bed, she removed the plastic tray in which the remaining chocolates sat.

The box underneath was full of pills. All different shapes and colours: some small and round, some larger and tablet-shaped. Some bicoloured capsules. Most of them looked slightly fuzzy, as if they'd got wet.

The woman nodded at Sarah smugly.

'We have SSRIs. We have laxatives, anti-sickness pills, seda-tives... We have painkillers. We have antipsychotics.' Like a market seller touting her wares. 'We have tramadol. That's really popular as a combo with the SSRIs. Drug-drug interac-tion, they call it. You're not meant to take them together because... Whoo!' She grinned. 'Fiver a pop, but I can give you a free sample, a try-before-you-buy kind of thing?'

Oh God.

'How did you get all these?'

'They're not all mine!' she laughed. 'I'm heavily medicated, in theory anyway, but they're not all mine! I buy as well as sell. What you have to do, right, is push the pill between your teeth and your cheek, so when nursie makes you open your mouth to check you've swallowed it – nothing to see here! Then when she's gone, slip it out, slip it into the box, choccies go back on top.' She replaced the plastic tray. 'Simples!'

'Ingenious.'

The woman nodded. 'I'm Marianne. You're Sarah, yes?'

'Yes. Please... I'm really tired. I don't want anything.' The last thing she needed was more drugs swilling around in her system.

The woman's obvious pride – she wasn't just touting for business, she was showing off, showing off how clever she was – it was horribly depressing. It was just so, so awful that what counted as an achievement, a win, in this place was an illicit hoard of sucked pills.

Marianne snapped shut the box of chocolates with a wink. 'I've been messing with you. I know what you really want. Julia told me.' And, like a conjuror, she brought a black, shiny, rectangular object from behind her back.

A phone!

Sarah reached for it, but Marianne pulled it away with a grin. 'Uh-*uh*! You want to make a call, it'll cost you.'

'Okay. Fine.'

'Eighty quid.'

'Okay.' Sarah reached for it again.

'And I don't do credit.'

'But I don't have any money with me here! *Please!*' She stared into the woman's face. 'I need to call my sister because my little boy is missing. I need my *sister!*'

'Okay. I'm not made of stone – we'll say sixty. But that's the death, as they say. Take it or leave it.'

'*I don't have any money!*' she sobbed. '*Please!* I can get you it, I can get a lot more than that, but not right now.'

'Ha! If I had a pound for every time I've heard that one, Sarah! You get a visitor to bring you in some cash – cash, mind, not a cheque – and we can do business. I'm in Room Fourteen. Just down the corridor.'

When Marianne had gone, humming cheerily, Sarah curled on her side, away from the door, and gave in, finally, to tears, her face pressed to the pillow so the nurses wouldn't hear.

SHE DIDN'T KNOW how long she'd been asleep when she woke, heart pounding.

Something was telling her she had to move. To get out there.

She shot out of bed, not stopping to put on her robe or slippers. She staggered into the corridor on her bare feet.

'Sarah!' Isla, a nurse with scraped-back ginger hair, beamed at her. 'You've got a visitor, my love! Visitors, in fact! Why don't we get another chair through and you can talk in your room, eh? If you –'

But Sarah wasn't listening because she had seen who it was, she had seen her at the end of the corridor – a young woman in a green puffer jacket and jeans, an ordinary, average-size woman with a face that was pleasant rather than pretty – although she had rather striking blue eyes – with ordinary mouse-coloured hair pulled back in a ponytail –

'*Evie!*'

She ran, her bare feet slapping on the grey vinyl, she ran into her sister's arms, and Evie was holding her, she was stroking her hair, she was sobbing with her: 'Oh *Rah-Bee*! It's all right, it's all right. Everything's going to be all right.'

'Are you real?' Sarah sobbed.

'Of course I'm real, silly!'

'Where have you *been*?'

'I haven't been anywhere.'

'But – last night – You weren't *there*!'

'I was at Chrissie's.' Evie pushed her gently away and got out a tissue, with which she started to wipe Sarah's face. 'Rah-Bee, I told you I was going to Chrissie's.'

It was a cliché that looking at your twin was like looking in the mirror, but in their case it was true. They were mirror twins, as were about quarter of all identical, monozygotic twins. The mirror thing happened when the embryo split late, after it had developed a left and a right side, so Sarah and Evie were mirror images of each other, the small deviations from symmetry replicated in each face, but where Evie's left earlobe, for instance, was very slightly wider than her right, with Sarah it was the opposite way round. And Sarah was left-handed and Evie right-handed. Mirror twins were meant to be closer than any other kind, because, psychologically, it really was like looking at yourself. It was as if the identical-ness had been designed for the twins themselves, so that when you looked at each other, you saw yourselves as being even more similar than did the rest of the world.

Sarah took Evie's right hand in her left and squeezed it, and Evie squeezed back. For a moment they just stood there, being together, and then Sarah had opened her mouth to tell her everything, to tell her about Oliver, when:

'Mummin,' said a small voice.

Sarah whipped round.

She hadn't seen the buggy at first because of all the fat nurses standing around it, but now she could see it and she could see *him*, she could see *Oliver*, sitting there looking up at her, his honey-coloured hair as unruly as ever in the Tintin quiff it went into no matter what you did, his cherub mouth an O, his little face turned up to her with a half-hopeful, half-worried look of enquiry.

The face that, in her blackest moments, she had thought never to see in this life again.

And the relief of it, the joy of it whooshing through her had her falling to her knees on the hard floor, a supplicant, a penitent, a worshipper, sobbing:

'*Oliver!*'

She swooped on him, hands fumbling with the belt of the buggy, and she grabbed him up into her arms, the solid little body pressed into hers, his hands gripping the collar of her pyjamas. 'Oh darling, my darling, it's all right, Mummin's here, my *darling!*'

The wonderful weight of him! The sweet smell of his skin, the tickle of his fine hair on her cheek, the rise and fall of his little chest...

'No, ah too!' he complained – meaning she was holding him too tightly.

'I'm sorry, I'm sorry.' She loosened her grip, laughing and crying all at once, and then he started to cry too, arching back away from her, and suddenly he was gone, the warm weight of him was gone, and Evie was hefting him on her hip and saying, 'Rah.'

Sarah shook her head; swiped at her face. 'You took him? *You took him to Chrissie's?*' Chrissie was one of the mums in the baby and toddler group that Evie took Oliver to twice a week. Oliver and Mikey, Chrissie's little boy, were best friends. '*Why?* Why didn't you *tell me?*'

Evie looked at her for a long moment, and then she turned to the nurse hovering a discreet distance away and said, 'Would you mind taking him while we –'

'Oh, it would be my pleasure, wouldn't it, young man?' She beamed at Oliver and he turned his face away, into Evie's shoulder.

But Evie lifted him off and the nurse took him and he started to cry again, and Sarah went to go to him but Evie took her arm and drew her away back down the corridor.

'Vee-Bee, we have to tell them!' Sarah tugged against her.

'We have to take him, show him to Dr Laghari!' She laughed, shakily. 'I'd like to see him try to claim that Oliver's a delusion when he can't hear himself think over that racket!' She stopped and turned. Poor Oliver was writhing in the nurse's arms, staring after her. 'Vee, I have to go to Oliver!' And: 'It's all right, darling!' she called.

'No. Sarah.'

Evie spoke so sharply that Sarah was stopped in her tracks. 'He's not "Oliver". His name is James, and he's my son. You know that. You don't have a child. You've never had one. You have this – this recurring delusion that James is yours, but that's all it is. It's a delusion.' Her face crumpled. 'I'm so sorry, Rah.' And she reached for Sarah.

Sarah flinched back. 'Oh my God!'

'Sarah – I'm sorry, but he's... I have to get him out of here...'

Oliver was bawling now, his face red, and Evie ran back to him. She snatched him from the nurse and dumped him down into his buggy and wrenched it round without stopping to do up the straps, and she was pushing him away, back down the corridor, and Sarah was running, running after them, but then hands grabbed her, too many hands, and she struggled, she kicked and she tried to punch and slap and she screamed:

'*Don't let her take him!*'

'Sarah, you need to calm down.'

'She's stealing my baby! My *sister's* stealing my *baby!* Stop her, *please stop her!* He's not hers, he's mine, he's my son Oliver and she's *stealing him!*'

Evie and the buggy whipped round the corner out of sight, and in front of her now there was Carol's fat mean face, telling her no one was stealing anyone's baby, and

'She's taking my child without my permission! If that's not *fucking stealing him*, what is? You need to stop her! She's getting away!'

'Calm down and stop shouting!' shouted Carol.

And now Isla's voice: 'We're going to get you back to your room now, Sarah.'

'Get your fucking hands off me you *fat fucking bitches*! Let me *go*!'

'Sarah, take a good long breath for me, all right?'

'*Evie!*' she screamed. '*Evieeee!*'

'We're going to turn you around, and you're going to walk nicely back to your –'

'Like fuck I am! Get your *fucking hands off me!*'

4

W hy?
Why was Evie doing this? Why was she pretending that Oliver was her own child?

But her brain wouldn't let her do anything more than frame the question; it wouldn't let her think about it, as if it was desperately trying to protect itself the only way it knew how, like What Happened to Mum and Dad. It wouldn't let her face it.

It wouldn't let her find an answer. *And she needed an answer!*

She curled up on her side under the covers; she curled into the smallest ball she could and howled, not bothering to muffle the sound.

'Sarah,' said a voice. 'Sarah, my love.' And she felt a pressure on her arm.

'Such a fucking drama queen,' said another voice.

And then she was sinking down, and the next thing she knew it was presumably morning – Carol was banging about the room opening the curtains.

'Toilet,' said the nurse. 'Then you can have your breakfast, if you can be trusted not to throw it at me like a two-year-old.'

A two-year-old.

'My sister,' Sarah said, her voice a dry croak. She swallowed. 'Yesterday...' Had it really happened, or had she just imagined it? 'Was my sister here? Did she come to see me, with Oliver?'

'Your sister and nephew came for a visit, yes, but I doubt they'll be back after the reception they got. All that yelling and shouting and carrying on. And in front of the wee one, too.'

'I DON'T CARE WHAT "EVIDENCE" you might have,' said Sarah, digging her nails into her palms. 'I don't know why she's – why this is happening, but nothing you can say, nothing you show me is going to make me believe I'm not his mother. When Oliver was gone, when I looked in his cot and he wasn't there, when I couldn't find him... It was as if the world had stopped turning. Or, no – it was as if I'd left the real world behind and stepped into some awful parallel one.' She stared past Dr Laghari to the photograph of mist wreathing a pine-clad mountain. 'That must have been what precipitated the delusional episode. It was like I wasn't Sarah Booth any more. Without him, I'm not really anyone, if that makes sense. I'm his mother, and that's the only part of me that matters. *I'm his mother.*'

Although she didn't look at him, she knew his expression would be carefully neutral.

She took in a long, ragged breath. 'He's not "James", he's Oliver. He said "Mummin". When he was here, he was in his buggy and he looked up and saw me, and he said it. *Mummin.* It's his version of Mummy. You can ask the nurses.'

'Was he looking at you, or at Evie?'

The name was like a physical blow.

'*Me!* Of course he was looking at *me!*'

For a long time, he didn't say anything. Probably a trick to get her to look at him.

She played along. She met his sympathetic gaze.

'Have you noticed something different about what you've been saying today?' he asked, diffidently, as if he was suggesting something that she may or may not agree with, and that was fine. 'Compared with when I first saw you?'

'No,' she said heavily. 'Enlighten me.'

Another long pause. Then: 'Yesterday… when I wasn't steering the conversation, when you were the one to choose the subject, it was always the child. Today, you're talking about yourself.'

Oh God.

'What do you think that could mean?'

She could feel the blush, suffusing her face. 'I'm only trying to tell you why I know I'm his mother.'

He smiled, a genuine smile this time. 'Sarah, I'm not accusing you of being selfish. Far from it. All I'm suggesting is – do you think the explanation could be that you're not worried about the child any more? And could that be because you know he's with your sister, and she'll take good care of him?'

'No,' she said. 'No.' She wasn't sure if she was trying to argue with him or just trying to stop him, stop him talking about her, about Evie, because she couldn't do that, she couldn't say her name or even think about her.

'Could it be that you know he's perfectly safe with –'

'No,' she said.

But she couldn't fight him. If he wanted to talk about this, there was nothing she could do to stop him. She felt as if a huge weight was pressing down on her, on her head, on her arms and legs, making it impossible to move or even think, much less fight this man, this clever man in the sharp suit with the easy air of authority, of knowing exactly what was right for her, of being completely in control.

And now he was setting printouts down on the coffee table between them, dealing them in front of her like a pack of cards, like he was a magician about to amaze her. *Pick a card, any card.*

He tapped the printout on her far left. 'James Booth, date of birth 10th of July 2017. Last attended Golspie Health Centre for earache in December, which cleared up with a course of antibiotics.'

The room at the periphery of her vision was spinning, and it was impossible to focus on the paper, to read what was on there.

How could this be? She didn't understand. How could this possibly be?

'No. That was Oliver. *Oliver* had earache.'

'And this is an email I've received from your GP, Dr Gibson.' He indicated the last sheet of paper.

She pushed it away. 'Lewis is lying through his teeth. You can't trust anything that man says.'

'Can I just read it out to you?'

She didn't respond. The whole room was tipping now. She closed her eyes, but that didn't help. She was having to grip the arms of her chair as if she were on a ship in a rough sea.

'Okay,' said the doctor's voice. 'I'll read it, shall I? "Hi Jagan. I'm sorry to hear that Sarah's delusion about her sister's child has not yet resolved. Her delusional disorder, as you'll see from her EPR, is generally mild, with hospitalisation only having been required once before, when she experienced an episode of severe psychosis with bizarre delusions. Although the non-bizarre delusion concerning James is persistent, manifesting regularly, it has until now been manageable on an outpatient basis with cognitive behavioural therapy. Most recently, in November of last year, she spoke to Fiona Cameron at Raigmore, whom I think you know. This was via a video consultation, as Sarah's agoraphobia precludes her from attending appointments. In the EPR, you'll see that Fiona describes Sarah talking about her recurring confusion as to whether her sister Evie's son James is indeed her sister's son or is Sarah's own child, whom she calls 'Oliver'. The delusion is, as I say, persistent, with extreme levels of elaboration – for example, she talks about her 'memories' of giving birth.'" He paused. 'I think you get the gist.'

She opened her eyes, trying to focus on his face.

He set the sheet of paper back down on the coffee table.

She didn't say anything. She looked down at herself, at her chest rising and falling.

'I've looked at your EPR – your electronic patient record – and everything he says in that email checks out. Do you remember talking to Fiona Cameron, your psychiatric consultant, via a video link?'

'Yes.'

It had only been a few times, about her agoraphobia and panic attacks, not about a 'delusion' that 'James' was Oliver.

And the thought of him, suddenly, was a little shot of strength running through her, through her veins and her muscles and her brain, letting her lift her head and look him in the eye and say, 'Not about Oliver. About my agoraphobia. And of course I remember giving birth! Who could ever forget it?'

And, oh God – how could she have been so stupid! So *stupid stupid stupid*!

All this time she'd been trying to convince him that Oliver existed, she'd been carrying the evidence around with her, *on her own body*!

She stood and opened the waffle robe, pulling up the pyjama jacket to expose her stomach.

'Stretch marks! See?' She started to walk round the coffee table to give him a closer look, but he put out a hand to stop her.

'Stretch marks can have many different causes. And they are very faint, aren't they?'

'They're not that faint!' She certainly was never going to be wearing a bikini again.

She thrust her stomach at him, and he reared back and said, 'Sarah, please, sit down.'

She stayed right where she was, breathing as if she'd just run a marathon.

'You experienced significant weight loss in your early twenties, didn't you, after the deaths of your parents? But, according to your notes, you rapidly returned to a normal weight following treatment for PTSD. Stretch marks are very often caused by rapid weight gain.'

She looked down at her stomach, at the faint white lines like little waves on a stormy sea.

'A scan,' she said, as the strength left her body, leaving her legs weak, her knees threatening to buckle under her. 'Or whatever. Isn't there a scan you can do that can prove I've given birth?'

'Delivering a baby does change the shape of the cervical os – but such changes can also be produced by abortion of a foetus or a miscarriage.' He pushed his chair back, away from her, the legs scraping on the floor. 'So a scan would not be definitive proof of a live birth.'

'But I've never had an abortion or a miscarriage!'

How could she prove that, though? And Evie had had several miscarriages when she was married to George. So scans wouldn't differentiate between them, even if Sarah could persuade the doctors to carry them out.

And as if thinking about Evie had cracked open her defences, it hit her again like a sledgehammer:

Evie has taken Oliver.

Evie.

'Sarah,' said Dr Laghari gently. 'Please sit.'

She pulled the pyjama top down and went back round the coffee table to her own tub chair, sinking onto it, feeling all of a sudden so shaky that standing wasn't really an option anyway.

'Would it be possible to have a drink of water?'

'Of course, yes. I'll fetch you one.'

When he'd gone, she sat and stared at the documents ranged in front of her. Ranged against her. She didn't care what so-called evidence he produced. She *knew* she was Oliver's mother. Never mind memories, never mind evidence – she knew. Right down to her core, she knew. It was the only certainty she had left.

It was as if becoming Oliver's mother had caused a physical change in all the cells in her body, all the neurons in her brain. Before Oliver, she used to enjoy crime series on TV, not really caring about the age profiles of the characters. Now, she needed to check that harming of a child wasn't involved before she started watching. And nature programmes were equally fraught. She felt so sorry for reptiles and insects, being abandoned as eggs by their mother, never even seeing her; how could it be built into their life cycles that none of the little ones would ever know a mother's love? Through millions of years of evolution?

Being a mother had changed her in every way possible.

When Dr Laghari came back and she'd taken a long drink of cold water from the plastic cup, she thought he might say she could go back to her room, but he sat back down and asked her, gently, if she felt able to tell him about the trauma that had precipitated her mental health problems.

'I understand that it happened in the summer following your graduation from university? When you were twenty-two? Nine years ago?'

What Happened to Mum and Dad.

'Yes.'

She didn't want to remember, but of course, unbidden, the images came.

Sitting with Evie in Evie's car, carefully wiping away, with the fingers of her left hand, the thin layer of dust on the slightly textured plastic of the dashboard – somehow it had been vitally important to clear that dust away. Not looking outside the car, at the high hedge bounding the front of the vicarage, their childhood home; not looking at the blue and white police tape fluttering across the gate. Wanting to go but wanting to stay. It had been an unspoken compromise, to sit there in the lane and wait for the bodies to be brought out to the ambulance that was parked up at an angle on the grassy verge in front of them.

Sitting with Evie on Mrs Bowles's sofa the next day, as the policewoman passed Evie the plastic evidence bag with the sheet of A4 inside and one of Dad's thick, creamy, good-quality envelopes. Evie's voice, somehow far away and not Evie's, reading the printed words: "'To whom it may concern. We cannot continue.'" *Cannot*, not *can't*; Dad would never use a contraction in written English. "'For various reasons, our lives have become insupportable. I hope that, in time, Evie and Sarah will come to understand our actions, if not condone them. I am deeply sorry for any upset caused. Yours, Michael Booth.'"

Any upset caused. As if he'd been addressing a Parish Council meeting.

Standing in the glebe behind the house, on the flat part of the meadow where the buttercups were thickest, studding the green with yellow. The shotgun, half-concealed in the tangle of grass and wild flowers. Mum and Dad, on their backs, flattening the grass under them, their faces gone, their heads like jagged, misshapen bowls into which a thick, bloody, curdled broth had been poured –

Tipping back her own head as a skylark suddenly began to pour its song down on the glebe, down on meadow and river and the spreading beech trees that dipped low along the hedge, on the honeyed stone and the church spire beyond, on this Cotswold idyll that Mum had called her 'little piece of paradise'.

Knowing that there was no beauty here, that the skylark's

song was a song not of joy but of fear, designed by indifferent evolution to draw off a predator. Knowing that, for her, the beauty had gone out of the world, completely and forever.

But she had been wrong.

Because she had had Oliver.

'Sarah?' Dr Laghari prompted her. 'Do you think you could tell me about it?'

'No. I'm sorry. I don't think I can.'

He inclined his head. 'That's perfectly understandable. But I wonder if I could ask you...' A diffident smile. 'I wonder if I could ask you to tell me one, just *one*, memory from that terrible time that is good.'

She closed her eyes.

'My sister,' she said slowly. 'Evie. She – The day it happened, the day I... I found them, she never let go my hand. Well, apart from when one of us had to go to the bathroom, obviously.' A shaky laugh. 'And all night, she held me in her arms. She saved me. No exaggeration.' She opened her eyes. 'I sometimes think, when the embryo was dividing to make the two of us – you know that we're identical twins? – somehow the cells that became Evie got given the strength meant for both of us, so I ended up with none and she – she –' And she couldn't speak. She suddenly couldn't speak.

When they were children, they had decided that, instead of being Christians, they'd worship the much more entertaining Greek gods, and used to secretly offer up prayers to Zeus in church when they should have been saying the Lord's Prayer. Part of the Zeus mythology was that he had two urns, one filled with blessings and one with afflictions, and to every mortal he dished out some of each.

But somehow Evie had got all the blessings and Sarah all the afflictions.

'She's been a very good sister to you, I think. She's always looked out for you?'

'Yes.'

'Do you think,' Dr Laghari said, very gently, 'that this very good sister of yours, Evie, your twin, who, from what I can gather, has been there for you through thick and thin... Do you really think she would do something so cruel as to steal your child?'

The word *child*, although softly spoken, seemed to ring around the room, bounce around off the walls and the ceiling and the thick, shiny vinyl on the floor.

'No,' whispered Sarah. 'But she has.'

Dr Laghari exhaled a breath. It was the first time she had seen him come even close to exasperation, and she couldn't blame him. She knew that it sounded mad. She knew that the two things couldn't both be true – but they were. Somehow, they were.

The fact that Evie would never steal Oliver, and that fact that she had done so.

'Your sister,' said Dr Laghari eventually, rubbing his fore-head. 'Your sister would like to come and see you again. I think that might be a great help, but it is, of course, entirely up to you. Would you like to see Evie?'

'No,' she said, and then, immediately: 'Yes.'

He smiled. 'Which is it, Sarah?'

Which is it?

Obviously, she needed to confront Evie. Obviously. What else was left to her? If she was going to fight this, if she was going to get Oliver back, she needed to talk to Evie. But even the thought of it was almost more than she could bear. If Evie really had stolen Oliver...

But why? *Why?* Why would she do it?

Evie always wanted a child.

The thought unfurled itself in her mind, as if it had been waiting there all along, waiting as a tender green shoot waited for what it needed, for the rain to seep down into the soil, before pushing up from the dark into the light.

Evie always wanted a child, but was unable to carry a baby to term.

But he's not your child! She sent the thought out to Evie. *He's mine, he's mine, he's mine!*

And he needed her. Oliver needed his mother. That was the important thing in all this.

'Yes,' she said. 'I'll see her.'

5

'Where's Oliver?' said Sarah at once.

Evie came into the room but stopped just inside the door, holding a huge satchel in front of her like a shield, her gaze flicking from Sarah standing by the bed to the invalid table to the wipe-clean wing chair. She didn't say anything.

And it occurred to Sarah that maybe she'd just thought *Where's Oliver?* rather than saying it out loud. That had been happening, with the drugs. She'd be sure she'd said something when she hadn't, or, worse, she'd be sure she'd only thought something when she'd actually said it out loud, like someone with Tourette's.

Her head was pounding and she felt weird and floaty and not in control, but at the same time her emotions were flattened out, as if she were a spectator watching Sarah Booth and all the bad stuff that was happening to her but not really caring about any of it except for one thing, except for the one thing that cut through the fug like a knife.

So she said – maybe again, maybe for the first time – 'Where's Oliver?'

'James is at Chrissie's. He's perfectly safe.' Evie offered a weak smile, but Sarah couldn't have lifted her lips in response even if she'd wanted to.

'Here we are, now,' said Isla, bustling in with a chair from the dining room, which she set by the window opposite the wing chair. And as she left: 'Enjoy your visit, girls.'

Neither of them made a move towards the chairs.

'He's not *James*,' Sarah said. 'He's Oliver. Why are you pretending that my child is yours?'

'Oh, Rah-Bee.' In a few steps Evie was standing in front of her, smiling the smile that always made Sarah feel better, even now.

But that was ridiculous.

As Evie reached for her, Sarah smacked her hand away. And now, as if at the flick of a switch, the emotions were back, coursing through her so she could hardly speak, she could hardly push the words out through the blockage in her throat. 'I don't understand. Vee-Bee. Why are you doing this?'

And before she quite knew what was happening she was sobbing in Evie's arms, and Evie was rocking her, crooning, and Sarah felt the tightness in her chest ease, some sort of muscle memory telling her it was okay now. It was okay, because Evie was here.

'Is it because you want – a child of your own?' Sarah got out. 'Is it because you can't carry a child to term? Why not just adopt?'

Evie kept rocking her. 'I *have* carried a child to term, Rah-Bee.' Her voice was so soft, so gentle, so dearly familiar.

Sarah pulled back so she could look her twin in the eye.

Her mirror twin.

But Evie wasn't just a mirror image of Sarah – she was her own person, a completely separate person with her own mind, her own needs and desires, her own agenda. None of which

Sarah could ever really know. Not really. She couldn't know what was going on inside that head.

'You've always looked out for me. I thought it was because you loved me, but was it – was it just because you felt it was your duty? Do you resent me? Have you hated me, all this time? You must hate me, to do this.'

'Oh!' Evie wailed. 'I could never *hate you!*' She grabbed hold of Sarah's hands. 'We've lived through everything together, haven't we, *everything* – from the time we were just a collection of cells inside Mum? How could I hate *you?*' Her lips quirked in an attempt at a smile.

For a long moment they just stood, holding hands. Left to right, and right to left.

And the fug descended again, and Sarah knew she was crying but the emotion felt distant now, at one remove, as if it belonged to someone else, as if the tears on her face, the tears she could vaguely feel, were not hers at all.

Evie was touching Sarah's face with both hands and singing, waveringly, '*Now the day is over...*' She wiped the tears from Sarah's face, and then she put her hands through Sarah's lank hair, pulling her fingers right through it, scalp to ends, scalp to ends, and Sarah stood there and let her do it, and Evie started singing again, under her breath, so quietly that Sarah could hardly hear the words: '*Now the day is over, night is dropping by...*'

When they were very small, not more than four years old, and Sarah was lying miserably in bed after some upset, unable to sleep – suddenly Evie would be there, cuddling into her and stroking her hair and face and singing that hymn, her own garbled version of it – it should have been *night is drawing nigh*, not *dropping by*, but Evie wouldn't have known the word *nigh* at that age, and the idea of night dropping by for a visit must have seemed logical to the two tiny girls. And Sarah would fall asleep soothed by Evie's voice, by her calming touch, by the comforting thought that her troubles were leaving her with the day's ending, that here was the friendly night dropping by, and tomorrow all would be well.

All would be well...

But it wouldn't be. Nothing was *well*. How could it be?

She slapped Evie away. Slammed her back against the wall.

'I'm his *mother!*' she screamed, right into Evie's face.

Evie flinched and turned her head.

'*I'm his mother! I* am, not you. *I* am!'

And she hit her, she hit Evie, she used her fists on her, on her arms and her shoulders, she flung her hard against the side of the sink and Evie gasped, and then the door was flying open and Carol was using her bulk to corral Sarah back into the space next to the bed, to force her against the wall, big hands gripping Sarah's arms so tight that pain shot up into her shoulders, shot down into her hands.

'No!' Carol shouted. Like Sarah was an animal. 'No!' She shook Sarah in time with the words: 'Calm – *down!* Right – *now!*'

Sarah's head bounced back against the wall.

'Stop that!' a sharp, authoritative voice rang out. 'Leave her alone!'

Carol released Sarah and took a step back, and then Evie was between her and Sarah, enunciating, clearly and firmly: 'Get away from her. Get *away!* You call yourself a nurse? A member of the *caring profession*? If I ever hear of you laying hands on my sister like that again, I will take it up with Dr Laghari.'

'I was only restraining her according to the guidelines.' But Carol couldn't meet Evie's gaze.

'Get out,' said Evie.

When she'd gone, Evie put her arms around Sarah, so gently, as if Sarah were a piece of infinitely fragile, infinitely precious china, and Sarah clung to her, she sobbed into Evie's fleece, she tried to gulp something and Evie said, 'It's all right. It's going to be all right. Come and sit down. Shall I get us some water?'

Sarah subsided into the wing chair and then she was sipping cool water as Evie perched on the chair in front of her and took her other hand, her right hand, in her left.

'I have some things to show you, okay?'

Evie let go her hand and opened the satchel and offered Sarah one of those flip-over card folders, with 'Conceptitoi' on the front in a blue, sciency-looking font, and a woman's smiling face looking down at a gurgling baby. 'I conceived James via a sperm donor. This is all the documentation.' She placed the folder on Sarah's lap.

Sarah opened the cover. The first document was a sheaf of pages clipped together – a contract, detailing all the terms and conditions involved in using Conceptitoi's services to obtain 'donated sperm for home insemination'. Evie had signed the last page. It was dated 22 November 2016. Under the contract was an invoice, stamped 'Paid,' for £950.

Evie took the folder away and replaced it with a thick sheet of paper: a birth certificate from the National Records of Scotland, watermarked and official-looking. She stared at the black text.

James Patrick Booth, born 10th of July 2017 to Eve Frances Elizabeth Booth.

Evie must have pretended there was a mistake with his name and got the records changed.

It was so enormous, so terrible a betrayal that she couldn't begin to get her head round it. Evie. *Evie* had done this? Yes, she had – this was an official document, wasn't it, an official document bearing witness to the impossible fact that Evie had stolen Oliver and was pretending he was her child.

'You got the records changed,' she said, dully. 'By pretending there'd been a mistake?'

How could she hope to get away with it? Okay so she'd altered some records, somehow faked the sperm-donor thing, somehow persuaded Lewis to help her, but –

It just didn't make sense. It didn't make any sense at all.

'No,' was all Evie said.

She took a laptop from her bag and opened it on the windowsill, typing something in from a little card. A Wi-Fi code.

'Here's the Scotland's People site,' she said eventually. 'It lists births, marriages and deaths in Scotland from 1513 to the present. You can search it yourself. Search for *Oliver Booth* and *James Booth*.'

In the search boxes, Sarah typed 'Oliver' and 'Booth' and selected records since 2015.

The result popped up in big blue letters:

We found 3 results in 2 categories

Heart pounding, she clicked through to the births category. A table came up showing surname, forenames, gender, a reference number and 'RD name', which seemed to be the town or city where the birth was registered There were two entries:

BOOTH OLIVER ANDREW M 1954 307/19 Hawick
BOOTH OLIVER WILLIAM M 1989 177/96 Dundee East
and West

Sarah pushed the sheet of paper away. 'These databases are never a hundred per cent accurate, are they?'

'Now try James.'

This time, there were thirty-one results, broken down into births, deaths, divorces and marriages. There were eight records in the births section. The last, most recent entry was:

BOOTH JAMES PATRICK M 2017 231/44 Golspie

Golspie was the nearest town to Achnaclach, where they lived. Golspie was where Evie had registered Oliver's birth, because Sarah, of course, wasn't able to.

'You went back to the registrar and said you'd made a mistake and – and got his name changed.'

'No I didn't.' Evie leant over and tapped on the keyboard, and suddenly the screen was filled with his smiling face, Oliver's smiling face, and Sarah moaned an animal noise and reached out to him, pressing her fingertips to the screen –

And then she saw what was filling the top of the photograph over his head. A yellow banner with jaunty red lettering, strung across the kitchen in Evie's cottage. *Happy Birthday James!* it proclaimed. Oliver was in Evie's arms, beaming at whoever was taking the photograph.

'His first birthday party,' Evie said quietly, tapping the keyboard to start the slideshow. 'You weren't there, of course.'

A series of happy images filled the screen – mums and dads and babies, party hats and birthday cake and a big frieze pinned to the wall of smiling animals, a tiger and a porcupine and a rabbit and a goose. And there was Margaret from next door, dabbing a hanky at a little girl's face.

'No,' said Sarah. 'For Oliver's birthday, it was just me and you and him. At my house. Obviously. We had a cake and party food and – and we played games with him –'

'We had a separate party for just us, yes. But James had a kids' party too. You've seen these photos before.'

'No. I haven't. You took him – and – and pretended to all these people that he was James, that he was your child.'

Evie exited the slide show and brought up a video. The echoing, high-pitched voices of very small children suddenly filled the room. 'Baby and toddler group,' she murmured. 'You know I take him to that.'

And there was Oliver, toddling towards the camera, pulling behind him an enormous stuffed panda which was bigger than he was, his little face so proud, and a woman's voice, not Evie's, said, 'Oh, look at James! Oh wow, James, *what* a strong boy!' And Oliver opened his mouth and shouted with happiness.

'Rah-Bee,' said Evie, taking her hand again. 'I know you love him so much. You love him like he's your own. You're not just his aunt. It's almost like you're his other mother. I think of you that way, and so does he. Remember when he was born, and you said it felt like he was your own child?'

Sarah remembered giving birth herself, and *Evie* saying that.

But all their lives they had shared their experiences, as if what happened to one of them happened to them both. It was a twin thing. In a way, identical twins were one person, not two. 'You're natural clones,' she remembered Lewis saying once with rather disturbing enthusiasm, as if she and Evie were specimens he'd like to study, a weird natural phenomenon. One person who had split into two in the womb.

Sarah couldn't be out in the world, she couldn't live like other people did, but it almost didn't matter because Evie was out there having all those experiences for her.

Borrowed light.

Was it possible – was it just possible that Sarah, in the grip of a delusion, had borrowed *Evie's child*, inside her head? Was it possible that Oliver was actually James, Evie's son? That all her memories of being his mother were borrowed from her twin? That she wasn't his *mother* but his *aunt*?

'Can I see that again?'

She watched him move across the echoey space, his laughter sending a thousand little needles into her heart. As whoever was filming tracked him from a sunny patch of floor into shadow, the image darkened so Sarah could see, in the surface of the screen, Evie's face reflected back at her, watching him too.

Evie said this was James, her own child.

Evie would never take Sarah's child.

There was only one way in which those two facts could be reconciled. And this was the reason why, all this time, her brain had been refusing to confront the possibility that Evie had stolen Oliver.

Because it wasn't a possibility at all.

When the video had finished: 'Again?' Sarah said, numbly.

As it played for a third time, as Oliver dragged the panda across the floor yet again, as he shouted again in glee and the picture darkened, Sarah watched not the child but the reflection of Evie, her wonderful, kind, selfless twin Evie, smiling as she watched the little boy.

Her little boy. Not Oliver, but James. His name was James, and he was Evie's child.

6

'Put up your hood,' said Evie.

Evie had brought Sarah's big coat to the hospital, her man's Barbour with the hood that she could hide inside, like Kenny in *South Park*. It was ridiculous, really. Yes, it was raining, but they were inside Evie's car. Swishing through the wet in their cosy dry little bubble, swishing along the A9 to Golspie, a skeletal wintry wood on one side, the grey North Sea on the other. Only twenty minutes of the journey left to go.

But that was starting to feel like twenty minutes too long.

She put up her hood and closed her eyes.

Evie always knew. She always knew what Sarah needed.

When her twin had arrived at the hospital to take her home, the regulation twenty-eight days after Sarah had been admitted, she had brought with her two cards and two boxes of Hotel Chocolat, one for Dr Laghari and one for the nurses. Sarah and Julia had giggled over the card for the nurses, with its cute illustration of a cat taking a dog's temperature, as Sarah had written an outrageous message inside: '*Thank you all for taking such good care of the patient from hell! (Except for Carol, who's a bloody sadist and needs sacking, TBH.) Lots of love, Sarah.*' And they'd sealed it up, like naughty children, before Evie could read it. One of the few benefits of having a mental health problem was being able to do that sort of thing and get away with it.

At the door, one of the nurses had patted Sarah's back and said, 'You look after yourself, my dear,' which Sarah would have found patronising at the age of a hundred, let alone thirty-one.

She had caught Evie's eye. The Look, they called it – that constant catching of the other's eye, that wordless communing between them, not to check that the other person thought the same – because that was pretty much a given – more just to touch base, like doubles tennis players doing a fist-bump.

Dr Laghari had taken her hand in both of his fleshy ones.

'I am very pleased with you, Sarah Booth,' he had said, with a twinkle in those black eyes. 'You have come on in leaps and bounds. You are stronger than you think.'

But he'd kind of spoilt it by reminding her of the coping strategies they'd been working on, and impressing on her the importance of telling Evie or Lewis if she began to feel 'confused or agitated' again. She had assured him that she would, standing in the lobby smiling, trying to stop her legs from shaking as she pulled on the Barbour over the soft navy cashmere dress that Evie had brought her to wear.

What she wasn't telling him, what she wasn't telling Evie and never would, was that she still felt like a mother who had lost her child. The need for him, the need to hold Ol – *James* in her arms, to look into his face and feel that pull, that ache of love – it still came upon her in waves, flooding her brain, sweeping away all logic.

But she was very glad that Evie hadn't brought him with her.

As one of the nurses had remarked, Evie had thought of everything. She had produced a blue leather make-up bag into which she'd put Sarah's medications, along with a note she'd

got Dr Laghari to write with the names and dosages of each –
quetiapine, the antipsychotic, one 150 mg tablet to be taken
each night without food, and phenobarbital, the sedative, one
30 mg tablet to be taken once a day with a full glass of water.
They had tapered her dose of phenobarbital from the 120 mg
daily she'd been on when first admitted, and the plan was to
wean her off it completely eventually.

Standing in the lobby, Evie had picked Dr Laghari's brain
about the best apps for Sarah's phone to remind her to take her
medications. Sarah had let it wash over her – she had just taken
her dose of phenobarbital and she'd had difficulty concentrat-
ing. How did people being discharged manage, if they didn't
have an Evie?

Now, sitting in the passenger seat of Evie's car, she slowed
her breathing right down, as Dr Laghari had shown her, in an
attempt to ward off the panic attack that was crouching on her
back, ready to engulf her if she let it in. *It's fine, it's fine*, she told
herself. *You're with Evie and she won't let anything bad happen.*
Evie had brought Sarah's two phones – Sarah never went
anywhere without her two phones, both fully charged, each
with a different network provider, to double the chances of
getting reception in an emergency – and she was clutching
them, one in each hand. If anything happened, she would be
able to call 999 immediately and someone would come and
help them.

She was desperate for the journey to be over, but at the
same time she didn't want to think about what would happen
when they got to their destination. She had confided only in
Julia the fact that she wasn't sure she wanted to go home. She
had got used to her little room with its bleak outlook.

'*Literally* bleak,' Julia had said as she'd shoved Sarah's
toiletries into her case. 'You're institutionalised, you silly bitch.
You'll feel so much better when you're home, with Evie and

James just down the road. And the hunky doc. You're going *home.*'

Yes.

That was what she had to hold on to.

She was going home.

SHE DIDN'T WANT to get out of the car. She couldn't get out of the car.

Evie had the passenger door open and was leaning over her. 'Give me one of the phones and take my hand. I'm not going to let you go. I'm going to be with you all the time.'

Sarah let go the O2 phone and gripped Evie's hand.

'We're going to get wet, but hey.' Evie smiled at her. 'I lit the stove before I left, so it should be nice and cosy by now.'

'What have you done with the phone?' Panic cut through the sedative fuzz.

'It's here, see? In my pocket.'

Sarah swung her legs out of the car and stood, and then it was possible to walk across the apron of gravel in front of the house to the door, clutching Evie's hand and the EE phone.

'Right then.' Evie smiled, handing Sarah the key as they stood at the door, rain pouring off their hoods. 'You do the honours.'

Her hand shaking, Sarah turned the key in the lock.

And then they were through the door and Evie was shutting and locking it behind them, and yes, oh yes, it *was* good to be home, it was *so good* to be back in her own space, the only space in the whole world she could control, absolutely. She actually stumbled, and had to steady herself with a hand to one of the columns of the cloister, as her whole body slumped with relief.

She didn't feel happy, exactly, because the phenobarbital fuzz flattened out all the highs and lows – it was more a rightness, a feeling of the pieces coming back together, of her life resuming its proper shape.

She was in her own home with the door locked. No one could come in here unless she said they could.

Home.

The Roman House.

The surprise, the 'stroke of genius', as one of the RIAS – Royal Incorporation of Architects in Scotland – judges had put it after the Roman House had won its award, was that this outer door opened not into a hallway but into a cloister around an open space: the atrium.

Sarah had designed the whole house using a Roman villa as inspiration, but she had agreed with the RIAS judges that the atrium was the best bit. Water burbled over the granite urn in its square granite pool in the centre of the space, open to the elements, so now raindrops spattered the surface of the water and the mosaic surrounding it was slick with rain, although cleverly concealed drains prevented water from sitting anywhere.

The cloister was faithful to its Roman prototype, with a pantiled roof supported by simple stone columns. Ivy and, in summer, a hop twined up the north range, and as they walked around under the cloister, a gaggle of sparrows shot out from the eaves.

Oliver – no, *James* loved it here; he loved the birds especially. Whenever he saw them he would run at them, squealing, wanting to be friends, and when they flew off in alarm he would turn to her, puzzled and slightly offended, although he was unable yet, of course, to articulate this.

Sarah stepped out into the rain, across the mosaic to the edge of the pool, where she just stood, enjoying it, letting it work its magic, this beautiful, simple, open space, filled with light from the sky above even on this grey day.

It was one of the many misconceptions about agoraphobia,

that it was a fear of open spaces. For Sarah, it was more a fear of what might happen out there, out in the unpredictable, uncontrollable world. What people might do to you, or demand of you, or even say to you. How you yourself might react.

She loved open spaces, as long as she knew no one and nothing could come into them unless she wanted them to. As long as she knew she was safe in them.

Evie – Evie, who always knew what she needed – had disappeared, she realised when she turned, eventually, to apologise to her. Sarah crossed the atrium to the inner door.

The house proper was built around two large courtyard gardens. The first courtyard, which contained the big living room in the west range, the kitchen in the south, and a gym and storeroom in the east, had a series of glassed-in arches, the central arch in each range enclosing glass doors that slid smoothly, at a touch, into the walls on either side.

Evie was bending over the wood-burning stove at the far end of the living room, throwing on a big log. There was a beautiful big bunch of white lilies on the long walnut table behind the sofa with its back to her. The three big comfy sofas, covered in pale oatmeal linen, were arranged in a U, with the focus the stove rather than the modestly sized television set to one side.

A memory leapt into her head of Oliver's toys, scattered over the floor and sofas; of his ride-on London bus and his pull-along dog; of his roll-and-ring ramp tower, with the chunky wooden cars he loved to watch rolling down from one ramp to the next; of his little 'shop' set up against the far arch, which she'd made for him out of painted cardboard boxes and old food containers: cereal packets and ice-cream tubs and coffee jars. And they'd made fake fruit and veg for it together at the kitchen table, although more of the papier-mâché and paint seemed to have ended up on Oliver than on their creations.

Was that even a real memory, a memory of James, or had it never happened at all?

Did James have a play shop? Had Sarah made it for him, or had Evie?

She wanted to know, but now wasn't the right time to ask.

She set the EE phone down on the walnut table next to the O2 one Evie had left there.

Evie turned and grinned at her. 'Welcome home, Rah-Bee!' She came across the expanse of rug and folded Sarah in her arms. 'I've made you mac and cheese. It's in the fridge. You just have to blast it in the microwave.'

Sarah's favourite.

'Thank you,' she gulped into Evie's fleece. 'You're so good to me.'

'I know, I'm such a treasure.'

'You are! I'm so sorry, Vee. I'm so sorry about everything. Putting you through this.'

'Don't be silly. I'm just glad to have my old Rah-Bee back.' She took a strand of Sarah's hair in her fingers. 'I'll cut it tomorrow. Remind me to bring my scissors.'

In London, when Sarah had stopped being able to go out, Evie had taken a hairdressing course so that she could cut Sarah's hair. She was really good at it. And she would go round the shops trying things on and sending Sarah the photos so that Sarah could choose the clothes and shoes she wanted, the pretty dresses, tailored trousers and flowery tops that she loved and Evie hated. 'Laura Ashley circa 1984,' Evie would text along with a photograph of herself in a drop-waist floral dress looking mutinous, and Sarah would text back: 'Hideous on you, but yes, will look great on me. Get it!' And it had been a tonic to watch Evie tottering around a shoe shop in high heels, the picture shaking because the shop assistant holding the phone couldn't stop laughing.

Sarah gulped back the flood of tears that threatened. She accepted a tissue from Evie and blew her nose.

'Give me a call, okay, if you want me to come and spend the night. But I'll leave you in peace now. Let you...' Evie stopped.

'... get my head together,' Sarah finished. They were always finishing each other's sentences. When they'd been at uni, studying architecture together, it had been something that used to amuse and infuriate their friends in equal measure.

'I didn't mean it that way.'

'I know. Thanks, Vee-Bee. You're the best. You really are.'

When she'd gone, Sarah wandered through the house, touching surfaces, sliding the glass doors open in her bedroom and stepping out into the rain, into the most private of the courtyards, the one onto which the bedrooms and bathrooms and study faced. She had planted a knot garden here, and after three years the box hedging was filling out nicely, knitting together, shiny green even in the depths of winter. There were gravel paths and bushes of lavender and rosemary and curry plant in the triangles and rectangles and rhombuses – were they rhombuses? – formed by the little hedges. And in the centre, a birch tree, and low planters which in summer would be a riot of thyme and wild strawberries and pot marigolds.

She sat down on one of the benches there, never minding the damp that soaked, immediately, into her dress, glad that Evie had gone, glad that she wasn't here to worry about Sarah sitting out in the rain like a mad person. She closed her eyes, letting the fug of medication and the rain and being here, *just being here*, soothe away all the stresses of the morning.

She took a shower, afterwards, luxuriating in the stream of deliciously, decadently hot water caressing her hair, her shoulders, her back. Then she pulled on a fluffy robe and padded on bare feet down the carpeted corridor, lit by skylights, that ran around the blank outer walls of the house.

All the rooms faced inwards. She had designed it that way, much to the builder's bafflement.

'There's a sea view from here,' he'd objected as they'd stood on the foundations.

And yes, there would have been a sea view from this spot in the corridor, through a gap in the pine trees that surrounded and sheltered the building. But she didn't want any views of the world outside this house. Outside her sanctuary.

She opened the door of the room next to her own bedroom. In her delusion, this had been Oliver's nursery. Dr Laghari had made her describe it. The cot, the mobile above it, the changing table, the Victorian wooden chest full of his toys. The sunshine yellow walls. The floor-length window.

And then he had shown her photographs of the room as it really was. The photographs Evie had emailed him. Photographs of this beige spare room, with its king-sized bed and matching bedside tables, its long free-standing mirror, all painted a tasteful duck-egg blue. Its Georgian mahogany chest of drawers.

Only the window was the same.

But she remembered, surely, repeatedly having to clean that window because Ollie would stand there, his grubby little hands on the glass? Sometimes he'd even lick it, as if he were trying to eat the garden, as Evie used to say –

But it must have been James who did that.

And the nursery was a figment of her imagination.

Both she and Evie were blessed with 'a wonderful imagination', as they were always being told when they were kids. But it wasn't a blessing – it was a curse. Sarah was sure that it was her 'wonderful imagination' that made her susceptible to mental health problems; that allowed her to retreat from reality whenever she needed to.

When they were children, the twins were always disappearing into imaginary worlds, whether their own or those created for them in books. They'd get a book from the vicarage library and run down the garden to the old rotten hammock under the sycamore which the previous family had left there. They'd squeeze into it together and, while Evie read aloud, Sarah would lie back and look up at the branches and the leaves and the sky, or just close her eyes and rock.

Mum and Dad hadn't held with contemporary children's fiction, so it had mainly been the classics they'd devoured. *Tom's Midnight Garden* had been a favourite – how they had cried, when they'd finished it and had to leave that world behind! They'd started it from the beginning, immediately, all over again. And *Kidnapped*. They'd been in love with both David Balfour and Alan Breck Stewart. And Sarah, in particular, had adored the E. Nesbit stories about the Bastable family, Dora, Oswald, Dicky, Alice, Noel, and H.O. Sarah had identified strongly with Oswald, the (mostly) well-intentioned but rather feral narrator. 'It is one of us that tells this story,' he said, near the start of *The Story of the Treasure Seekers*, 'but I shall not tell you which: only at the very end perhaps I will. While the story is going on you may be trying to guess, only I bet you don't.' It was really easy to guess, though, because the narrator was always saying how brave, clever and kind Oswald was.

The characters had all been so real to them that it had been a terrible wrench to say goodbye; for Evie to read the last line, and close the book, and say the words of doom:

'That's the end.'

That's the end.

Sarah had so been looking forward to reading those books to Oliver, when he was old enough. But she never would, because Oliver didn't exist.

It almost felt as if she'd suffered a bereavement. As if she'd lost a child.

Her boy.

Her own little boy.

Gone.

SHE WALKED SLOWLY BACK to the kitchen and opened the fridge. And forgot what she was looking for. She stared at the shelves, trying to think. Evie had stocked the fridge with all Sarah's favourites, olives and mango juice and pine-nut pasta and smoked salmon...

Food. She was looking for food. Obviously. That was why she was standing here with the fridge door open.

Evie's mac and cheese.

It was in a Tupperware box. She took it out and set it on the worktop.

Evie had left the little blue make-up bag with her medication in it next to the sink because she should take her next dose of sedatives, this evening, with a glass of water.

Sarah shook her head.

The destructive emotions were blunted by the drugs, but so was her ability to think. The drugs had her in a permanent cloud of woolly thinking, hardly able to put one butterfly thought after the other.

Oliver didn't exist. She knew that. Theoretically, she knew that. But how could she confront the delusion, how could she beat it, if she couldn't even think about it clearly because she was drugged up to the eyeballs every minute of every day?

She zipped up the make-up bag and pushed it behind the toaster.

All day snow had been falling, big fat flakes that drifted into the knot garden from the square of sky above, slowly blurring away the gravel paths and the box hedges and the mounds of lavender and rosemary, until by five o'clock, in the early dusk, nothing remained but a series of pale mounds looming in ranks on the other side of the glass doors of her study.

Sarah got up from her desk to put on the top light, and the garden disappeared entirely, replaced by a reflection of the room: Sarah herself, dressed in black jeans and a scoop-neck black cashmere jumper, the severity of the outfit lifted by a chunky silver choker and bangle; her drawing board; her desk, which she knew did not contain any documents detailing Oliver's birth or vaccinations, because she had checked; the shiny chrome and contrasting soft stone-coloured leather of the Eames-style chairs; the pale green walls; the high bank of drawers that held the architectural plans, the specifications, the reams of correspondence with clients and builders and Highlands and Islands Council.

Because this wasn't just Sarah's study – it was the hub of

their architectural practice. Evie had a 'satellite office', as she called it, in her cottage, where she saw clients very occasionally, but mostly she met them on site or at their own homes.

Evie knew where the keys to her desk were. She could have removed all Oliver's documents and thrown them in the wood-burner.

No. *No.* She *knew* she was his mother. But she also *knew* that this was a delusion.

She sat back down at the desk, on which she'd placed the blue make-up bag and a full glass of water. Her whole body was trembly and shivery, although the heating was whacked right up.

She'd Googled withdrawal symptoms for quetiapine and phenobarbital. If you suddenly stopped taking phenobarbital, you could experience shivering and anxiety.

Check.

Withdrawal of quetiapine, like any antipsychotic, could lead to a return of the psychosis initially targeted by the treatment.

Check.

How could she have been so stupid? How could she have thought she knew better than Dr Laghari? Far from letting her confront the fact that 'Oliver' didn't exist, her decision to stop taking her meds had allowed the delusion to come creeping back again, a little more each day, in the week since she'd stopped taking the tablets.

She unzipped the bag and took out the packet of quetiapine. Popping a tablet from the foil onto her palm, she stared down at it for a second before putting it in her mouth and knocking it back with a swallow of water. Then the phenobarbital. She drank the whole glass of water, although her throat wanted to gag on it. She hated these drugs, she hated what they did to her head, but anything was better than this – than the fantasy, the terrible, wonderful fantasy, that Evie's child was her own.

After she'd swallowed the drugs, she just sat there, her hand going instinctively to the drawer in which, in the delusion, she'd kept Oliver's important documents.

She opened it.

Leaflets about roofing materials. Leaflets about skylights and windows. A thicker booklet about the new cladding system they were thinking about for one of their clients. She took it out and tried to read it. To channel her thoughts away from where they wanted to go.

How had Evie managed, alone, while Sarah had been gone?

They had been running at capacity as it was, commissions coming out of their ears, first and foremost thanks to their unexpected success with the RIAS award, and the glowing feature in the property section of *The Scotsman* about the 'innovative young Booth twins at Sister Archt'. But also, they were riding the zeitgeist with their niche designs for clients with mental health problems. These days, it was finally not just acceptable, but almost fashionable, to be in some way impaired or damaged.

Evie had been horrified when Sarah had said that to a client on the phone. But the client, a lovely guy with Asperger's, had definitely seen the funny side. And, as Sarah had pointed out to Evie, she was allowed to say that, being so impaired herself as to be virtually housebound.

Which left Evie with all the heavy lifting: the meetings with clients, the site visits, the appointments with council officials, the field trips to quarries and carpenters and suppliers of weird taps, while Sarah got to do the fun bits, the research, the design, the internet browsing for ideas and products.

From time to time, Evie broached the idea that she buy Sarah out of the partnership.

'You could still go on working, only you could pick and

choose what you do, and you wouldn't have the stress of joint responsibility for everything. I'd take over all that. You could do as much or as little as you liked. I could recruit another architect –'

It had been kindly meant, although it hadn't been an entirely altruistic suggestion from control-freak Evie. But Sarah needed to keep her stake in Sister Archt. She needed to feel properly involved. And so, for once, she had stood firm and not let Evie talk her round. It wasn't as if there was a problem as long as she could work from here, in her own space, a safe space where no client or builder or supplier ever set foot.

But today she had done zero work.

She had just drifted round the house, from room to room to room, seeing him everywhere, Oliver, *her Oliver*. When she opened a door, she'd remember how he'd reach up and whack the handle to open it, no matter how often she showed him how to do it properly. When she sat on a sofa and opened a book, she remembered how this would always be a signal for Oliver, jealous of the book for claiming her attention, to clamber up onto her lap, and how she'd pull him against her and breathe him in, her little boy, her Oliver, her child who wasn't, in fact, her child at all.

In the last week, since her release from Marnoch Brae, Evie had brought James to see her six times, but had never left her alone with him. In the evenings, Sarah had got into the habit of poring over the hundreds of photos of him on her laptop and phones, trying to remember the occasion on which each had been taken. There was one, in particular, of Evie holding James swaddled in a blanket when he must only have been a few days old, taken in the living room – Evie said that was the first time Sarah had seen him, but she couldn't shake the false memory of lying, spent, drenched in sweat, on the bed in her own room, her heart exploding with love as she heard his cry for the first time; as Lewis lowered that warm, impossibly fragile little scrap of humanity – *her* scrap of humanity, her very own little human – onto her chest.

A false memory.

The brain was a mysterious organ, Dr Laghari had said. 'We're only beginning to understand it. False memories seem real because every memory, in a way, is false – selected, revised over time, reimagined.'

There were no photographs of the play shop she remembered. And none, of course, of the nursery that had never existed, although the false memory remained, stubbornly trapped in her brain.

Sarah didn't blame her sister for not trusting her with James. It would take a while, she supposed, to earn back Evie's confidence. To prove herself to be someone with whom she could leave her precious baby.

In a way it was a relief, because, although she loved spending time with James, being around him was still almost unbearable. And yet she hated it when he wasn't here, when the house was empty and silent and somehow purposeless, and her damaged mind would fill it with all those 'memories' of Oliver.

Her head said that he was Evie's son James, but in her heart he was still her own darling, her own Oliver, her baby.

And of course, with her twin's sixth sense, Evie had probably picked up on that, no matter how carefully Sarah had tried to hide it. Evie must be terrified that Sarah would spiral down again, down into that murky place where the real and the imagined collided and merged.

But it would be okay now. It would be okay now that Sarah had started back on her meds.

The phone on her desk buzzed.

Evie.

'Hey, sis,' said Sarah.

'Hey, sissy. Listen, I've just bumped into Lewis. Is it okay if I invite him to supper?'

Apart from Evie and James, Lewis was the only person who ever set foot in the Roman House. There was the time the RIAS judges had had to see inside, of course, but that had been a one-off. She had a large safe-box outside for deliveries.

Was it okay, to have Lewis here?

She wasn't sure how she felt about him now. She knew it was completely unfair and irrational of her, but the kind, funny Lewis she'd almost thought of as a friend had morphed in Sarah's damaged mind into the Lewis of the night of the storm, a Lewis who manipulated and lied and had her carted off to the loony bin.

'Rah-Bee?'

'Yes. Yes, Vee, that would be fine.'

'I'll leave James with Margaret.'

Margaret, Evie's next-door neighbour, did not, of course, have dementia. When a mad-haired, mad-eyed Sarah had turned up on her doorstep in the middle of a storm, raving aggressively about an imaginary child, she had naturally been scared out of her wits and shut the door on her. Sarah couldn't blame her for that. She'd written a card as an apology, which Evie had passed on. Sarah had hoped that Margaret might have sent a note back, or an email, or maybe called, but there had been no response.

She didn't blame the poor woman. Mental illness was a scary thing, and a lot of people just couldn't handle it.

She didn't blame her at all.

WHEN THEY'D FINISHED SUPPER, when Sarah had finished apologising to Lewis for the night of the storm, when Lewis had finished apologising to her, Evie got up from the table and went to the glass doors and slid them open, letting in the frigid air.

'Why is it,' she mused, leaning on the stone archway to look out at the garden, 'that there's something so strange and magical about the dark? Is it because your imagination has to take over from your vision – and conjures up all kinds of weird stuff? You know when you're driving at night, or in the twilight, and all you can see is the shapes of trees and hills and houses, maybe a light in a window – do you ever imagine that you've travelled back in time? That if you went up to that window and looked inside, you'd see a Georgian family gathered round a table playing cribbage?'

Lewis laughed. 'Uh, *no*?'

'And you thought I was the delusional one,' smiled Sarah. 'We're both –'

'– crackpots,' finished Evie.

Lewis's grin stiffened, and the twins exchanged the Look and burst out laughing, which seemed to discomfit poor Lewis all the more.

Evie insisted on clearing up in the kitchen while Sarah and Lewis 'adjourned'. On their way through to the living room, which connected to the kitchen, Lewis stopped outside the door to the cupboard that was built into the angle between the two rooms, where, on the walls to either side, framed photographs of Achnaclach were arranged.

'Are these your relatives?' The word 'these' sounded more like 'dese'. His nose had obviously been broken at some point, probably playing rugby, hence the nasal twang, although the slightly non-symmetrical nose only added to his rugged good looks. Sarah supposed that she would probably have been attracted to him if she hadn't kind of given up on men when her mental health had become an issue; and if it hadn't been so abundantly clear, right from the start, that he liked Evie.

At one time, Evie and Lewis had gone on a couple of dates, but it hadn't worked out. Evie said he was lovely, but he wasn't for her. Too intense. 'He treats me like a china doll,' she'd complained. And then, rather guiltily, she'd admitted that 'There's the nose thing too. He's kind of...'

'... snuffly,' Sarah had finished.

'Yeah. It probably gets blocked up because it's got that kink in it. In the restaurant, when he thought I wasn't looking, he *picked his nose and ate it!*'

'He did not!'

'Well, I'm not absolutely *positive* that he ate it. He had his napkin up to his face.'

They both knew from experience that, once the two of them started giggling over a date's personal habits, the romance was effectively over.

'Yes,' Sarah said now. 'Some of these are our family.'

The top photograph was a grainy image of the harbour in 1910, a small fishing boat in the foreground with four men in it. A skiff, Grannie had called those boats. Behind, on the quayside, was a line of people, mostly children, the girls in snowy white pinafores over their dark dresses.

The cottages were in most cases unchanged now from their appearance in the photo, hunched behind each other in their little rows of three or four that radiated out from the harbour, all sheltering behind the gable of the lowest 'end' house, the one nearest the sea. The cottages like Evie's were least prized as holiday homes, but used to be the most desirable to the fisherfolk because they were furthest up the row, furthest from the sea, tucked under the grassy bank that had constrained the tiny village to the space between the sea and this abrupt rise in the land – hence the name Achnaclach, meaning 'awkward' in Gaelic. The bank reached up higher than the chimneys of Evie's house, allowing just a pocket handkerchief of garden in the space between it and the gable.

'This is Evie's cottage?' Lewis pointed at one of the other photographs.

'Yes, that's Grannie with her brothers. She was born in that cottage.'

'They had huge families back then, didn't they? I was looking at the census for 1901, and there were something like a hundred kids in Achnaclach. Now we're down to one.'

James.

Sarah nodded. 'Grannie would be horrified by what's happened to Achnaclach. Just Evie's cottage and Margaret's still owned by the "old" families.'

When Grannie had died, Mum had decided to let the cottage rather than sell it, and there had been local tenants in it ever since, until five years ago when the last ones had moved out and Evie and Sarah had decided to make their big move from London and live here themselves, on the far north-east coast of Scotland, as far from London as it was possible to get in every sense.

Evie had just been through the divorce and Sarah – well, Sarah had been finding coping with London increasingly difficult. Even though she never left the flat, it was the *sounds*. The *noise*. The constant reminders of people, of traffic, just outside the walls. When buses or lorries went by, the whole building would reverberate. And when she had to leave the flat, to go to the dentist, or that awful time she'd visited a friend in hospital – it had been a nightmare. Panic Attack Central, as Julia would say.

Moving to Achnaclach had seemed like the answer. They had absolutely loved it as children, this tiny village built around the equally tiny harbour at the end of a single, narrow road so quiet that cats used to sleep on it in the sun and sometimes refuse to move for Grannie's car, much to the twins' delight. The road hugged the shore at one end of a long, quiet, perfect sandy beach backed by dunes and rolling fields of barley.

They'd come in December, and for a while it had been good. Sarah had even managed to go for fairly regular walks at that time, always with Evie. In such a tiny village, it was surprisingly easy to get lost. In the oldest part, there weren't proper streets but very narrow little lanes called pends between the short runs of cottages, just wide enough to drive a horse and cart along, most straight but some twisting back on themselves. You'd come out of a pend into a more open area, a patch of gravelly ground with a few houses around it, and wonder where on earth you were.

There was nothing happening in Achnaclach in the winter. There was no shop, no pub, no village hall even, after it had been sold and converted into a house a few decades ago. There was no call for a village hall, with most of the villagers gone. From November to April, the place was desolate, the cottages, once so full of life, now shrouded and shuttered and disconnected from one another, the tiny rocky harbour deserted and the campsite by the dunes closed.

But Sarah had been glad of it. She had loved the loneliness of it, at first.

She had loved the feeling that with the departure of the tourists, the ghosts had returned. You always felt as if you might turn a corner and come face to face with Grannie as a little girl, running home with the morning milk, a grinning little girl in woollen stockings and tweed skirt and Shetland jumper, wiping her mouth and swinging a small metal pail with rather less of a topping of cream than when it left the farm.

But then Sarah had got the idea in her head that the ghosts that inhabited the shadowed cobbled pends, the empty smokehouse, the grassy brae rising behind the village were sad ghosts. There was a mournful feel to the silence, she'd decided, as if the ghosts that lingered there were full of grief, full of yearning for what was gone, for what was lost, a long-dead child's eager steps, a long-dead mother's smile.

And then spring had turned to Easter and then summer, and the holidaymakers had returned, and she had wondered how she could ever have felt oppressed by ghosts. These people were horrendous! So noisy, so shouty, so disrespectful, somehow, of the history of the place, leaving their plastic inflatable Loch Ness monsters and miniature wetsuits everywhere. They came and they went. They weren't a community. Sarah had had a lot of sympathy with Margaret's pursed lips, the tone she used when talking about the 'incomers', although she was ready enough to accept their money in return for her keyholder duties.

It had been too much.

And so Evie and Sarah had bought the small pine plantation in the dip behind the brae, just inland from the village, and built the Roman House here, designed by Sarah to suit her needs.

Lewis's gaze was lingering longest, she saw, on the only colour photo in the group, taken a couple of years ago and showing Evie and other members of the kayak club lined up in their kayaks in the harbour. Men always did like Evie. Men and women and children and cats and dogs. How could they not? She might not be beautiful, but she glowed with health and energy and fun, and had an unforced, natural exuberance about her that was very appealing. While Sarah was closed in on herself, Evie was opened out, radiating a friendly, kindly interest in people that Sarah lacked entirely.

She glanced past Lewis, back into the kitchen, and yep, Evie had clocked him staring at the photo and was giving Sarah the Look.

Evie brought them coffee and a plate of dark chocolate ginger biscuits, and said she was off; she'd better relieve Margaret of James. Lewis looked up at that, his face unreadable. Things had been a little awkward since Evie had dumped him, but Sarah knew that wasn't why she was making herself scarce. And she supposed it wasn't a terrible idea to talk to Lewis, properly.

When Evie had gone and the house was quiet, apart from

the faint sound of the dishwasher, Lewis sat back on the sofa opposite, coffee cup cradled in his long, strong fingers, and said, 'So. How are you really?'

'Mm.' She sighed. 'Don't tell Evie, but...'

He shook his head with a smile. 'Doctor-patient confidentiality applies.'

'I stopped taking my meds.'

He went very still. 'You what?'

'I know, I know. I'm back on them now. I know it was stupid. Really stupid.'

'And potentially dangerous. Why on earth...?'

'I was having these thoughts... I was still having these thoughts about being Oliver's – James's mother. My hope was that if I stopped the medication I'd be able to address that, to think everything through more logically – because with the meds, I'm just so spaced out. But after I stopped taking them, the delusion about James... It came back, with a vengeance. All these false memories.' She twisted the silver bangle on her wrist. 'I still have a "memory" of giving birth. I've no memories of James as a tiny baby, Evie breastfeeding him, any of that... But I "remember" breastfeeding *my* baby.'

He nodded. 'That's because, in the delusion, those memories of Evie are warped – the neural connections in your brain are switched around, so those memories become associated with you, rather than Evie.' He grimaced. 'The fact that you're twins won't help. You're pretty much genetically identical, so Evie's child kind of *is* your child, technically, or as close as makes no difference. There have been studies showing that twins favour the children of their identical twin to almost the same degree as they favour their own kids.'

'Yes, I can appreciate that. I guess I love James so much because I'm so close to my twin, and he's her child. It's like James is a part of me. All my memories of him – I remember him as Oliver, my own little boy.'

'The important thing is that you recognise that these "memories" aren't real.'

But they felt real.

So, so real.

'Sarah, I can't stress to you enough the importance of following Dr Laghari's treatment plan. He knows his stuff. Don't you trust him to do the best for you?'

'I do trust him, yes. I'm sorry.'

'Okay, well, the plan is to keep you on the antipsychotic for the foreseeable future while the phenobarbital is gradually tapered, but given that you were having problems with anxiety and so on, even before you stopped taking the meds, I think it might be an idea to put you back up to 60 or 90 mg a day of phenobarbital. I'll run it past Dr Laghari and let you know tomorrow. And don't worry too much about the false memories. Now that you're back on your meds, they should fade.'

'Good,' she said, nodding as her stomach plummeted.

While her head recognised the desirability of this, her heart didn't want those memories to fade. Didn't want to lose them. To lose her little boy, her *own* little boy. But that was a dangerous, dangerous road to go down, and she must turn away from it. She knew she must turn away.

8

When the snow had finally melted and three days of sun and wind had dried out the ground a bit, Sarah suggested to Evie that they might take the short walk along the coastal path to Unster Castle, an atmospheric ruin perched on the cliff edge. It was the only walk Sarah had been managing to do in the last few years – probably because it was so entirely predictable. She knew that nothing unexpected was going to happen. They might see people, but usually at a distance. They might get jumped on by a dog, but she could handle that. The worst that could happen was that someone might smile at them and remark on the weather.

This was what she always told herself. But even so, the prospect of it had her chest tightening and her pulse racing, despite the fact that she'd taken her midday dose of phenobarbital a few hours early to dope herself up a bit. Lewis had told her that Dr Laghari had agreed about increasing the dose of phenobarbital, and she was now on 90 mg daily. She hated the sluggishness that came with it, but at least the delusion seemed to be receding.

Evie worried that maybe it was too soon for her to go out, but Dr Laghari said it was good for Sarah to push herself. This would be good for her.

She sat on the bench in the atrium, lacing her walking boots. She was wearing her navy lined trousers because they had two zipped pockets, one for each phone, and under her North Face jacket was Evie's cream-coloured fleece – when she went out, she always wore something of Evie's as a sort of comfort blanket. This fleece had an Evie smell on it, the fresh lemony smell of her moisturiser.

The sun was streaming into the atrium, making the water tinkling in the pool glitter. She leant back, idly watching it, her eyelids beginning to droop.

'*Hello-hello*, Auntie Sarah!' Evie's voice came drifting from the other side of the door.

Sarah didn't dare to hope that this meant what she thought it meant.

But when she opened the door, there he was.

Oliver.

Beaming at her from the BabyBjörn on Evie's back, his feet kicking out to either side in a pair of adorable little trainers she didn't recognise. In one hand he was clutching Dubby, the yellow dumper truck, his constant companion.

'Well, hello!' Sarah smiled at him, and took his other hand in hers. So soft. 'Are we going on a big adventure?'

'Aow-woww-im,' he said, suddenly serious.

'Yes, we're *all* going!' The tightness in her chest eased a little. The sun felt so good on her face. This was going to be a good day. 'We're *all* off on an adventure!' she told Ollie.

James. He was *James*.

Evie was beaming at her too. 'Okay! Let's go, people!'

'Don't go too fast,' Sarah said at once, her pulse starting to race again. 'You need to be close enough –'

'– that you can reach me at all times. I know, Rah.' Evie frowned at her. 'Are you sure you want to do this?'

'I'm sure.'

Evie, as usual, went in front, and a couple of times Sarah had to call to her to slow up when the path dipped downhill. Evie had to be within touching distance. That was a must. Every so often, Sarah had to physically reach out and touch her, or at least the back of the BabyBjörn. And Sarah couldn't go fast because she had to keep to the same stride length and the same rhythm – another comfort-blanket thing. Sometimes she counted in her head as she walked, up to a hundred and then back up from one again. But it was hard, putting one foot in front of the other. She just felt so tired. She could hardly keep her eyes open, and a couple of times she realised she'd had them shut, just for a few steps.

Maybe this had been a mistake.

But with the two of them walking so close together, James was right in front of Sarah, and all the way to the castle she'd be able to look at him, to drink him in. What she needed to do was concentrate on James. That would keep her awake. He was quite the fashion plate, dressed in a white bobble hat, a blue hooded jacket with white and yellow dinosaurs on it, cosy khaki trousers and those darling little trainers, which were bright red with luminous yellow go-faster stripes. Their soles, she noticed, were pristine.

The path wasn't at all dangerous. There was a gradual grassy bank leading down to the rocks and the sea on one side, and fields on the other. As they got nearer the castle, the path climbed until they were high on the cliffs, the shore a series of rocky promontories and gullies where they could hear the sea rushing and breaking, but the path struck away from the edge at this point, into a tangle of brown winter brambles and gorse.

James kept dropping Dubby, and Sarah had to keep picking the toy up again. It was a huge effort to bend down to get it, and when she straightened, she felt weird and light-headed. Just as she'd decided to put it in her pocket for safekeeping –

'Maybe Auntie Sarah should put Dubby in her pocket to keep him safe,' Evie suggested. 'So he doesn't get lost.'

They so often had exactly the same thought at exactly the same time.

What Lewis had said last night, about identical twins – was that what this was? A combination of a disordered mind and a biological pull, telling her that Evie's child was hers because, from the point of view of the bigger picture – the passing on of genes to the next generation – he *was* as much hers as Evie's?

'I love his new trainers,' she yelled at Evie.

It was hard to converse in single-file mode – the breeze off the sea whipped your words away.

Evie turned. 'I know, aren't they the cutest? I wish they'd do adult sizes in the toddler fashion ranges. I would *love* trainers like these! He's been running about the cottage in them all morning, but this'll be their first proper walk. I'll let him down at the doocot.'

The dovecote, or doocot in Scots, had been built in the 1500s to supply pigeons and their eggs to the inhabitants of the castle. Shaped like a giant old-fashioned beehive, it stood in the middle of a field with a wide path up to it. When they reached the path, Sarah found her breath coming in gulps – something to do with knowing the car park was just over the rise of the field. There was no one in sight, but people might very well appear at any moment.

'Vee-Bee,' she gasped.

'You're fine, Rah, you're fine.' Evie pulled her into a tight hug. 'Breathe *out*... Good, that's great! Now hold it... And... *slowly* in.'

Sarah took a long gulp of air.

Evie was rubbing her back. 'If we see anyone, we'll turn and go the other way. No interaction will be required. No one's going to get near us. I promise. You're fine, Rah-Bee. You're perfectly fine. Now hold it. Hold your breath. Okay. *Good*, that's really good. You're doing so well, sissy. Now out again.'

What would she do without Evie?

As the panic attack receded, a single thought flooded her brain: *I love you so much.* But there was no need to say it. There had never been a need.

They just held each other close.

On Evie's back, James reached past her head to touch Sarah's hair. 'Mummin.'

'I know, I know, James!' Evie laughed. 'You can't wait to be free!'

Sarah helped her to release James from the BabyBjörn, and he shouted with pleasure to be set on his feet, to have the whole path with its infinite possibilities stretching out in front of him. The contrast between his view of the world and Sarah's couldn't have been starker.

He waddled forward with that slap-footed gait toddlers had, as if they were so delighted to be finally walking that they wanted to emphasise every step. Sarah breathed slowly in, slowly out. He was just so adorable, his Tintin quiff and his short legs in those relatively wide trousers making him look like a cute little cartoon character.

When he'd gone a few paces, he looked back with a mischievous grin.

'I'm gonna get you!' sang Evie, and he squealed, breaking into a trot as Evie pretended to run after him, taking tiny steps to let him keep ahead of her. 'I'm *co-ming*! Better look *ou-out*!'

She finally caught him, swinging him up and kissing him, and then Sarah took his other hand and they walked along with him between them, swinging him up off his feet every few steps, making him chortle and shout with delight. Sarah smiled. His little hand in hers was better than any amount of anti-anxiety medication.

Evie stopped, and threw her head back, and intoned: '*Close to the sun in lonely lands.*'

Sarah grimaced. Tennyson, if she was not mistaken.

'But it's not really *lonely*, is it?' Evie smiled. 'In London, you're just another person who's washed up there; another piece of flotsam and jetsam. But here, you get talking to your hairdresser and you find out she's Margaret's great-niece and her boyfriend is the nice guy in the garage! Everyone's connected. And when I think of our ancestors, our great-great-great-grandmother maybe coming to work in this field, coming to help with the haymaking... I feel I can almost reach out and take her hand!'

'Mm,' said Sarah.

At odds with Evie's control-freakery, but equally annoying at times, was this romantic, poetic side to her. As children, they'd had free range in their father's library, which he'd inherited from past incumbents, but no access to contemporary children's books, TV or the internet. So they'd kind of grown up like 1950s children. Previous vicars had been big on Wordsworth, Tennyson and Thomas Hardy.

The vicarage seemed a million miles away. A million years. Never mind the 1950s – the place had hardly changed, in its essentials, since before the First World War. Mellow Cotswolds stone, mullioned windows, gently sloping lawns and rhododendron-dominated shrubberies... The occasional distant sound of ball on bat – 'Leather on willow,' as Dad used to say – from the cricket ground on the other side of St Stephen's.

Sometimes Dad would stroll down there on a Saturday evening to catch the end of the match, and a deckchair would be brought out of the pavilion for him, and there he'd sit, Panama hat shading his eyes, holding court as the ladies of the village hurried to bring him a cuppa and a plate of sandwiches and cakes left over from the cricket teas. 'Mrs Bowles, you make the best cup of tea in the county,' he would exclaim. 'But don't tell Deirdre!' Mum, Deirdre, would sometimes join him for ten minutes, standing behind his chair like a servant, droopy and weak-eyed, squinting at the men in their cricket whites and making inane comments about not understanding leg before wicket.

They were both completely different people in public, as if they had disguises they would put on and take off at the vicarage door.

She pushed away *What Happened to Mum and Dad*, which always snuck up on her, ambushed her, whenever her parents popped into her head.

At the doocot, Evie opened the door and held James up to the locked grille that stopped people getting inside.

'See all the little rooms for the pigeons?' Sarah said. 'For the birdies?'

'Buddies,' he breathed, looking up and up at the honeycomb of little cubbyholes all round the walls where pigeons still roosted and laid their eggs – safe, for the last four hundred years, from human incursions.

'Yes, birdies!'

Evie put him back in the BabyBjörn for the walk to the castle. As they returned to the coastal path, a seagull swooped low over them and out to sea, and Oliver bounced in the Baby-Björn excitedly.

No.

James. *James.*

'Buddie!'

'Yes, see all the buddies!'

The castle was perched on the very edge of the cliff, but the path to it was perfectly safe, leading through a scrubby area of rough grass which, in spring, would be covered in wild primroses. There had been a castle here since the 13th Century, but it had been abandoned in the 1600s. The inhabitants had moved inland and built a more civilised mansion for more civilised times, leaving Unster Castle to the gulls and the kittiwakes.

There wasn't much of it left. The upper storeys had tumbled into the sea, or the stone had been robbed to build farmhouses and cottages. The walls now were mainly less than ten feet high, but you could still walk through the ground-floor rooms and see where the fireplaces would have been and even a loo, a vertiginous hole in the stonework at the end of a short, narrow passage.

She always felt better once she'd got inside the castle. For some reason it felt safe here.

'Well done, Rah-Bee!' said Evie, hugging her. 'Would you be okay to explore with James?'

'Yes,' she said at once.

'Okay, while you guys do that, I'm going to take some photos.'

Sarah groaned. 'Yes, because you might just have missed some vitally important detail in the couple of thousand you already have.'

Evie gave a mock pout. 'It's called –'

Being thorough. Evie's mantra. Sarah didn't even bother finishing that sentence.

'Yeah yeah. We're out of here.'

Evie was obsessed with this place. They periodically discussed designing another house similar to the Roman House, but based on the layout of Unster Castle and built, this time, around a single courtyard. But Evie was never quite satisfied with the designs they came up with.

Sarah and James went off together to explore, at James's pace, his little hand in hers, but Sarah was quite content to bumble along. Maybe it was the relief at getting here, but her energy levels had crashed. James, though, was not a demanding companion. Typically, he seemed more interested in a tiny woodlouse he found on one of the walls than in the castle itself.

Transfixed, he stood watching its progress across the stone and under a piece of moss.

'That's a woodlouse,' Sarah told him.

He looked up at her and pointed at the moss.

'Yes, I think that's maybe where he lives.'

He stooped for a better look at this unusual home, but he didn't poke it or pull at it. He was a good little boy in that way, even at this early age, respectful of the other creatures with which he found himself sharing his world.

'Figh-end.'

'No, I don't think we frightened him. We stood nicely and we didn't make a noise or hit, did we? He's maybe just tired and wants to have a little nap.'

A little nap. What wouldn't she give for a little nap?

She lifted James in her arms and walked across the room to one of the wide, empty window embrasures in the north wall that was built right on the edge of the cliff and afforded unobstructed views out to sea. She set him down on the stone sill facing the sea, his little legs sticking straight out in front of him. The wall was so thick that his feet in their snazzy trainers were nowhere near the edge, but she kept a tight hold on him nonetheless. 'Look at all the birdies!'

There were a dozen or more seagulls soaring on the thermals that rose from the cliffs, their calls like babies' cries. She pressed her face against his soft cheek and sang, quietly, 'The sun is coming out to play...'

He began to bounce in response, his mouth lifting in a smile. 'Sun as cowin *ow* an pay!'

It was a weak, low winter sun that left the line of cliffs in shadow, but still – it was a lovely day. And in that moment, she knew, suddenly, that everything was going to be all right. She was leaving the delusion behind her. She was grounding herself back in reality –

And then, suddenly, he was gone. Snatched from her grasp.

She wheeled round.

'What were you thinking!' Evie gasped, clutching James to her. He started to wail, the sound echoing round the castle walls. 'He could have fallen!'

'Of course he couldn't!'

'It's a *sheer drop* from here!'

'So? I had a tight hold of him. He was in no danger of falling whatsoever! Evie! You're being *ridiculous!*'

But Evie was already striding away.

9

Sarah set and lit the wood-burning stove and made herself a cup of strong coffee, sitting watching the fire roar away, before attempting to call Evie again. For the last three days, she'd been trying to apologise for what had happened at the castle, but Evie was having none of it. Apparently Sarah had 'crossed a line'.

Which was ridiculous.

It was true that she hadn't exactly been thinking clearly when she'd put Oliver – *James* up on that windowsill. She'd been so dopey from the sedatives. In fact, the whole excursion had been much more difficult than it needed to be because she'd been like a brain-dead zombie.

The sedative just hadn't been working for her.

Okay, so she knew Dr Laghari and Lewis had her best interests at heart, and they were the ones with the medical knowledge, but, as Julia would say, it was Sarah's body. Sarah's mental illness. Surely she was the one who should get to decide how to handle it? Surely she was the one who knew best what was working and what wasn't?

So – just as an experiment – she'd stopped taking the sedative altogether, without, of course, telling Evie or Lewis. Her hope was that the antipsychotic medication would keep the delusion at bay, while her unsedated brain would be less of a liability all round.

Although James had never been in danger.

As if she would put him in danger! But Evie was always right – Sarah should know that by now. And, rather than fuming over the injustice of it, she should just accept that of course Evie would overreact about something like this. She'd always been risk-averse to the nth degree. This was a plus in their line of work, of course, as she always checked and rechecked that their designs and specs met all the health and safety requirements. The Building Control officer loved her. He always said that he knew whenever one of their applications came in that he hardly had to look at it, he was so confident it would conform to all the regs.

Sarah was sitting on the sofa that faced the courtyard garden. This was a lot wilder than the knot garden, designed with wildlife in mind. She always left it alone in the autumn so that the seed heads and hips and berries were there for the birds through the winter, and there was a feeding station by this window with sunflower seeds and peanuts. There was a flock of goldfinches squabbling over it now, their exotic red and yellow and black plumage splashes of colour on a grey winter day.

Before she could even lift her phone, it buzzed on the cushion next to her.

Evie.

This happened too often to be a coincidence – one of them would decide to phone the other, but before she could do so, the other twin would pre-empt the call.

'Hi,' she said.

'Oh, hi Sarah. Look, I'm sorry, okay? I'm sorry if I over-reacted.'

Hmm. That 'if' had not escaped Sarah's notice. But she smiled, and said, 'I'm sorry too. I'm sorry if I scared you.' Two could play at that game.

'Listen, I'm wondering if it would be okay if James and I came over today? We could have a nice lazy Sunday. I could bring his paints and stuff.'

It was a peace offering she was more than ready to accept. 'That would be great. Come now. I'm just about to open a packet of Biscoffs.' Evie's favourite.

'OH MY GOODNESS!' exclaimed Sarah when Oliver handed her the sopping wet piece of paper that was his 'painting', runny blue poster paint dripping from it onto the plate of biscuits, which Evie snatched away a second too late. The sisters grinned at each other. The kitchen table looked like a dozen children had been painting at it, not just one small boy.

It gave the room such life.

The kitchen was beautiful, with its sleek white units and granite tops, its quirky open shelves, the antique dresser and the big old pine table positioned facing the glass doors in the central arch, but it needed *this*, it needed the chaos that only a child could create, to make it a home.

'That's *amazing*, Ollie!'

'James,' said Evie quickly.

'Sorry, *James*.' Sarah took the wet A3 sheet in her hands. 'Is this a birdie?' It was a safe guess.

He nodded vigorously, pointing at the centre of the paper. 'Amond imon.'

She looked at Evie, who laughed and shrugged.

'That's *really* good, James. Aren't you clever?'

He smiled complacently and reached for a biscuit.

'No, darling, that one's all paint, see?' Evie prised his hand off it. 'Have this nice clean one instead.'

But Ol – James wanted *that* one. His mouth wobbled.

'Okay,' said Evie. 'Here's the deal. You really shouldn't get a biscuit at all because it's almost time for your lunch. But if you really want one, it's this one or nothing. Your choice, James. What's it to be?'

He slowly closed his hand round the non-painty biscuit. He probably hadn't understood half of that, but he'd got the gist. He was such an intelligent child. He already had a huge vocabulary of words he understood, and was adding more to those he could say every day.

When they'd fed him and put him down for his nap on one of the sofas, they made a sketchy lunch for themselves of houmous and bread and tomatoes and ate it at the cleared table, from which they could see through the garden into the living room. Both of them sat gazing at James's tousled Tintin quiff peeping above the blanket on the sofa.

Their boy. Their darling little boy. Only he wasn't *theirs* – he was Evie's.

And she hadn't left Sarah alone with him once since they'd arrived.

Was it unreasonable of Sarah to think there was more to this than Evie's risk aversion? That was part of it, no doubt, that she couldn't bring herself, yet, to trust Sarah with him. But even as children, Evie had always had to be the one calling the shots.

When they were ten years old, Lissa Edwards had moved in to the cottage next door to the vicarage, one of the few children in the village of their own age. To the rufty-tufty, rough-and-ready tomboy twins, Lissa, a year older than they were, had seemed the height of glamour. She was allowed to paint her nails. She had a little black handbag on a gold strap that she took everywhere, the strap slung across her body so as not to present an impediment to such activities as climbing trees and fording the brook at the bottom of the garden – Lissa had been glamorous, but she had also been fun and up for anything. The first time she'd forded the brook with them, although she'd screamed like a banshee when Sarah had jumped on her midstream for a piggyback, she'd struggled gamely on to the other side.

The contents of Lissa's bag had been another source of wonder. There was a little sparkly purse – Lissa had *her own money*, which she spent generously on icepoles or crisps or Mars bars for them all in the village shop. And a nail file, and a pack of tissues, and usually a packet of wine gums, an illicit treat – Dad felt that anything with alcohol in its name, as a matter of principle, should not be available to children.

Lissa had become their best friend within seconds of their meeting, but Evie had laid down the law later that day, as they waved Lissa off down the vicarage drive, marvelling at the way her skirt swished as she ran.

'You can't play with her unless I'm there too.'

And Sarah had known better than to argue.

Even at the age of ten, Sarah had been aware that one twin was usually dominant, but, as she'd run back inside after Evie, she had reflected that Evie really did push her luck with that.

She had complied with the Lissa rule, though. Sarah always did comply, in the end, with Evie's rules.

Mainly, it was fine. Mainly Evie's laying down of the law was for Sarah's own good, but occasionally, just occasionally, like with Lissa Edwards, Evie's own self-interest came to the surface; her exploitation of her power over Sarah. Their twin relationship was definitely a dictatorship rather than a democracy, and sometimes the fact that the dictatorship was benign wasn't much of a comfort.

'He's getting so big.' Evie pulled another tomato off the little bit of vine on the plate. 'He's at the eightieth percentile for height now. I do sometimes wonder about his – not his *father*, I don't think of the donor as his *father*... His genetic heritage, I suppose.'

As if he knew they were talking about him and didn't like it, James woke, the blanket agitated as he fought it with his arms and legs.

'Okay, sweetheart, Mummin's coming,' called Evie.

After a turn round both courtyard gardens and a very brief splashing of hands in the very chilly fountain in the atrium, they settled in for an afternoon in front of the fire, Evie ostentatiously checking that the child guard was properly in place around the stove.

She had brought a big plastic storage box full of James's toys, and had set it down on the floor for him to rummage in. The toys were now, of course, scattered all over the rug between the sofas, and he was crawling about happily, bashing dinosaurs together and demolishing the houses Evie and Sarah constructed with the Duplo bricks.

'He's such a *boy*,' Evie laughed, snatching back her hand as T-rex pummelled the little penguin she'd been voicing, the penguin's overtures of friendship evidently not meeting with approval in the dinosaur camp.

Satisfied that the penguin problem had been appropriately dealt with, Oliver sat back on his nappy-fat little bottom and contemplated his surroundings with a critical gaze.

Sarah couldn't take her eyes off him. Everything he did was fascinating to her. She could happily spend her whole life just sitting here watching him.

'Dubby oddy,' he said.

Sarah could see the little yellow dumper truck under the sofa opposite. This was his favourite toy and needed to be in sight at all times.

'Dubby *oddy*,' he repeated, a note of worry in his voice.

Sarah scooted over to the sofa, extracted the truck from under it and put it into Ollie's chubby, slightly damp little hand.

He beamed at her, immediately thumping the truck on the rug.

'Oh, careful, James,' said Evie. 'You'll not be so happy if you break Dubby, will you?'

Sarah just sat there, suddenly frozen, as Evie put her hand over the little boy's in an attempt to demonstrate how to play nicely with the truck, pushing it along on the rug.

Dubby oddy.

Dubby, of course, was his name for the dumper truck. And *oddy...*

'Oddy' was his attempt at his own name.

Just before she had been hospitalised, he had started to attempt his own name, but only in combination with 'Dubby', his most prized possession. He was trying to say that Dubby belonged to him.

To Ollie.

Dubby Oddy.

Sarah stood, so abruptly that Evie looked up at her in surprise.

She made herself breathe. She made herself think, as she walked slowly around to the kitchen, telling Evie she was going to make them a peppermint tea.

Oh for God's sake!

That wasn't a memory.

James wasn't calling himself 'Ollie.' It was just the gibberish he talked all the time. It was just her mind, her stupid, unreliable, unpredictable mind, up to its old tricks.

But this was worse than it had ever been. As she waited for the kettle to boil, running her hands over the pale, smooth, cool granite of the worktop, she let the dismay wash over her. She'd stopped taking sedatives, but she was still taking quetiapine, the antipsychotic, religiously every day – so why was the delusion getting *worse*, not better? Surely the antipsychotic was meant to stop that happening? Had her disorder progressed to a new, more severe phase?

If it had, how was Evie ever going to be able to trust her with James again?

How was she ever going to be able to trust *herself*?

WHEN EVIE and James had gone, out into the early dark, she moved about the house, switching on all the lights. Not very ecologically friendly, but tonight she needed brightness; she needed to banish the shadows, the unknown, the ambiguity of things half seen, half recognised.

She needed to get back to what was real. To reclaim her real memories. To push out the delusion.

She ended up, of course, in what had been the 'nursery' in the delusion, but in reality was a bland adult bedroom that, apparently, was only ever used by Evie when she stayed overnight. She stood in the middle of the room and turned a slow three-sixty, imprinting what she could see on her mind. A king-sized bed. Duck-egg blue bedside tables. A long mirror. The beautiful, glowing mahogany of a Georgian chest of drawers with swan-neck brass handles that were, from a distance, like smiling mouths: the circular bases of the fixings were the eyes and the handle suspended from them was the mouth.

She didn't remember ever pointing this out to James, but she must have done, surely?

The awful truth was that she didn't remember this room, at all, in its current form. Not at all. But the delusion version of it was very vivid.

She could see, in her mind's eye, the white cot that had stood over by the window, where the bed was, and the mobile above it that she'd bought online, a beautiful Japanese mobile with brightly coloured birds constructed from strips of silk woven together, so light that they moved in the slightest current of air. Blue and red and pink and orange and green. And the walls – she remembered them being painted a cheerful sunshine yellow.

She put out a hand to the nearest wall and scratched at the beige paint with her fingernail. Some paint came off under her nail, and she examined it. Only beige, with no hint of yellow.

She examined the scratch she'd made on the wall, the tear in the lining paper. Sarah hated plasterboard – it was in her opinion flimsy, brittle stuff with poor soundproofing qualities and, being made with cement, bad for the environment – and hadn't wanted it anywhere near her own house. The walls had been constructed using a modern version of lath and plaster, the laths coming in panels that the carpenter just attached to the stud frames of the walls before the specialist plasterer had come in to cover them with lime plaster, which she had finished herself with lining paper and paint.

She pulled off a sliver of paper. There was no yellow paint under it. No one had repapered and repainted, unless they'd first gone to the trouble of removing all the original yellow-painted lining paper – and why would they do that?

She walked round the room, trailing her hand over the chest of drawers, the fitted wardrobe, the cool expanse of the window. When she reached the bed, she flopped down on it and stared up at the smooth white ceiling. This was where the cot had been, in the delusion. Right here, so Ollie could look out at the garden and watch the real 'buddies' as well as the silk ones in the mobile.

Stop it.

She had to stop dwelling on all those fake memories. Push them out. Let the real ones back in. Otherwise... If she couldn't do that... That way lay the descent into madness she'd always dreaded; that Evie, she was sure, dreaded too.

But right above her, right over where the cot had been, on the ceiling, she could see –

She scrambled up and stood, wobbling, on the mattress, peering at the ceiling.

And there it was.

The tiny hole where she'd pushed in a tack to hold the mobile in place.

TWO HOURS LATER, the room was a mess of plaster dust, torn lining paper everywhere. She hadn't bothered to protect the bed or the other furniture, she'd just gone for it.

She'd got the steamer and a scraper from the storeroom behind the kitchen and attacked the walls, peeling off whole sections of lining paper in one go, poking the scraper behind the architrave around the door and window, where someone stripping the previous wall covering might have left awkward edges behind.

Nothing. Just the beige-painted lining paper throughout the room, and the lime plaster under it. Until she reached the built-in wardrobe.

There, when she poked the scraper under the edge of the framing around the doors, it came out with a narrow sliver of paint-caked paper on it.

The left-behind edge of a piece of lining paper that was painted bright sunshine yellow.

10

The next morning, Sarah woke in a horrible state of confusion, and it wasn't until she'd stumbled from her bedroom to the 'spare' room next door that she was able to convince herself that she really had found them: the telltale pinprick in the ceiling and the ragged strip of yellow-painted lining paper, still on top of the chest of drawers where she'd dropped it, last night, in shock.

She picked it up and ran it through her fingers. It hadn't been yet another delusion. It hadn't been a dream. 'James' really was her own son Oliver, and Evie really had taken him.

Evie –

Evie!

Her own, lovely sister!

It was so unbelievable that she couldn't begin to contemplate Evie's motivation. Rather, she found herself focusing on the details of how she'd managed it.

That night of the storm, Evie must have used her key to get into the house, and sneaked into the nursery and taken Oliver. When Sarah had found him missing, she'd played into Evie's hands by running to the village, to Lewis. But if she hadn't, if she'd called the police from the house, she supposed the police would have contacted Evie at an early stage in the search, and Evie would have told them that poor deluded Sarah didn't have a child, that the nursery and baby stuff and toys in the Roman House belonged to her own son, James. And then Lewis would have got involved, as Sarah's GP, and Sarah would have been carted off to Marnoch Brae.

But it had worked out even better than Evie could have hoped. Sarah had run to Lewis, and he'd managed to get her sectioned without anyone checking her own house at all. Then, while Sarah was in Marnoch Brae, Evie had had plenty of time to remove all – or almost all – traces of Oliver from the Roman House.

Sarah had made it easy for her.

No. She had made it *possible*.

By shutting herself away in here, by never seeing anyone, by not having any friends – why would she need friends when she had Evie? By letting Evie take Oliver out to the baby and toddler group, to his medical appointments, to playdates – anywhere, in fact, he needed to go – she had given Evie absolute control of him. She had allowed Evie to pretend that he was her own son James.

She had been so grateful to her sister. So thankful that, between them, they were able to give Oliver a pretty much normal life despite Sarah's limitations. When all the time... All the time, Evie was forcing poor Oliver to take part in a masquerade, calling him James, playing at being his mother. How confused he must be. No wonder it had taken him so long to say his own name – for a lot of the time, it *wasn't* his name.

Sarah's disorder wasn't worsening – yes, she'd had a delusional episode, probably precipitated by Oliver's disappearance, but, like the one she'd had before, it had lasted only a day or so. She'd soon come back to herself, and to the sure and certain knowledge that she wasn't imagining Oliver; that she really was his mother.

Why had she let them dope her up with drugs? Why hadn't she trusted her instincts? Surely a mother's instincts were the strongest, the surest of all?

Running back to her own bedroom, she yanked open a drawer and shoved the sliver of lining paper, the evidence, under a pair of socks.

She wanted to confront Evie. To shout and scream and demand him back. Her child! *Oliver!*

But she made herself shower, and dress, and drink a glass of water, her hands shaking so much she could hardly hold it steady. If she confronted Evie, only one thing was going to happen – Sarah would be carted off back to Marnoch Brae so fast her feet wouldn't touch the ground.

No. She had to think this through. That should be easier now that she'd stopped taking the antipsychotic as well as the sedative.

Evie was clever, but then so was Sarah. They were twins, weren't they?

But Sarah had never, really, tried to match Evie in anything. She had always let Evie be the one to achieve, to impress, to shine – the one to win. She had been happy to step back, to leave the limelight to her much more confident, much more vivacious sister. Even when they'd won the RIAS award, even though the Roman House had been Sarah's design, she'd been happy for Evie to take at least equal credit.

But there was no way Sarah was going to let her win this time. Oliver was her child, and she was going to get him back. Whatever it took.

Whatever it took to win, Sarah would do it.

. . .

'Hi, sissy!' she said brightly when Evie answered her phone. 'You're probably sick to the back teeth of me, but would you and James like to come over again today for lunch?'

She had to see him.

She had to see Oliver and know that he was safe. To watch Evie with him – really *watch* her – and satisfy herself that she wasn't a danger to him, this woman who had stolen a child.

Evie had always wanted a child. Sarah didn't know for sure, but she suspected that one of the reasons why Evie and George had split up had been that she wanted kids and George didn't – Evie said she was sure George had been relieved when she'd had her miscarriages.

Evie had always wanted a child, and now she had one.

'Uh, sure,' said Evie. 'Just let me get on top of this ironing and we'll be right with you. Say, half an hour?'

The ironing. All Oliver's miniature clothes, the adorable little T-shirts and jumpers and trousers.

'Perfect! See you soon.'

Belatedly, she realised that there was no time to clear up the mess in the spare room – no, the nursery – before Evie arrived. If Evie happened to go in there, Sarah would just have to say that she'd decided to redecorate.

There was time, though, to do a little digging.

How had Evie managed it?

Lewis must have agreed to change Sarah's medical records, to forge the notes from the consultant. To have Sarah sectioned! And presumably he'd changed Evie's records to make out that *she'd* been pregnant and had a child. Why would he risk so much, to enable Evie to perpetrate such a horrendous deception?

Was he really so infatuated with her?

Sarah walked slowly through the house to the display of photographs on the wall just outside the kitchen. Lewis's expression when he'd stared so fixedly at this one of Evie with the other kayakers... Had it been a look of love, or just the opposite? Did Evie have some sort of hold over him? Was she blackmailing him over malpractice or something?

She rang the health centre and told the receptionist that she wanted to see her medical records.

'Sorry – your *records*?'

'My medical records,' Sarah said slowly, as if to an idiot. 'My EPR. I'm entitled to see it. It's a legal requirement that you let me see it.'

'Riiiight. Okay then...' As if she was doing Sarah a huge favour.

'Can I access the EPR online?'

'No. If you want to see your records, you'd have to make an appointment to come in to the health centre.'

'But – I can't do that. I'm agoraphobic.'

'Well, I'm sorry, but there is no online access.' A pause. 'I can offer you an appointment with Dr Sutherland for tomorrow at 11:15?'

Sarah closed her eyes. She felt shaky and light-headed at the very thought. How would she even get there? Evie couldn't take her. She couldn't do it.

'Ms Booth? Do you want the appointment?'

No!

'Yes, thank you.' She had to do this. She had to do this for Oliver, no matter how impossible it seemed. She could take a dose of phenobarbital just to get her through it.

She shut her eyes and summoned Oliver's expectant face.

It's okay, Ollie. It's going to be okay. Mummin's going to get you back.

When she'd ended the call, she sat down at the kitchen table, opened her laptop and began scrolling through all the photographs of him on there. There were no photos of Oliver in the nursery, of course. None of him in Sarah's arms right after he'd been born. Evie must have deleted them all.

But what about her Google Photos account?

She went online and logged in. But it was the same story – any incriminating photographs had been purged. Evie must have been in here too.

Could Sarah take the laptop and her phones to a computer geek? Nothing you deleted was really gone, was it?

But then she looked properly at the laptop. The letters printed on all of these keys were clear and black. But she remembered being annoyed that the letters had started to wear away – the S, A, C and D had become virtually illegible. She remembered thinking this was pretty shoddy, as the laptop was only a couple of years old.

It wasn't her laptop. It was the same HP model, but it wasn't the same machine.

Evie – and Lewis? – must have transferred all her software and files from her old computer to this new one, minus anything incriminating. They'd probably done the same to her phones. But there was no way she could prove it.

She closed her eyes.

Okay. She needed to focus. She needed to find evidence that Oliver was Oliver, not James. She needed something to take to the authorities, the police, that would mean they had to take her seriously. Something Evie and Lewis had overlooked or hadn't been able to distort for their own ends.

She registered on the Scotland's People website and ordered a copy of the birth certificate for 'James Patrick Booth,' whose birth in 2017 had been registered in Golspie. It was possible that Evie had forged the certificate she'd shown Sarah because the real one showed an alteration of the name. Sarah paid extra for the priority service so that it would arrive tomorrow.

The doorbell trilled.

Evie – oh-so-considerate Evie – never just let herself in. She always rang.

'We're travelling light today,' said Evie as she breezed into the atrium, pushing Oliver in his buggy, a big canvas shopper hanging from her elbow. She had her hair scraped back in her usual jaunty ponytail and looked fresh-faced and healthy. The blue eyes they'd inherited from Dad always looked somehow brighter in Evie's face than in Sarah's. They sparkled.

Sarah wanted to grab Oliver and push Evie back out of the door. Lock it against her. But that would be boarding the fast train to Sectioned-ville, as Julia would say.

'Here he is!' Sarah exclaimed instead, smiling at Oliver and hefting him up from the buggy. 'What a big boy you're getting!'

Oliver smiled at her.

'No wonder, considering the amount of porridge he had for breakfast,' Evie called back over her shoulder, already making her way into the house proper. 'He'll probably be sick on you.'

Sarah whispered into his soft little ear: 'You're not going to be sick on Mummin, are you, Ollie?'

'There's a programme about crows on at eleven I think he might like,' Evie said as they settled Oliver in the living room. 'Oh Rah-Bee, you've not lit the stove! It's a bit chilly in here for him.' She turned on Sarah the fond but exasperated, *why-am-I-not-surprised* look that she gave Sarah whenever she had fallen short of Evie's standards.

And Sarah wanted to take her by the shoulders and shake her, to slap that smug face, to pull that neatly brushed hair –

But most of all she just wanted to ask her *Why*? Why had she done it?

Had she, *really*? Or had Sarah made a mistake? A tiny pinprick in a ceiling... A small sliver of painted lining paper... Did those things really add up to her sister, her twin, stealing her son?

But as Sarah sat on the sofa and lifted Oliver onto her lap, as she breathed in his lovely biscuity smell, as she felt the solid weight of him lean into her, she wondered how she could ever have doubted that he was her child, when every particle of her being, every cell, every nerve ending in her body was saying that he was *hers*, he was *hers*, he was *hers*.

Her little boy. All her memories of him had been real. Of course they had been.

She had been right about Oliver, and catastrophically wrong about Evie.

How could Evie love her, and do this? It was as if the sister she'd thought she'd known all her life had gone, in a puff of smoke: a mirage, a dream, a fantasy. The real Evie was someone controlling and domineering and utterly, utterly selfish.

Not Evie.

As the woman scrunching up newspaper for the stove turned and smiled at them, Sarah smiled back but in her head she was screaming:

You're not my Evie!

Eve. She would think of her, from now on, not as Evie, and certainly not as Vee-Bee, but as Eve. A different person entirely. A stranger she was going to have to get to know, to second-guess, to outmanoeuvre, to defeat. Her much-loved twin Evie was gone, and she wasn't coming back.

AFTER LUNCH THE SUN APPEARED, and after the inevitable 'Sun is coming out to play' routine, the three of them ventured out into the wild courtyard garden to see the clump of moschatel that had come into flower unseasonably early. It was situated in a particularly sheltered part of the garden, facing south, snuggled against a little mossy log, which presumably explained the early flowering.

'You see, darling,' Sarah said, taking Ollie's hand. 'It's called the town hall clock because these tiny green flowers – they're really more like leaves, aren't they? – they look like four clocks, one facing in each direction.'

Of course he didn't understand, but he liked it, Sarah was sure, when she talked to him as if he did. It made him feel grown-up and included in the adult world, which must, she often thought, be a frightening place to a small child constantly trying to work out what was going on; whose only fixed point, whose north star, whose only sure guide through it all was his mother.

What did he think had happened?

Why did he have to stay with Evie? Why had Mummin abandoned him? Why was he sleeping in a different bed in a different house?

She had to move away, to hide her face from them both.

Eve, ever perceptive, said, 'Rah-Bee? You okay?'

'Yeah yeah, fine,' she said brightly, widening her eyes and swallowing and plastering a smile to her face as she turned. Eve stood, hands on hips, frowning. Behind her, Oliver was squatting, fat little bottom stuck out behind him as a counterweight as he brought his face down towards the tiny town hall clock flower.

'Oh, darling, I don't think it has much of a smell.'

She saw it happen in slow motion – distracted, Oliver looked round, overbalanced, and fell face-first onto the mossy log.

There was the usual two-second delay before the howl of indignant anguish began, echoing around the courtyard. Squirming onto his back – there went the town hall clock – he held his arms out to Sarah, his face brick red.

'Mummmm-innnnn!'

But before Sarah could get to him, Eve had scooped him up. 'It's all right, darling, Mummin's here.'

It was the hardest thing she had ever done, to stand still and watch them. To watch Eve comfort her child. To watch his face, the momentary confusion, the stiffening in Eve's arms before he pressed his face against her.

She loved him, at least. Eve loved him. There could be no doubt about that. He was safe with her.

But oh! How her body and heart and soul ached for him, how she ached to hold him, to give him the mother's comfort he instinctively knew Eve wasn't supplying, even while not quite knowing what it was that was lacking.

She ached with love for him, and with hatred for Eve.

And in a rush, a series of images from their childhood flashed across her mind.

Evie, rocking Sarah in the old hammock at home, pushing too hard and too high so that it almost looped-the-loop and tipped Sarah out, all the time shouting, 'Promise!' – what, Sarah couldn't now remember – until Sarah would have promised her life away to make it stop.

Evie, taking a hammer to Sarah's old tea caddy, her box of treasures, because Sarah wouldn't give her the key. The wood splintering while Sarah sobbed.

The two of them as kids in Achnaclach, on the first day of the glorious two weeks in summer they used to spend with Grannie. In those days, local families had still lived in a lot of the cottages, most of them with children, but Evie, her hand resting warm on the back of Sarah's neck, had guided her on past a group of children at the harbour, although Sarah had longed to stop and join in their game, which had seemed to involve jumping off the quay into the water. It had looked like so much fun, but it was too dangerous, Evie had said.

And then a much more recent memory: Eve, her hand over Oliver's to show him how to play *nicely* with Dubby the yellow dumper truck.

Was Eve, in private with him, as controlling as she'd always been with Sarah? It was more than likely. She might love Oliver, she might never knowingly hurt him, but there were ways and ways of hurting someone. Damaging them in ways that no one could see. Damage that left no scars. Damage so subtle that you might not even know it had happened to you until one day the monster, the whipped beast crouched at the back of your head, reared up and pounced.

11

S he couldn't get out of the taxi. The fucking sedative was having zero effect. Every time she plucked up the courage to make a move, something stopped her opening the door. She just sat there shaking and staring out at Golspie Health Centre. From the front, it looked like a dormer bungalow, with dark green windows and guttering, and had a backdrop of school playing fields and trees and a gently rising field.

There was nothing to be afraid of in there.

Nothing was going to happen except that she was going to chat to Dr Sutherland ('Dr Sutherland, who lives in Sutherland!' Evie used to laugh) about her medical records. No big deal. See the records, come back to the taxi, get taken home.

Lewis wouldn't be in there because Tuesday was his day at the cottage hospital, where he carried out minor surgical procedures like removing warts.

She had both phones in her bag. She had a small bottle of water for one of the coping strategies Dr Laghari had taught her. But she wasn't wearing anything of Eve's because that was more likely to make her want to claw her skin off than be any sort of comfort. And, of course, Eve wasn't here.

Of course she wasn't.

The thought, and the little spurt of anger that came with it, gave her the strength she needed to open the door and get out.

Hanging onto the door: 'You'll wait for me, won't you?' she asked the driver for maybe the third time.

A nod.

That wasn't enough.

'Will you wait?' she almost shouted.

'Aye,' he muttered.

She shut the door and started walking, taking long, steadying breaths. Okay, so her legs were shaking, and at any moment she felt it was entirely possible she'd crash to the tarmac in a faint, but she managed it – she managed to walk to the door of the health centre.

She was ten minutes early for her appointment.

But all day she'd felt like she was racing the clock. She'd been up before it was light to tackle the nursery, bagging up the stripped wallpaper, hoovering like a demon, then pushing the furniture to one end of the room and setting up a trestle table for pasting the lining paper. She'd remembered there being maybe six or seven rolls of lining paper in the storeroom, but had only been able to find four – the rest must have been used by Eve. Four was more than enough for the small area of wall she needed to tackle, though – one whole wall was window and another was fitted wardrobe. She'd managed to get one half of the room papered. This afternoon she'd do the other half, then apply the beige paint she'd found in the storeroom, presumably left there by Eve. It wasn't a full tin, but should be just about enough to do the whole room.

The white mist descended as she entered the lobby, and she had to glug most of the water in the little bottle to fight it off, to banish the grey spots that threatened her vision. She managed to walk to the desk and check in with the receptionist, and attempt a normal smile. She was wearing her confidence outfit, a tailored dark chocolate trouser suit that had cost over four hundred pounds, a floral Liberty scarf and dark-red heels, and she'd spent ages going at her hair with the curling tongs. She was pretty sure she didn't look like a madwoman.

She took a seat in the waiting area and grabbed a magazine she knew she wouldn't be able to read. Her brain was going haywire, jumping from one thought to the next, and her whole body was reacting like she was running a race, her lungs desperate for air, her back slick with sweat under the cashmere jersey that had *so* been the wrong choice.

It was boiling hot in here.

Was it? Or was it just her?

She took a gulp of precious water from the bottle she was clutching. And then a small, slower sip. One of Dr Laghari's calming strategies was to sip water, and concentrate on each part of the process – putting the bottle to your lips, taking the water into your mouth, feeling it there on your tongue, swallowing it, imagining the cooling, soothing liquid travelling right down inside you...

'Sarah Booth,' said a voice, thank God, and now Dr Sutherland was smiling at her and remarking on the unseasonably warm weather they were having for March, although that had been quite a spell of snow a few days ago, hadn't it? She was close to retirement, Sarah guessed, in her early to mid-sixties, grey hair cut sensibly short.

'It is warm in here,' Sarah got out.

Dr Sutherland's office looked out on the car park. Sarah could see the taxi driver, sitting in the taxi with a newspaper and a chocolate bar. He was a dour sort of a man, but that was fine. She couldn't have made small talk on the journey here if her life had depended on it.

'... all digitised now in EPRs – electronic patient records,' Dr

Sutherland was saying, swinging the screen round so that Sarah could see. 'Everything that was on paper has been scanned in. So here are your notes from when you were a child. They're quite difficult to read in places.' She moved the keyboard round. 'You can zoom in here.'

This wasn't what she was interested in, of course, but Sarah pretended to read. She recognised old Dr Ashmead's crabby handwriting. He'd been a doddery old man with big nicotine-stained fingers, and she and Evie had hated him.

'You've troubled the medical profession remarkably little, in terms of physical problems,' said Dr Sutherland. 'Only the usual childhood illnesses and a broken arm. And a gash that needed stitching.'

Sarah remembered Dr Ashmead's shaky old hand stitching the cut on her leg while Evie chattered throughout to distract her and Mum stared off.

Eve. She could get through this by thinking of Eve. By getting angry.

'Yeah, but I've kind of made up for that by being a nutter,' she rapped out.

A pause. And then: 'A mental health issue is nothing to be ashamed of, Sarah.'

Sarah sat back from the screen and looked at her, this no-nonsense woman in the smart M&S blouse and trousers for whom everything in life had probably been a breeze. 'I know it's not – but why would you say that, unless you actually think the opposite?'

These old-school docs, in her experience, were often in the pull-yourself-together camp. But she shouldn't have said that. She needed her help.

'No, Sarah, I don't think that at all,' said Dr Sutherland, distinctly frostily.

Damn.

She and Evie used to have a code word – 'mumble' – for

such situations, to be used by Evie if she deemed what Sarah was saying, or was about to say, to be inappropriate. When they were teenagers, there'd been this girl Callie in another class who'd had blonde streaks in her hair and freakishly shaped eyebrows – *really* freakishly shaped, pathologically freakishly shaped, with big extra hairy bits over the middle of them. She'd looked like a permanently surprised badger. Whenever they were about to encounter Callie, walking along the corridor or in the school grounds, Evie would say, 'Stop *mumbling*, Sarah,' just in case Sarah was thinking about making another helpful suggestion about tweezers.

'Can I see the stuff for 2016 and 2017?' Sarah asked. Sweat was running down her spine. Why was it always so hot in these places? She needed to get this over quickly before she passed out or something.

Dr Sutherland reclaimed the keyboard and screen to scroll down to the relevant part of the records, and then turned the screen back round. 'Here's 2016.'

That was the year of the bad episode, of the random toilet man incident when Oliver had been conceived. At the end of 2016 and into 2017, Lewis had monitored her during her pregnancy – always at home, because her agoraphobia had precluded attendance at the health centre.

Sarah quickly scanned the notes for 2016. The 'psychotic episode' was described – Sarah hated that term, *psychotic*, which was used by the medical profession to describe a mental disorder where the patient had lost touch with reality, but which everyone else associated with dangerous psychopaths. The suspicion that the episode had been precipitated by antidepressants was noted. But there was no record here of a pregnancy at all. She scrolled down to July 2017.

No record of the home birth.

She couldn't breathe. The tightness in her chest was stopping her lungs from inflating...

'I feel – a bit weird,' she gasped, pushing herself up from the chair. 'I'm sorry, I need to go outside for a second.'

Standing on the area of grass behind the building, looking at the calming view – it *was* a calming view, wasn't it? – of trees and fields, she chugged the last of the water and pulled in gulps of unseasonably mild air.

Lewis had wiped it all. All the stuff about her pregnancy, the birth...

On the way back to Dr Sutherland's room, she detoured into the loo and refilled the water bottle. Just the sight of the full bottle in her hand was somehow reassuring, and she was able to march back into the room and sit, to apologise briskly, to resume reading through the records.

There were details about her previous stay in hospital provided by Dr Laghari's predecessor at Marnoch Brae, a humourless woman Sarah hadn't liked nearly as much. And notes from Fiona Cameron at Raigmore, the consultant she'd had video chats with. They described Sarah's recurrent delusion that her twin sister Evie's son James was her own child, whom she'd named 'Oliver'. The delusion was sometimes fleeting, lasting only a moment, but at other times could last a day or more. Sarah was, the consultant noted, cooperative and 'willing to engage' in strategies to recognise warning signs and try to prevent the onset of delusional thoughts.

Those notes were a complete fabrication.

'I'd like to speak to Ms Cameron, if that's possible,' Sarah said.

'Ah, I don't think she's at Raigmore now. But I can refer you to another consultant there if –'

'No,' she said, rudely. 'It has to be her. Where is she working now?'

'I really don't know. I can't refer you to Ms Cameron, but –'

How convenient.

'Okay.'

Was Dr Sutherland somehow part of it? Was she covering for Lewis? It wasn't easy to attract young doctors to practices in remote areas, so keeping Lewis here would presumably be a priority, whatever he'd done.

Lewis must have added the stuff about her 'Oliver' delusion to her EPR, somehow also logging in as Fiona Cameron to fake the consultant's notes, and deleted all the parts detailing her pregnancy and Oliver's birth. And in Oliver's records, he'd probably changed the patient's name to James.

'Is it possible to tell whether records have been altered?'

Dr Sutherland blinked. '*Altered?*'

She couldn't do this much longer. She had to get what she needed out of this awful woman and go. She needed to *go.* 'At a later date,' she snapped. 'Whether someone's gone in and changed them. I think I'm probably entitled to know that. There's probably freedom of information legislation covering this kind of situation.'

'Yes,' Dr Sutherland said grimly.

Sarah waited, not bothering to hide her impatience.

'There's what we call an audit trail, which shows the date on which any changes were made and whom they were made by.' She explained that the original records were still available to view even if a change had been made. 'Let me show you an example from my own records.' She tapped on the keyboard and looked over her reading glasses at the screen. 'I had a small operation in June of 2018, but the date of my hospital admission was entered incorrectly as July for some reason, and had to be changed later. As you can see, the audit trail shows that a change was made by my GP. And there's the date the change was made. And we have the option to look at the original record, which shows the original entry with the incorrect date of admission.'

'Yes, I understand.' Sarah took a breath. 'But my own records –'

'If we go back to your own EPR and go into the audit trail...
You can see there are no such changes to your records at all.
They're actually quite rare. There's no reason to go back and
change anything unless an error has been made.'

Oh God. Did that mean that Lewis had somehow hacked
into the audit trail system?

But if he'd done that, how would she ever prove it?

12

H er phone buzzed when she was up the stepladder
with a small brush in the 'spare room', touching up
the areas she'd missed. She descended and set the
brush down on a piece of newspaper before taking the phone
from her pocket and turning off the radio.

'Hey sissy,' said Evie's – *Eve's* – voice in her ear. 'I'm just
outside. I've been ringing the bell – did you not hear me?'

'I'm in the loo. Give me five minutes.'

Sarah shoved the brush, newspaper and stepladder into the
wardrobe, pulled the furniture back into position, and flew to
her bedroom. She pulled off her painting gear – a holey T-shirt
and old jeans – and selected thick black tights, a denim dress
and boots.

'Hi, sorry!' she gushed at Eve as she unlocked the door.

No Oliver today.

Eve came into the cloister. The breeze had whipped colour
into her cheeks, and her blue eyes were shining. It was a physical effort, to look her in the face; a physical shock, to see her
own face mirrored back at her, this face that belonged not to
Evie but to Eve, a stranger she didn't even know. Her thoughts

began to race, her heart pound, her lungs labour... the telltale early warning signs of a panic attack.

As she fought it, as she smiled at Eve and racked her brain for something to say, the irony wasn't lost on her – the presence of Eve precipitating a panic attack, when once it had been able to stop the symptoms in their tracks.

How close they had always been. How they had depended on each other. Well, Sarah had depended on Evie. But she thought Evie had also leant on her, in her own way, especially in those early London years, when Evie would come back from a night out and maybe something upsetting had happened, she'd fallen out with a friend, or her boyfriend had said something unforgivable, and the two of them would sit up into the early hours, rehashing and dissecting and mulling over what had happened, and planning a course of action.

It hadn't been a one-way street.

'This was sticking out of your postbox,' said Eve.

'Thanks.' It was an Edinburgh postmark – must be James's birth certificate. She pushed it into one of the big pockets of her dress.

'What's that on your face?' In the shadowed cloister, Evie – *Eve* squinted at her.

'Hmm?'

'There.' Eve's finger touched her cheek.

Sarah swatted the hand away and rubbed at the place. 'Probably a spot.' She knew it would be paint. Damn. She turned away and strode across the mosaic, the shortest route to the door, trying to control her breathing. Her back to Eve, she licked a finger and rubbed again at the place. Sure enough, her finger came away with a light smudge of paint on it. She hurried inside. 'Go through – I'm just going to fumigate the loo!'

In the bathroom, she pulled the blind up and opened the window and stood for a while, looking out at the sun on the knot garden and holding her breath. When she'd beaten back the panic attack, she glanced in the mirror to check that the paint smudge had gone.

Then she took the envelope from her pocket and ripped it open.

According to the National Records of Scotland, James Patrick Booth had been born on the 10th of July 2017 to Eve Frances Elizabeth Booth. It all seemed to be in order, with no later amendments. There was no father's name, as, conveniently, Eve was claiming to have conceived the child using a sperm donor, and of course donor names were never recorded on birth certificates.

Eve had registered Oliver's birth because Sarah couldn't.

Or so she had said.

In reality, she must have registered the birth of her own fictional son James. So even at that very early stage, right after Oliver had been born, Evie – *Eve* – had been planning to steal him. It hadn't been a case of Eve falling in love with Oliver and pretending to herself that he was hers, and the pretence getting out of hand, Eve telling people he was her son James... No. She had planned it from the day Oliver was born.

Her hand tightened on the paper.

All that planning... The cold calculation required...

She sat down on the loo, and dropped her face into her hands.

'Hey, Rah-Bee?' came a voice from the corridor. 'That's Lewis on the phone. He's in the garden centre, and apparently there are some box balls on special offer. He's wondering if you'd like some – you wanted some more for the knot garden, yes?' Her voice faded as she walked away. 'I'm just going to have a look and check what sizes would be good.'

Sarah jumped up and wrenched open the door.

But Eve wasn't in sight.

She ran down the corridor, almost skidding round the

corner, just in time to see Eve opening the door to the spare room. She had her phone to her ear, and rolled her eyes at Sarah with a smile. 'Yeah, just hold on,' she said into the phone. 'I'm just going to have a squiz at the garden now.'

What could Sarah say? There was no good reason to stop Eve going in there.

She followed her into the room. Still chatting to Lewis, Eve walked past the end of the bed to the floor-to-ceiling window that looked out on the knot garden.

The room smelt of paint. Didn't it? And the bed was squint! And the radio was sitting on the chest of drawers!

But Eve was staring out at the garden, telling Lewis to go for the 40 cm box balls rather than 30 cm. She turned to Sarah. 'How many do you think? Just four for the corners, or eight, so you could pair them either side of the end of the paths?'

'Four would be fine.'

'Yeah, we don't want to go mad!' Eve grinned. 'Just four, Lewis, thanks! Nice ones, mind. Okay... Okay, see you in a bit.' She ended the call.

Before her attention could wander from the garden to the room, Sarah put a hand to the end of the bed and sat down heavily, pushing it back straight against the wall as she did so.

'I feel a bit *bleh*.'

'Rah!' Eve sat down next to her and put an arm round her shoulders. 'What's the matter?'

'Could have been the two-weeks-past-its-sell-by-date fish pie I had for lunch.' She got up again and walked out of the room, so Eve, of course, had to follow.

She hadn't noticed anything, had she?

In the bathroom, Sarah held a damp facecloth to her forehead. 'I'll be fine after a lie-down.'

'Okay, Rah-Bee.' Eve rubbed her back. 'You have a lie-down. I'll chill here till Lewis arrives, then I'll go. Do you want anything?'

'No thanks.'

'Lemonade?'

'No.'

'Paracetamol?'

'I said *no*! I don't want anything!' *Not from you. Not ever again.*

'Okay, okay.'

'Sorry.'

Eve was looking at her narrowly.

She was going to have to be careful. Keeping anything from Evie had always been a nightmare – one twin seemed to know what the other was thinking almost at the same time as the thought popped into her own head.

'I'll be fine after a sleep.'

Eve hugged her. 'Poor Pooh-Bee. Okay. You go and sleep.'

Pooh-Bee. It was ridiculous, the infantile twin-speak they still used. Sarah found herself in sympathy, for the first time, with their father's fury when he'd overheard them still using it in their early twenties one Easter holiday. 'You are no longer five years old!' he'd thundered at them. 'Anyone hearing you would think you halfwits!'

'The Bible teaches us tolerance, doesn't it, Dad?' Sarah had countered.

'Actually, no,' Evie had said, for once letting rip. 'I don't think the Old Testament, in particular, can be said to be big on that. Not with all that smiting.'

Sarah had run with it. 'Yeah, but let's be fair. Halfwits are welcomed into the church with open arms. It's practically a requirement for membership.'

That had earned them banishment from the house; they'd had to get the bus back to London, to their student digs, that afternoon.

But Dad had been right: the childish twin-speak was cringy.

Sarah made herself smile; made herself not flinch away. 'Thanks, Eve.'

'*Eve!*' Eve chortled. 'We're very formal, all of a sudden!'

Sarah grimaced. 'I can hardly get my words out.'

'You certainly don't look too good.'

'Thanks.'

'See you on the other side. Sweet dreams, sweet sis.'

Sarah got her laptop from the study and holed up in her room with the blinds shut. Eve was suspicious; she was sure of it. She might not have noticed anything amiss about the spare room, but she was suspicious. Sarah wouldn't put it past her to come bursting into the bedroom to check up on what she was doing. So she lay propped on one elbow on the bed, back to the door, laptop open on the covers next to her. She stared at the Google screen, but couldn't focus on what she needed to do for thinking about Oliver.

Eve had presumably left him with Margaret. Was he even safe with that old woman? Was she up to looking after a small child?

How dare Eve accuse *Sarah* of putting him at risk, that time at the castle?

She wanted to run to the village. Snatch Oliver. Just *go*. But where? The police would catch up with her and she'd be sectioned again.

She had to find the evidence she needed to prove that Oliver was her son; to have Oliver returned to her by the authorities.

She typed: 'child's identity doubt evidence' and clicked on a few results, mainly reports of court cases where a woman was trying to get child support and first had to prove paternity.

It all seemed to come down to DNA.

That didn't help her, of course, because she and Eve had virtually identical DNA. Yes, there might be a few tiny differences, but any maternity test was unlikely to pick them up.

But what if she could get a DNA sample from Oliver's father? That would prove that Sarah must be his mother, because how likely was it that the man she'd had sex with in an Inverness pub toilet happened to be the sperm donor who'd fertilised Eve's eggs? Find Random Toilet Man, get him to supply a DNA sample, and she'd have the evidence she needed to prove, categorically, that Oliver was her child.

You couldn't argue with DNA.

It was simple enough to find a company offering paternity tests. She ordered a DNA testing kit for £99. It seemed all you needed was a sample from the child and one from the putative father – a swab of cells from the inside of the cheek. You then sent the samples off to the lab and they compared them and emailed you the results.

The problem was that she didn't even know Random Toilet Man's name, let alone his address. But she remembered what he looked like – tall, sandy-haired, stubbly, with eyes that were quite close together. He was probably in his mid-forties. And she seemed to remember that he was a carpenter, subcontracted to work on various building projects in Inverness. Or had she imagined that?

She tried Googling 'carpenter Inverness building sites' and got a list of joinery and carpentry businesses in and around Inverness, but, frustratingly, none of the websites featured photographs of the carpenters in question. She had a bit more luck when she looked under Images, but none of the grinning men in T-shirts was Random Toilet Man.

She shut the laptop.

And she must have dozed a little, because when something woke her it was dark in the room, just a faint light filtering through the blinds from the corridor across the garden that led into the other part of the house.

She got up and slipped on her moccasins.

When she reached the corridor, she could hear voices in the

living room. Lewis and Eve. She padded closer to the half-open door.

'... seems to be on a short fuse,' Eve was saying.

Three guesses who she was speaking about.

'I'd better check she hasn't stopped taking the medication again. That might be the issue.'

'Yeah.' A sigh. 'I don't know... I'm not sure she's actually accepted that James is James.'

'Has she said anything?'

'She's made a mistake, once or twice, and called him Oliver.'

'Hmm. Bound to happen.'

'I guess.'

Silence for a bit. Then Lewis again: 'I'd better be off, then.'

'How much do we owe you for the box balls?'

They moved out of Sarah's hearing. She scooted back to bed, and eventually she heard the door slowly open. She turned over sleepily, and Eve perched on the bed, and reached to push Sarah's hair off her face, crooning softly: '*Now the day is over...*'

Sarah sat up, away from her.

'Feeling better now, my silly old mouldy-fish-eating Pooh-Bee?'

Sarah smiled. 'A bit better, Vee. Listen, I forgot to ask you. Do you have a free day this week?'

'I could have. Why?'

'I had Jenny Anderson on the phone today, asking how we're getting on with the design.' A complete lie.

Eve made a face. This was one of the clients she'd had to stall while Sarah had been in hospital.

'I fobbed her off, but I'm thinking we'd better get the cladding choice finalised. Would it be possible for you to go down to Edinburgh and suss that out?' This new cladding system, designed to look like traditional butt and board but meeting all the new insulation requirements, was made in

Norway, but there was an outlet near Edinburgh they'd been in contact with. They really needed to see the stuff, handle it, talk to those guys, before making a decision.

'Yeah, could do, if it's urgent.'

Sarah grimaced. 'It kind of is. But what about James?'

'I'll take him with me.'

'It's a long journey for him.' And before she could stop herself she was saying, 'You could leave him here with me.'

The lure of the chance of a whole day alone with Oliver was too much to resist, never mind that it would completely scupper her own plans for the day. Plans that were vital for his future well-being.

What was she thinking?

But: 'No, it's okay,' Eve said. 'He'll be fine. He'll probably sleep most of the way.'

And it hit Sarah, all at once: it wasn't that Eve didn't trust her with Oliver. That nonsense about endangering him at the castle was just a smokescreen. The real problem with Sarah spending too much time with him was that their connection was re-establishing itself. Something instinctual in Oliver – poor, confused little Oliver – knew that Sarah was his mother. Eve was keeping them apart as much as possible to limit their opportunities to bond, because she knew that what she was up against was a force that swept all before it, a force against which all Eve's clever schemes and plots and stratagems would count for nothing if Sarah could harness it.

The most powerful force on Earth.

A mother's love for her child.

13

Oh God oh God oh God.

She couldn't do this. There were just too many people, too much happening, kids dashing in front of her on the platform so she had to stop suddenly, people shouting and pushing past – And she was too hot, she was sweltering in her long, very fitted pale-raspberry padded coat. The weather had turned even milder, but she needed this coat, she needed the tightness and the warmth of it; it comforted her in the same way, she supposed, that babies were comforted and soothed by being tightly swaddled. It was like walking around inside a big hug.

She managed to get onto the train and shut herself in the toilet.

She needed Evie.

She couldn't do this without Evie.

Of course she could. Evie wasn't Evie, she was *Eve*, and she was the reason Sarah was here, standing here in this weird little toilet with the metal loo, in the middle of a train with maybe a hundred or more people on it.

She sat down, fully clothed, and put her head on her knees, her arms round herself, until her heart stopped bumping.

What if she had a heart attack in here? What if she died? What would happen to Oliver? No one but Sarah knew who he really was. He would grow up, his whole life, not knowing, and at Eve's mercy.

Breathe, breathe, breathe.

There was some sort of tinny announcement being made out there, but she couldn't hear it. What if it was something important, like the train had to be evacuated because there was a fire? But they'd check the toilets, wouldn't they, in that case? Surely?

She sat still, senses straining to catch a clue as to what was happening, but then she heard a raucous braying of laughter. People wouldn't be laughing if the train was on fire, would they?

She had planned this trip meticulously. She'd booked a taxi with the same firm and requested the driver who'd taken her to the health centre, smiling when the woman at the other end of the phone said, 'Jimmy? You *want* Jimmy?' Not quite able to disguise her surprise.

But Jimmy suited her fine.

Sometimes a lack of social skills was a definite plus. They had exchanged not a single word throughout their interaction, apart from at the end, when Sarah had paid him and asked him to confirm that he would meet the 15:35 train from Inverness that afternoon.

'Aye,' he'd managed.

She'd planned every step of the journey, but if she couldn't hold it together, if she couldn't even get to Inverness...

But the train was moving. It was too late to change her mind and get off.

· · ·

As she approached the taxi rank at Inverness station, she went through the steps of Dr Laghari's *What's the worst that can happen* coping mechanism. The worst that could happen was that she fainted and the driver had to take her to hospital. Not a big deal. Or she might have to ask him to take her somewhere quiet and peaceful, maybe a park, and wait for her as she took a walk, sat on a bench by a pond or something. Not a big deal either.

And she had her water. She took a little sip, held it in her mouth, then let the cool liquid slip down her throat. And she opened her bag and checked that both phones were still there, and closed her fist around the packet containing the testing kit, to remind herself why she was doing this.

She selected a taxi with a driver who looked like Jimmy – big and dour with a fat belly – and told him, truthfully enough, that she was looking for a tradesman she knew was working on a building site in Inverness, but she didn't know which one. She had printed out the addresses of the building sites in Inverness she'd managed to find with a bit of Googling. She gave this list to the driver.

'If you know of any others, we could try them too?'

'Aye, you could try the development up on Glenurquhart Road. That's good-quality houses that're being built there, you know? If your man's a good 'un, he might be there. My pal's wife, she works in construction, and she says...'

It looked like the resemblance to Jimmy was purely superficial.

She said, 'That'd be great' and 'Oh, right' at intervals, while begging him silently to *just shut up.*

The first building site was on a road that contained mainly bungalows. There were lots of trees and gardens full of greenery, and the traffic wasn't crazy. The building – a block of flats? – was at foundation stage, so there wouldn't be any carpenters on site yet, but it would be worth asking nevertheless.

She got out onto the dusty pavement. White clouds scudded over her head in a sky that was more like a summer than a spring one, bright and breezy. She took a long breath and fumbled in her bag for her sketch. She'd always been good at drawing. The pencil sketch was, she hoped, an accurate likeness of the toilet man.

She would have to stop thinking of him as that. He was Oliver's father, after all.

There was a labourer shovelling sand into a barrow behind the fencing panels.

'Hi,' she called through the grille of the fencing. 'I wonder if I could ask you something? It's a bit of a strange one.'

The man – well, he wasn't much more than a boy – looked at her suspiciously.

She waved the sketch at him with what she hoped was a cheery smile. Her heart was bumping away, and her mouth felt sticky and dry. What if he attacked her?

Why on earth would he attack her?

She took a quick sip of water.

He came to the fence, and she held up the sketch. 'I'm looking for this man. He's a carpenter.' And she trotted out the story that had seemed reasonable at four o'clock in the morning when she'd been planning what she'd say, but now seemed ridiculous. 'He did some work for my friend, subcontracted to her builder, and he was really brilliant and I'd like him to do some work for me, but she's fallen out with the builder and doesn't know the carpenter's name, only that he does a lot of work for builders in Inverness. So I was hoping... Do you recognise him?'

He looked from her to the sketch, naked disbelief on his face. 'No.'

'Okay. Thanks anyway.'

She dived back into the taxi. She would have to think of a better story.

The next place they tried was deserted. At the next, a much larger development, an expansion of a new housing estate, there was a site office, a portacabin. As she was fighting a panic attack outside, a burly man clomped past her in big work boots, saying in passing, 'Looking for the show house?'

'No. I'm looking – for someone – who might work here.'

He opened the door of the portacabin, pulled off his hard hat, and made a sweeping gesture with it, inviting her inside.

She really didn't want to go in there.

But she smiled, and walked past him into the overwarm fug of plaster dust and microwaved beef noodles and tea. There were three men sitting round a table having an early lunch.

Okay. She could do this. She could do this, for Oliver.

She put the sketch down on the table in front of them. 'I'm looking for – a Good Samaritan. He helped me when I – I fainted in the street. A couple of weeks ago. I'm trying to find him to thank him... He was wearing a high-vis jacket and a hard hat, so I think he must work in construction somewhere round here. Do you know him? I've tried to draw him – he didn't give me his name.'

They didn't know him, but they seemed to accept her story.

At the next site office, with an audience of the boss man and his PA, both of whom welcomed her cheerily, she was able to warm to her theme, adding the embellishment: 'He came with me in the ambulance and everything! I'm sure he must have missed a whole afternoon of work. I feel really bad that I was too out of it to thank him properly.'

They had nothing, but suggested she try another construction site a couple of streets away where there were a lot of 'chippies' on site at the moment. Here, two men were sitting outside on a wall eating, appropriately enough, chips. This time, she found she couldn't get out of the taxi, and had to speak to them through the open window. She went through her routine, adding, for the hell of it, 'I think I might have hit him – I was pretty confused.'

Another blank.

'Going to have a break and a bit of lunch?' Graham, the taxi driver, suggested. 'I can recommend a pub or two.'

Sarah hunkered down in the back seat. She had been hoping to avoid the nuclear option, but she couldn't kid herself any longer that trawling round random building sites was getting her anywhere. And so:

'Can you take me to the Crown and Thistle, please?'

Graham sucked his teeth. 'Whoa. I'm not sure it's your kind of place, Sarah.'

ANYWHERE LESS REGAL OR, indeed, Scottish than the Crown and Thistle was hard to imagine. It was an old man's pub with lots of dark varnished oak and horse brasses. Ye Olde England. Entering the place was like the opposite of all those kids' stories, *Tom's Midnight Garden* and the Narnia Chronicles and Harry Potter – far from discovering a magical world of wonder, it felt like you were leaving the nice, bright, daytime world behind to enter a grim sort of purgatory where it was always a lock-in at one o'clock on a Saturday night and everyone in the place was a drunk, a racist, a misogynist, a sexual predator, or all of the above.

Was Oliver's father a sexual predator? He had, after all, taken shameless advantage of a woman who was drunk as a skunk and obviously not in her right mind.

But had it been obvious, in fact, that she wasn't in her right mind, at that point? Possibly not.

Or was she just making excuses for the person who had contributed half of Oliver's DNA? One thing was for sure – she really wasn't looking forward to seeing him again. She stood just inside the door and touched her palms with her fingers.

What's the worst that can happen?

Another sexual predator could take advantage of her fragile condition to rape her. *Put that in your pipe and smoke it, Dr Laghari.* What on earth would he say if he could see her now?

A fortifying little bubble of laughter rose in her throat, and one of the three short, round men sitting on stools at the bar looked up at her.

'You gonna share the joke, then, love?' It was a Cockney accent.

Eve said she'd been surprised, at first, to find that so many of the voices you heard up here were English. But she'd soon realised that part of the explanation was that the English were disproportionately represented in the more vocal subset of the population.

Jimmy the Taxi was typical of your average Scot, Sarah supposed. Possibly he was a real live wire at home and with his friends, and it was just that public displays of exuberance, or 'showing off' as Grannie would have said, marked you out to your fellow Scots as a pain in the arse.

I must tell Evie that little nugget of wisdom, Sarah thought, before remembering. Evie, the Evie she'd thought she'd known, didn't exist. She had no one, now, to tell these things to.

'I bet *she's* got a punch line worth hearing,' muttered Mr Cockney in a stage whisper.

The other two men on the barstools chuckled, shooting her raking glances.

Oh God.

The Three Little Sexist Pigs.

Wishing that she was wearing a coat that wasn't quite so tight, Sarah handed round the sketch and gave them a variation of her shaggy-dog story, this time including the information that she was sure he'd said this was his regular. The Third Little Sexist Pig put out a hand, wordlessly, for the sketch.

'Aye,' was all he'd said – or perhaps it was all he was going to say, being Scottish – when a man materialised behind the bar and pointed an aggressive and extremely large finger at Sarah.

He was an extremely large man.

And horribly familiar. A memory leapt to the front of her brain: of lying with her face pressed to the damp, malodorous carpet, of this man sitting on her back, supposedly restraining her, and feeling his hand, suddenly, between her legs.

'That's a load of shite,' he bellowed at her. 'Fainting in the street? More like passing out blattered out your fucking skull! You're Andy's fucking stalker!'

Andy. Andrew. That was Oliver's father's name.

'I'm not a stalker,' she squeaked.

'Last time you showed your face in here you caused eight thousand quid's worth of damage and scared the bloody punters witless. You're fucking barred!'

She took a breath. 'I'm sorry. I was mentally ill at the time.' She had nothing to lose, now, from telling the truth, and bringing an innocent child into the mix might garner her some much-needed sympathy. 'I need to find Andy to tell him... To tell him that he's got a son. I conceived a child that night. His name's Oliver and he's almost two years old.'

'Poor bloody kid,' muttered the Third Little Sexist Pig.

'A likely story! Get out!' yelled the barman.

'As if – I'd want – to stay in here – any longer than I have to.' Sarah could hardly push the words out for the tight blockage in her throat. But she needed to say this. 'Okay, so I caused a lot of damage – but I suffer from PTSD, and was having a delusional episode at the time. What's your excuse for taking advantage of the situation to cop a feel?'

Until then, she had wondered if it really had happened or if it had been part of the delusion, but his face, the defensive, shifty look in his eyes, gave him away.

'You're lucky I don't report you to the police for sexual

assault! Actually, I still might! These days the authorities are a lot more willing to believe victims. How do you reckon your "career" would progress with a conviction for sexual assault on your record?'

And now she had to get out of here.

What if I can't get out? What if they block the door?

Someone laughed, harshly, raucously, and she bolted for the exit, the white mist gathering, the laughter seeming unnaturally loud and close, as if it were hacking its way inside her head.

She hauled open the first door and staggered through the tiny lobby to the outer one, almost falling through it, gasping fresh air into lungs that were shrinking and shrinking...

Her legs had gone wobbly. She stopped on the pavement, a hand to the stone surround of the doorway. She could see Graham parked across the street waiting. Might she have to wave to him, to get him to come and help her?

The door opened behind her.

She wheeled round.

It was a woman, a woman with dirty blonde hair caught up in a messy cascade on top of her head. She was very heavily made up, with industrial black eyeliner and pale pink lipstick on trout-pout lips. 'Wankers,' she said. Then: 'Are you okay, there?'

Sarah nodded, heaving in air.

'I'm Mairi, by the way.'

Sarah managed to say her own name.

Mairi took a packet of cigarettes from her bag, a bag that was weirdly a bit like Lissa's, black with a gold strap, although this poor raddled woman, who was probably about fifty but looked more like seventy, couldn't have been less like Lissa.

She shook the packet at Sarah.

'No – thank – you.'

She shoved one in her mouth. It was the longest cigarette

Sarah had ever seen. 'I'm liking your work,' Mairi said round it. 'You told Billy.'

Something about the woman, an air of unflappability, as if nothing in the world could surprise or shock her, was very calming. Sarah found she could breathe, after all. She could speak. 'The barman?'

A dismissive nod as Mairi bent to her lighter.

'He really – he really did assault me.'

'Yeah, you and me both, doll, you and me both.' She inhaled and blew the smoke upwards, away from Sarah. 'Listen, Andy – he doesn't get out to play much any more, but him and his wife Steph, they're in here maybe one Saturday in two for a bar lunch. Haven't been the last couple of weeks, so chances are they'll be this Saturday? About one-ish?' Mairi narrowed her eyes at Sarah. 'You sure you're okay?'

'Yes. Thank you. That's – thank you for telling me.'

'He's an okay guy. Not like those wankers in there.'

Sarah exhaled, as if she too were a smoker. She'd known he would be. Oliver's father couldn't be a bad person. 'He's married?'

Mairi, looking off as the breeze whipped the smoke away, twisted her mouth in a world-weary grimace. 'I just said he's an okay guy – of course he's married.'

'Do they have kids?'

'Two. Boy and a girl.'

Oliver's half-brother and half-sister.

This was beyond weird.

'Thanks, Mairi. Thanks very much. I really appreciate it.'

Mairi waved off her thanks with the huge cigarette.

As she scuttled across the road to the taxi, as Graham folded his newspaper and gave her a thumbs-up, as she sank into the slightly mouldy-smelling upholstery, she shrank from the prospect of having to do this all over again – and on a Saturday, when the trains and the streets would no doubt be heaving with shoppers and teenage gangs and kids.

And then having to ask Andy, maybe in front of his wife, for a DNA sample to prove that he was the father of her child –

She dug her nails into her palms and leant forward. 'Are you working this Saturday?'

14

S arah was wearing a fleece and had pulled her hair back into a ponytail. It felt weird to have her face and neck exposed – she always wore her hair down. And she had no make-up on, apart from a dusting of blusher to try to emulate Eve's healthy glow.

She gave the bathroom mirror a perky Eve smile. It was going to be fine. It was going to be a breeze.

They had often swapped identities when they were kids. Once Evie had stood in for Sarah in a debate in front of the whole class. The real Sarah had sat in the audience, mortified, while Evie's version of her had stood pontificating in a voice by turns strident and barely audible. Did Sarah really sound like that?

Then there had been the time Sarah had been coming back from the village shop with vegetables for Mum, and had met Lissa, zooming along on a glittery scooter.

'Hi Evie!'

Usually it was Evie who went to the shop.

Sarah had played along. 'Hi,' she had greeted her, making her voice *lighter and brighter*, as Mrs Hayward the music teacher had once described Evie's voice in relation to Sarah's, before hurriedly making amends by saying Sarah's had more *gravitas*.

'Do you want to come to the Cotswold Wildlife Park on Saturday? Mum and Dad say I can bring a friend and I'd like you to come.'

'Can Sarah come too?'

'No. It's expensive, so it's got to be just you.'

'So why me and not Sarah?'

Lissa had shrugged. 'I really like Sarah, but I think you and me have got more in common.'

Sarah had fumed inwardly. Lissa liked Evie better, because Evie had sabotaged any chance of Sarah making proper friends with her. The rule was that Sarah wasn't allowed to play with Lissa unless Evie was there, but the opposite didn't apply.

'Please say yes! We're taking a picnic and everything.'

'I'd love that! Thank you, Lissa!'

So 'Evie' had gone with the Edwardses to ooh and ahh at the lions and the giraffes, and pet the llamas. She'd told Evie that Lissa had just invited Sarah, and Evie had *not* been happy about that. 'But you can't go without me!' she'd objected.

Sarah had, for once, stood her ground. 'But you're not invited, and Mum says I can go.'

All that day, the injustice of Evie's Lissa rule had gnawed away at her as she and Lissa had such a great time pressing their noses to the car windows to get a better look at all the amazing safari animals and clutching each other in the reptile house when a crocodile started staring at them 'Like we're on the lunch menu!' as Lissa had squealed.

'Evie' had waited until the end of the day, when they were driving home and Mr and Mrs Edwards were listening to country music turned up loud. She'd said to Lissa, 'Today's been really good. You know your mum was asking what was our favourite thing, and I said the rhinos? That wasn't *quiiiite* true.'

Lissa had raised her eyebrows, probably thinking a joke was coming, from the way 'Evie' was smiling at her.

'Because the funniest animal in the zoo was *you*. You are *thick as shit*, Lissa. I know we shouldn't mock the afflicted, but you are *sooo* funny you should be kept in a zoo for people to come and see.'

Lissa had blinked, her face falling comically into an expression of shock.

'Yeah. I mean, who doesn't know the difference between an antelope and a *fucking deer?*' And 'Evie' had laughed her tinkling laugh, and Mrs Edwards in the front seat had twisted round and smiled at them and asked if they'd like a lemon sherbet.

'Yes, please, Mrs Edwards.'

As Lissa had blinked back tears, Sarah had felt really bad. Poor Lissa! But at the same time, she'd been elated. For once, she'd thought, she had won. She'd got one up on Evie. No way was Lissa going to want anything to do with Evie now, so Evie would have no option but to let Sarah play with Lissa on her own.

And of course Lissa had avoided Evie like the plague, but she'd avoided Sarah just as assiduously. What Sarah hadn't reckoned on was the way people tended to think of the twins as a unit. If Evie had turned out to be horrible, then so must Sarah be.

Evie had turned on Sarah when it had become clear that Lissa didn't want to be friends any more. 'What did you do?'

Sarah had shrugged, feeling, in hindsight, horribly guilty about it. 'Nothing.'

She'd felt like such a traitor. Such an idiot. But Evie never did find out about that particular swap.

And this one was going to be a breeze.

She'd had to wait a few days until she could be sure that Eve would be away for a good couple of hours at least – she was taking Oliver to another toddler's birthday party. Meanwhile, her alter ego 'Evie' had an appointment with Dr Sutherland at 12:50. Eve hardly ever went to the doctor's, so hopefully Dr Sutherland wouldn't remember her well. Sarah had booked Jimmy to pick up 'Evie Booth' at the Roman House at 12:30.

SARAH'S HEAD was aching by the time Jimmy pulled up outside Golspie Health Centre. How did Eve do it? Her throat was raw from having to keep up a constant stream of inane, one-sided chatter, and she felt spaced out, a bit like being drunk. But one welcome side effect was that she'd had to concentrate so hard that there'd been no room left in her brain for the panic that always threatened to overwhelm her when she had to leave the house.

Who knew that the best coping strategy of all was to impersonate your twin sister?

She felt good. *Really* good. But just in case she lost it in there, she had planned an 'out' – she would pretend that her phone was buzzing, that she was getting a call from her poor mentally unstable sister Sarah that she had to answer right away. And then she could bolt outside and lose it in private. But hopefully that wouldn't be necessary.

'Evie' gave Jimmy a cheery wave and bounced across the car park on her Skechers to the door of the health centre. Lewis took his lunch hour from 12:30 until 1:30 and always went for a run, so she was confident she wouldn't encounter him.

When Dr Sutherland called her in, Eve gave her a huge smile.

'I'm sorry to take up your time – I have to confess...' She plomped herself down on the chair by the desk. '... It's a twin thing! When Sarah mentioned that she'd had a look at her medical records, I immediately wanted to check mine! What am I like! Time-wasting patient from hell!'

Dr Sutherland was like a different person from the reserved, rather dull woman who'd dealt with Sarah. She was all smiles and jokes as she turned the screen and keyboard so that 'Evie' could look through her records, saying she wished there was more of this kind of time-wasting and less of the other kind, people wanting antibiotics for colds and sniffles and broken fingernails.

Eve's records, as she'd expected, had lots of details about her pregnancy – *Sarah's* pregnancy. It had been pretty much trouble-free, so there hadn't been too much pressure put on her to attend clinics and have scans. She had, though, had a bit of constipation and indigestion and suffered from cramp. This was all described in Eve's notes.

She scrolled on down.

There were scans! But how was that possible?

Lewis must have filched them from someone else's records. She peered at one of them, trying to make out the text at the top, which was probably the name and date, but the image had been truncated and only the bottom of the text was visible, impossible to read.

Clever.

'I know Sarah checked hers for amendments – have mine had any?' She laughed at the ridiculousness of the question.

Dr Sutherland raised her eyebrows. 'It was an unusual question the first time round, with your sister. You don't have to tell me, of course, but can I ask why you and your sister would want to know that?'

'Just out of interest.'

Dr Sutherland raised her eyebrows even further and turned the keyboard so she could click through to the relevant part of the records. 'No. There are no changes at all. As I told your sister, later amendments aren't common.'

What if Lewis had written up these notes, and uploaded the scans, *in real time*? What if the plot to steal Oliver dated back not just to his birth, but to when Sarah *first found out she was pregnant?*

Oh my God!

That must be what had happened. The records were never changed because they didn't have to be.

And a lot of things suddenly made sense.

The medication Eve had picked up for her from the pharmacy, for the constipation, hadn't come with the usual sticker on it, with her name and the dosage. She hadn't thought anything of it at the time, but Eve must have had to peel it off because it had *her own name* on it, not Sarah's. Because Lewis had prescribed it for *Eve*, who was supposedly pregnant.

She wanted to blurt it all out, to tell Dr Sutherland what that bastard Lewis had done. But she managed to control the urge. She was Eve, and Eve was always a model of self-control.

Breathe.

Dr Sutherland was looking at the scans now, going on about 'James' and what a lovely child he was.

Sarah's phone buzzed in her pocket.

Eve.

As if she had sensed what was happening. As if she had sensed that she must intervene.

'Sorry,' she said, looking at it. 'It's my sister – I'm going to have to take this.'

'Hi,' she said in the corridor, hurrying down it and ducking into the loo.

'Hi. Listen, Susan Mackay is here at the party and she's asking me about the extension, about the height of the windows on the east elevation. Could you have a quick squiz?'

The Mackays were the clients from hell, always changing their minds.

Sarah shut herself in a cubicle and sat down on the loo. 'Um, okay, hang on...' She clumped her feet on the floor, like she was walking across the slate tiles in the kitchen. Damn.

What height *were* those windows? She wouldn't put it past the Mackays to have asked for some weird odd measurement. She gave it another thirty seconds and then said, 'Nine hundred, floor to sill,' hoping that they'd just gone bog standard.

'That's what I thought. They're wanting them lowered, for the views. Six hundred.'

'So we'll need to look at the whole design again. And we'll need to change the spec to safety glass.'

'Yep, I've explained that'll all add to the costs, but Susan's adamant.'

'Okay, I'll play around with it.'

'Thanks, Rah-Bee. I'd better go – James looks like he's getting more cake in his hair than in his mouth!'

'Okay,' Sarah managed. 'See you later.'

'See you, sissy.'

The corridor, when she stepped out into it, was empty.

And there was Lewis's name on the door opposite.

Before she had time to think, she was trying the handle, finding the door unlocked, and slipping inside. It was a neat, personality-free space, with a pale veneered desk and counter along one wall, and royal blue upholstered chairs. No ethnic knickknacks in sight. But on the wall behind the desk, as in Dr Sutherland's office, was an array of certificates. Quickly, she used her phone to take pictures of them all. Maybe they were fake. Maybe he was one of those conmen who pretended they were doctors and got away with it for years. Maybe he went to medical school but got chucked out, never qualified, and Eve had found out and was blackmailing him.

She could check with whoever had supposedly issued these certificates – the General Medical Council – that he really was qualified.

Back with Dr Sutherland, she apologised and asked if she could have 'a quick squiz' at James's records. As Dr Sutherland scrolled through them and Sarah looked over her shoulder, at all the height and weight measurements, the details of vaccinations, the notes about earache and rashes and colds, she imagined Eve in here with Oliver, pretending he was her own son. And who was there to contradict her? Sarah was conveniently shut away in the Roman House, seeing no one, going nowhere apart from an occasional brief walk along the coast. If Eve told everyone that she was pregnant, maybe wore a false baby bump... If she told everyone that the baby she subsequently took out and about on walks through the village and along the coastal path, to the baby and toddler group, to his appointments here was her own child James, who was to know any different?

This wasn't just a case of altering a few records. Eve must have lived and breathed the deception for months before Oliver was even born and for all those months afterwards.

All those times when Sarah had willingly handed Oliver over to Eve, so grateful that she had her sister to do the things she couldn't for him... All those times she'd been glad of the respite, relaxing with a herbal tea and trashy TV, making the most of a child-free morning or afternoon, or even a whole day... Sometimes Eve would take him overnight to let her have 'a proper break'... All the times she'd wondered what on earth she'd do without Eve, Oliver's doting aunt... Little did she know that Eve was perpetrating this incredible, unthinkable, unspeakable crime against her. What worse crime was there, than to take a child?

'All right, then?' Dr Sutherland said brightly.

'Yes, that's great, that's all *fine*.' Sarah smiled perkily, getting to her feet. 'Thank you *so* much.'

15

That was him. Andy.

She was sure of it.

The man walking along the opposite pavement, hung about with bags from expensive clothes shops. There was a thin woman clipping along on heels beside him, talking on her phone.

'That's him, aye?' said Graham.

She supposed Graham must have got a look at the sketch at some point. He must know, by now, that this wasn't about building work.

'Yes.'

She needed to get out of the taxi. She needed to speak to this man, this man who was Oliver's father, but –

'Want me to come with you?'

'Yes! Thank you!' The kindness made her want to cry.

As Graham opened her door and offered her his arm, she grabbed him, she grabbed onto his golf jumper, and he helped her out as if she were a pensioner.

'I – I have agoraphobia,' she whispered.

'Aye, m'dear. But don't you worry, eh? You're safe with me.'

'Thank you.'

She had her hair in a ponytail again, and was wearing jeans, jumper and fleece in the hope that putting on the Eve persona would have the same effect as last time, but it wasn't working. Her legs felt weak and shaky as she crossed the road on Graham's arm – she should have worn her Skechers instead of the grey suede boots with a wedge heel – and she found herself unable to think, unable to remember what her plan was, what she had decided to say.

Her thoughts were skittering about and she couldn't focus her eyes either; her gaze kept jumping from the parked cars in front of the pub to the grimy windows to the crow on the roof that was pacing slowly along the ridgeline.

'Andy,' she said, finally, when they were close enough.

The man's gaze flicked from Graham to Sarah and widened. He looked behind them and back down the pavement, as if she really was his stalker, as if he was afraid of her. The woman, presumably his wife, was walking on, oblivious.

'Give me five minutes,' he hissed at her. 'Park gates.'

And he followed his wife into the pub, shoulders hunched, as if cowering away from a physical blow. Of course they'd have let him know what had happened, Billy and the Three Little Sexist Pigs. That Sarah had been in the pub asking for him, talking about a child. But Mairi couldn't have let on that she'd told Sarah he came here on a Saturday lunchtime. Her turning up was evidently a big shock.

The park at the end of the street was a tiny one, just a triangle of grass abutting a wall along one long edge and the backs of houses along the other, the short end of the triangle fenced off from the pavement by high railings. There was a meagre kids' play area with graffiti on the swings. Someone had had a go at the ride-on chick with lighter fluid, and its once bright yellow face was singed brown and melted into a one-eyed leer.

The place was, understandably, deserted.

Sarah sat on a bench while Graham retreated to a discreet distance and lit a cigarette as he contemplated the graffiti. Sarah had finished her water by the time Andy appeared, hurrying along furtively. He wasn't a bad-looking man, apart from those too-close-together eyes, which Oliver, thankfully, had not inherited. He was tall and athletic and healthy looking, and dressed smartly in designer jeans, green jumper and navy jacket.

She could have done a lot worse for a sperm donor.

'I'm not interested in having any contact with your child,' he said at once, belligerently. Billy had probably told him that attack was the best form of defence. 'How do I even know it's mine? It could be anyone's.'

It.

She stood. 'Don't worry. The last thing I want is to have you in my child's life. All I need is a swab.' She took the DNA testing kit from her bag. 'You just rub a cotton bud thing on the inside of your cheek... And sign a form... It's called a chain of custody form.' She unfolded it. 'And I need your name and address, but only so I can prove that he's... That he's your son and not someone else's.'

He backed away as if she'd just pulled a gun on him.

'No. No way.'

'It's just a tick box exercise, to prove –'

'*You* are a *fucking nutter*,' he hissed, his gaze flicking from her to Graham's substantial back.

Anger flared. 'Oh, really? It takes two to tango, as they say. I wonder what your wife would say if I went and had a little chat with her and told her why I'm here?'

'You stay away from my wife.'

'Give me a swab, and you'll never see or hear from me again.'

He narrowed his eyes. 'Do I look like an idiot? There's no

way I'm giving you a DNA sample! You come near me again and I'm calling the police, even if it does blow up in my face and my wife finds out. I'm serious. Come anywhere near me again and I'm calling the cops.'

As she watched him hurry away and out of the park, she clutched the DNA sample kit and tottered across the park to Graham. When you were a virtual recluse, when the only people you ever saw were your twin sister, a dodgy doc and a small child, you were bound to be out of practice interacting with other human beings.

She'd blown it.

'STOP!' she yelled at Jimmy as he turned off the little single-track public road, nosing the taxi through the gates at the end of the drive to the Roman House. In the shadow of the pine trees up ahead, she could see a jaunty ponytail swinging.

Eve. Pushing Oliver's buggy.

'Reverse, reverse! *Now! Quick quick quick!*'

If Eve knew she'd been out, on her own – an almost impossible feat, only to be attempted in the direst of circumstances – she'd know that Sarah was up to something. With her twin's intuition she would guess, probably, that Sarah knew the truth about Oliver and was trying to prove it.

And she didn't want to think about what Eve would do then.

In a leisurely fashion, checking his mirrors, Jimmy reversed back onto the road.

She thrust a twenty through the seats at him. 'Keep the change.'

She got out of the taxi and pulled the strap of her bag over her head, settling it across her chest. Then she jumped the drystone wall, the dyke, into the field. And she ran.

It wasn't easy going, tussocky and uneven and treacherous,

but she flew across that field, adrenaline pushing away the panic, fuelling her leg muscles; she flew over the dyke at the other side of the wood, she flew through the trees, jumping mossy hummocks and fallen logs and branches.

The house faced away from the drive, thank God; the driveway kinked round the house to the apron of gravel in front of the atrium door. And so the house would be between her and Eve, hopefully, if she'd made good enough time.

She charged out of the trees and across the gravel, pulling her hair out of the ponytail, and fumbled in her pocket for the house key.

It slipped from her fingers.

Damn damn damn!

She grabbed it up, staggered to the door, and was just pulling it open when Eve's voice said, 'Hey, Rah-Bee!'

She turned and smiled. Made a funny face at Oliver. 'Hi, Vee-Bee! Hi, gorgeous boy!'

Oliver scowled up at her and threw the toy he was carrying, a headless owl, down onto the gravel.

'Aw, poor Mr Owl!' Eve picked it up. 'As if losing his head hasn't been enough of a trauma! Be nice, James!' She parked the buggy and mouthed *tired* at Sarah, before asking, brightly, 'Where are you off to?'

Eve had assumed, then, that she was leaving rather than coming back. Good. At least that was something. 'I was going to try the coastal path.'

'In those boots?'

Sarah looked down, as if in surprise, at her soft suede boots. 'Oh God, what am I like!'

'You look like you're off to the shops! What have you got in that bag?'

A DNA testing kit.

'You're going to ruin the shape of it, cramming it full like that.'

'Yeah, but I need water and my phones –
'– and extra water and an energy bar.'
They both laughed.
'Should have taken a rucksack, shouldn't I?' Sarah mugged at Ollie. 'Silly Sarah!'
He glared at her.
'I'd offer to come with you, but someone's in need of a nap. I think we're both in need of one, to be honest. *The certain knot of peace...* No, don't worry, we'll just go back to the cottage. I think he'd probably be best in his own bed anyway.' She looked at Sarah. 'Are you sure you want to attempt that walk on your own?'

Sarah sighed. 'No, not really.' She looked down again at her boots. 'I think I might have been subconsciously sabotaging myself.'

'If the weather's reasonable tomorrow, we can do it then. I'd better get Mr Grumpy back.' Another penetrating look. 'If you're sure you're okay? Do you want us to come in –'

'No.' She managed a smile. 'Thanks, no, it's fine. I'm going to watch some crap on TV and have a bath. I'll see you tomorrow.'

Oliver started to wail as Eve pushed him away, the sound clawing at Sarah's insides. She stood for a reasonable time out on the gravel, waving as they turned round the side of the house, and then she dived into the atrium and pushed the door to and leant back against it, closing her eyes, heart still pounding.

Eve knew something was up.

She knew.

16

It had been bound to catch up with her, having to make all those excursions. For the next couple of days, all Sarah could do was hunker down, not even getting dressed and barely getting out of bed. She sent Eve a text – she couldn't bear to speak to her – saying she was 'Having a few human-free days' and Eve had texted back, 'OK Pooh – shout when you've had enough of it.'

On the first day, all she did was sleep and doze and feel sorry for herself. Without Eve, she was quite alone. There was no one else. No one she could turn to for help. Not one single person on the face of this planet who cared what happened to her and Oliver.

On the second day, she attempted to watch some TV, but all that noise, all that movement, all those horrible things happening on the news... She thought a programme about the Romans might be interesting and distracting, but it was on Channel 5, full of loud background noise, dizzying camerawork and lots of *crash bang wallop*. The content seemed almost incidental. She supposed they were trying to appeal to a younger audience, but she couldn't imagine anyone older than Oliver having much truck with it. On the Ides of March, when all the assassins were gathering at the Senate House, suddenly the shot careered across the Forum to the steps of the building – *whoosh, bang!* – as if Julius Caesar wasn't stabbed to death but met his end in a tragic zipwire accident.

She switched off the TV and opened her laptop, settling it on her knee on top of the blanket she was snuggled under. She Googled 'paternity force man DNA sample'.

The first few results were about conducting a test without the putative father's knowledge, which was apparently illegal. Then there was the stuff she wanted, about women who were mainly looking for child support – which she definitely wasn't – but were up against the problem of the man denying he was the father of the child and also refusing to supply a sample. It seemed that you could get a court order, in such circumstances, compelling the man to provide a DNA sample. If he refused to take a DNA test as ordered by a court, he faced legal consequences, and the court could take the view that his refusal constituted an admission of paternity.

So that was what she needed. A court order.

She did a bit more Googling. Her problem, it seemed, was that James's paternity was not, as far as officialdom was concerned, in doubt, so getting such a court order was going to be an uphill struggle.

She snapped the laptop shut and dumped it on the floor, curling up on the sofa for another sleep.

When she woke, she got herself a cup of coffee and opened up the General Medical Council website. She was surprised to find that it was really easy to check a doctor out. You just had to type their name into the search box in the Medical Register page, and bingo. Lewis Mark Gibson, male, year of qualification 2007, was registered with a licence to practice.

Eve must have some other sort of hold over him. Maybe she'd found out about some sort of malpractice that would get him struck off? Doctors were surely a lot more invested than the average person in their career – all that training, all those hours, all that effort... You weren't going to throw all that away, and the social status that came with it, lightly. You were ripe for blackmail.

But she was clutching at straws here.

She pushed her feet into her moccasins and wandered through to the kitchen, blinking in the brighter light that flooded this room through the skylights. She must look a mess. She hadn't showered or brushed her hair for two days. She hadn't even looked in a mirror.

She went to the glass doors and opened them to the courtyard. With the scrubbing brush she kept by the door for the purpose, she removed a few bird droppings from the bench and sat down in the sun, face lifted to it, feeling at once marginally better.

What was Oliver doing now?

She wasn't wearing her watch, but she thought it must be just after lunch. He'd be in Eve's house, having his nap. Wondering why he wasn't at home with Mummin.

Oh God!

No. Surely he was too young to think that way.

Consciously, perhaps he was. But she had seen his confusion, his disorientation, his anger, out there at the front door when he'd thrown down the headless owl. What must he have been thinking as Eve pushed his buggy up the drive to the Roman House? Maybe he'd hoped that this time he was going home for good. Home to Mummin!

And then getting there, seeing Mummin, expecting her to lift him out of his buggy and hug him and take him inside – And all that had happened was that Mummin had talked to Auntie Evie and then he was taken away again! No wonder he'd been 'Mr Grumpy', as that bitch Eve had said, so dismissively.

Tears were rolling down her face, her mouth hanging open, a keening, howling sound coming from deep in her chest.

She jumped up and blindly ran inside, through the kitchen and along the corridor to her bedroom, where she flung off her robe and her pyjamas and dived into the shower.

She couldn't afford the luxury, the self-indulgence of retreat from the world, no matter how frightening it might be, no matter how difficult it was to be out in it.

Because Oliver was out in it.

Alone, and without her.

HER HAIR DRIED AND STYLED, dressed in skinny jeans and a fluffy jumper, she sat in the atrium to make the first call, in the square of sunlight by the fountain, with the front door standing open so she could see the apron of gravel outside, where she and Oliver had last met.

She stared out at the gravel. She thought she could see a little scoop in it, where the owl had landed.

Oliver couldn't tell anyone what had happened. He was completely at the mercy of the adults in his life. Completely helpless. He could do nothing, absolutely nothing, about what was happening to him.

'My little boy,' she said aloud. 'It's going to be all right.'

Was it?

She was running out of options. Should she just take him and go? Run? Obviously it would be a last resort, because what kind of life would that be for him, on the run from the authorities with a messed-up agoraphobic Mummin?

But it could be that she'd have no choice. She should at least plan for such an eventuality.

She took the EE phone from her pocket.

'Hello,' she said when she was eventually put through to a human being. 'I need to withdraw a large amount of money –

most of the balance, in fact – from my savings account, and I need it in cash. I was wondering how I would go about that? Would that be a problem?'

She was ready to fight. She was ready to get tough, to insist, because it was, after all, her own money. Her own hard-earned money.

But, 'No, that should be fine,' the woman said. 'When were you thinking of making the withdrawal?'

'As soon as possible. Tomorrow? From the branch in Golspie?'

To make the second call, she stood in the door between the hall and the atrium, watching the sparrows bathe in the fountain. They were ducking their heads under the water and flapping their wings to work it through their feathers. Oliver loved it when they did that. He used to imitate them in the bath, pushing his head forward, arms held stiffly back like wings.

'Hi, Vee-Bee!' she said into the phone. 'I'm feeling more or less human again and was thinking that maybe you and – James might like to come over for lunch tomorrow? And do you think Lewis might forego his run and join us? I'm thinking I'll make it a bit of an occasion. To thank the two of you, for everything.'

She grimaced at the sparrow standing, bedraggled, on the granite lip of the fountain. The bird returned her gaze inscrutably.

'There's no need to *thank* us!'

Indeed.

'Of course there is! *Your worth will dignify our feast.*' That was one of Eve's stupid quotations she was always coming out with. 'I'm going to make the Extravaganza.'

'Ooh! Ooh! In that case, how could I resist?'

17

'What the hell *is* this?' said Lewis. He almost sounded like he was putting on a silly voice. Why didn't he get his nose fixed?

Eve laughed. 'Hmm. Maybe not *quite* what the cook wants to hear?'

She was giving Sarah the Look, and Sarah hoped she was returning it convincingly.

Lewis laughed. 'Sorry, Sarah. Not casting aspersions on your cooking, just curious.' He lifted the top layer of pasta with his fork. 'It seems to be some sort of mad lasagne?'

'Yep!' Eve reached across the table to dab at Oliver's mouth.

Sarah had to stop herself grabbing her arm and pulling it away from him.

'Waffff!' said Ollie.

'We call it Evie's Everything Extravaganza, don't we, darling?' Sarah smiled at Oliver. 'It involves about ten hours slaving over a hot stove, and I don't think anyone but her doting twin would do it, but apparently she's worth it.'

'I so am!' Eve was delving into the depths of the massive slice Sarah had given her. 'Ooh, and there's butter beans!'

'Of course.' If Sarah had been the kind of person who knew where to find poisonous mushrooms, the temptation to add them to the Extravaganza would have been very strong. *Oh dear, what a silly mistake – I thought they were ordinary field mushrooms.*

'Cheese, tomato sauce, pasta, courgette, onion...' Lewis was cataloguing, dissecting with knife and fork. 'Chicken, white sauce, sweetcorn... *Chips?*'

'Got to have chips,' Eve and Sarah said in unison.

'My God.' He took a drink of water. 'I'm going to be falling asleep all over my patients this afternoon!'

And here was the opening Sarah needed. 'As long as they don't report you to the GMC!'

Nope, no reaction, other than a grin as he chewed his first mouthful. 'Mmm. I think it might be worth it!'

'Are you a convert?' from Eve.

'Possibly. I'm reserving judgement until my digestive system has delivered its verdict.'

'Ugh!'

The vibe between them definitely wasn't that of black-mailer and blackmailee. If anything, it was flirty, at least on Lewis's side. Eve was trying a bit too hard. Could Lewis have agreed to go along with the Oliver/James deception as a favour to someone he had a huge crush on, and now *he* had something to hold over *Eve*, and she was being forced to let him into her life? Could he even be forcing her to sleep with him?

No. Sarah was sure she'd have picked up on it if that had been the case. She'd have sensed Eve's discomfort, her distress around him. No question.

'He seems to be enjoying it,' said Sarah, as Eve spooned cut-up Extravaganza into Oliver's mouth. 'Obviously a chip off the old block. Ha!' She broke off a piece of chip from her own plate and held it out to Oliver, who accepted it gravely and crammed it into his mouth with the rest, some falling out onto his bib. 'A chip off the old block,' she repeated.

This time, she did sense a tension. A quick flick of Eve's eyes from Sarah to Lewis.

AFTER LEWIS HAD GONE BACK to work, Eve seemed set to linger after Oliver had had his nap, and Sarah was conscious of time ticking on. She'd booked Jimmy for 3:30.

'I hate to kick you out,' she said, 'but the amendments to the plans for Braehead – I really want to get them finished today.' Actually, the client *had* been bugging her about them, asking if she'd uploaded them to the planning portal yet, and she had lied and said she had, that they must be lost in the system and she'd re-upload them. 'Come back this evening if you like?'

'We can take a hint, can't we?' Eve plomped a sleepy Oliver onto her knee and gently pulled her fingers through his quiff.

His little head nodded over, his eyelids drooping... And then suddenly he bolted upright, eyes wide, as if to say *Me? Asleep? I don't think so!*

Sarah couldn't resist. 'Can I have a James-cuddle?'

Eve held him up and Sarah swept him into her arms. 'Oops,' she smiled. 'I think someone needs changed. It's okay, I'll do it. Where's his bag?'

When she'd put a fresh nappy on him, Sarah took her time dressing him as he lay drowsily on the changing mat on her bedroom floor. His legs weren't a chubby baby's legs any more; they were getting so long. This was the first time she'd been able to study him properly since she'd gone into Marnoch Brae. Even his toes seemed to have grown, surely? She bent and kissed them.

'Ig,' he said, half asleep.

'This little piggy went to market,' she chanted, taking one perfect big toe with its little perfect shell of a nail between her finger and thumb. Oliver was watching her from half-closed eyes. She tweaked the next toe. 'This little piggy stayed at home...' And the next. 'This little piggy had roast beef... This little piggy had none.' She wiggled his little toe. 'And this little piggy... went *wee wee wee*, all the way home!' She danced her fingers up his leg, up his nappy and tummy to the tickly place under his arm.

Ollie squealed with shocked delight. It was always a shock for him, no matter how many times you did it.

She hugged him to her. '*All* the way home!'

SHE HAD THOUGHT that the trip to the bank might not be too bad, that she might be getting used to going out, but it was horrendous. At one point she almost actually fainted, when she had to wait in the lobby and all those people kept walking past and the staff were cackling and calling out to each other... She had to sit with her head on her knees, and a chirpy staff member came and asked if she was all right.

Returning in the taxi – thank God! She was nearly home! – she asked Jimmy to drop her at the end of the drive. He probably thought she was having an affair or something. Up to no good, anyway. And his suspicions would be confirmed if he knew that the floral Cath Kidston shopper she was carrying contained twenty-five thousand three hundred and forty pounds in fifty-pound notes.

The money took up a surprisingly small space. She had brought two shoppers but hadn't needed the second one. She had double-bagged the money, and now, as she staggered up the drive in the shelter of the pine trees, she picked up cones and added them to the top of the bag, paranoid that she was going to see Eve here again.

But she got to the house and inside the atrium safely, collapsing at once onto the bench.

She felt like a bank robber. Where to stash the loot?

Not in her study. Eve was always in and out of there. She plumped in the end for the cliché of the back of the wardrobe, behind her heavy winter coats. Then she changed into leggings and her soft blue sweatshirt, lit the stove, and put a Miss Marple on the TV for background moral support as she booted up her laptop and opened Google.

A low battery notification popped up on the screen. Damn.

But when she'd shut it down this morning, there had been fifteen per cent remaining. She was sure, because she knew she was going to have to charge it soon and had checked just before powering off.

Someone had been on her computer.

Eve.

Could she have been suspicious about Sarah wanting her to leave promptly after lunch? Could she have watched the house? Let herself in while Sarah was at the bank?

What had she been hoping to find? Dreading, perhaps, to find?

Sarah hadn't cleared out her history, and there was a whole load of stuff in there about DNA and court orders. But maybe that wasn't what Eve had been looking at. Maybe she'd been checking her correspondence or something. Looking in her 'Letters' folder, checking her emails...

But if she'd seen that search history, it would have confirmed that Sarah had not, after all, fallen for the gaslighting; that she was secretly trying to find a way to prove that Oliver was hers.

And if Eve knew that, what was she going to do about it?

Sarah took the laptop through to the kitchen, found its lead in a drawer, and plugged it in to charge on the worktop.

She was going to have to change her password. Why hadn't she already done that? Idiot! For convenience, in case one of them needed to log in to the other's stuff, she and Evie had always used the same two passwords: TheBaron22 and LaBelleDame22.

There was something so sad about having to change those passwords; having to change them because they weren't those two little girls any more, those little girls who'd been so close that Sarah sometimes wasn't sure if something she remembered had happened to herself or to Evie.

But had she been kidding herself? All this time? Had she taken her twin so much for granted that she'd never really known her at all? All the times when Evie had come home and let Sarah relive her day with her, looking through all those photos... It had never even occurred to Sarah that what Evie was giving her was an edited version of her life. What had happened in between the moments that had been captured for Sarah's consumption? In the spaces that had remained unphotographed, undocumented?

The spaces, all the spaces in Evie's life to which Sarah had never had access?

'OH MY GOD,' said Eve three hours later, coming in out of the dark, pushing the buggy into the atrium. 'You're not going to believe this. The Mackays have decided they don't in fact want an extension *at all!* They just texted me.'

Sarah shut the door behind them and put her hand, gently, on Oliver's head.

'Why doesn't that surprise me?'

'I'll withdraw the planning application tomorrow morning. They'll change their minds again, though, so we'd better not bin anything. They're saying we should reduce our charges for the plans accordingly, even though we'd completed them –'

'– until we had to start making all their changes,' Sarah finished. 'God.'

When they'd put Ollie down on one of the sofas, Sarah

curled up next to him, facing their reflections in the arched window opposite, and tried to relax as Eve pottered, switching off the top lights so that only the table lamps illuminated the room, pools of soft yellow light that left their faces in shadow, before curling up on the sofa opposite Sarah and Ollie's.

'Oh, I've needed this,' Eve sighed. 'Sissy-time, at the end of a long hard day.'

Sarah had never realised before just how much time she and Eve spent in each other's company. How many times had they been together in the dark like this, talking? As children, lying in their 'twin' beds in their room at home or in Grannie's cottage, exchanging a few words before dropping off to sleep; as teenagers, talking late into the night; as adults, in the London flat, sitting up together while the world went to sleep and it felt like there was no one else in it but them?

But Sarah had never been frightened before.

She was *frightened* of Evie.

Her twin.

Her other half.

How was that possible?

She was glad of the dark, because she couldn't betray it, not by a look, or a gesture, or an inflection in her voice. She couldn't let Eve know what she was thinking.

If Eve found out about the money in the wardrobe... about her plans to escape with Oliver...

Her palms, cupped around her mug of blackcurrant tea, were slick with sweat. But she made herself give her own contented sigh, and say, 'Yeah.'

'Ohft!' Eve leant back, closing her eyes. 'I feel like I haven't slept for a week. James has got into the habit of waking at three in the morning and then at half-hourly intervals, to just give me time to drop off before I'm woken again.'

Poor Oliver! No wonder he wasn't settling. But part of her was glad. Eve didn't deserve a good night's sleep.

Kidnapper. That was what she was. A *kidnapper*.

'Feel free to have a snooze,' Sarah said lightly.

'Actually, I might.' Eve swung her legs up and grabbed a cushion for a pillow. 'Talk to me, Rah-Bee.'

It was what they always used to say to each other, when they wanted to be eased into sleep by the other twin's soothing voice, like listening to the radio only better: *Talk to me*.

But Sarah, suddenly, could think of nothing to say.

'Okaayy,' she stalled.

Something from their childhood. Something to lull Eve, to take her brain back to a place where they meant everything to each other, back to those two little girls to whom *this*, this awfulness, this complete betrayal of one by the other, would have been quite unimaginable.

'I put on *Songs of Praise* the other day by mistake. I don't know when I last saw the inside of a church. You know, it's mad, but I actually miss St Stephen's.'

She pushed away What Happened to Mum and Dad and summoned in its place the squat, pale limestone church with its battlemented tower, dating back, as their father would never let them forget, to the 12th Century. In the low, slanting light of a summer evening, St Stephen's used to glow pink, as if lit from within, as if it really was a 'beacon of light', as Dad had sometimes referred to it in his sermons. The graveyard surrounding the church, shadowed by huge, spreading elms and oaks and sycamores, had been a wonderfully atmospheric place, a feast for their imaginations, full of crazily leaning headstones, some so old they had sunk almost completely into the ground, as if death was reaching out 'to the very stones themselves,' as Evie had put it.

They had been under stern instructions to stick to the gravel paths and not to run about or, perish the thought, actually *play* amongst the graves. But Evie had come up with a brilliant way round this. Before entering the graveyard, they would pick big bunches of wild flowers 'for the graves', so if they were spotted off the paths, they had a ready-made excuse.

'Remember little Eliza?' Eve murmured. 'I wonder if anyone puts flowers on her grave now.'

It had been their favourite gravestone – just a little limestone square set into the ground between two normal-sized stones, so inconspicuous you could walk right over it and not realise. The grass kept encroaching on it, and they kept having to pull it away from the edges. All that had been written on it had been 'Eliza, aged 2 years. Safe with God.'

'I used to almost want to believe in God, for Eliza,' Sarah said. 'I wanted to think of her being safe with God rather than just a tiny skeleton in the ground. Two years old. Not much older than – James. Hardly here, before she was gone.'

'I think Dad thought we'd be *safe with God* in the church,' Eve said sleepily.

'Yeah, "safe" in the sense of safely contained.'

How many times had they run through the graves, the massive old Victorian key bumping in the pocket of one or the other of them? Let themselves into the vestibule... Into the nave, the high, hushed space that seemed to go on forever before it reached the rafters. The air had had its own very particular quality, as if what they were breathing in had been breathed out by Victorian ladies in fusty black bombazine.

They had never prayed, unless mockingly to Zeus and Hera.

They used to run about the place, up and down the centre and side aisles, up the stairs to the dusty gallery. They played climbing games on the stacks of chairs in the storeroom off the vestibule, and opened the cake tin in the vestry in the hope that there'd be enough ginger snaps in there that Dad wouldn't miss a couple. They let themselves out onto the roof of the tower and looked down over the trees to what they could see of the road into the village, playing at spies.

And best of all, they'd take it in turns to pretend to be Dad, pontificating from the pulpit, fingers laced together, gaze fixed, loftily, over the heads of the imaginary congregation.

As if reading her mind, Eve said, 'Sarah's sermon!'

Sarah's sermon.

It had been Easter Sunday. Dad had had 'a digestive issue' and, as the congregation had started to arrive, had locked himself in the toilet off the vestry. Mum had gone back to the house for the Andrews Liver Salts, leaving the twins sitting on the front pew in their Sunday dresses and cardigans. Sarah still remembered the dresses they'd been wearing – Evie's was pink and Sarah's was yellow, constructed from a sort of seersucker material. White knee socks and sandals, although they were thirteen and none of the other girls their age wore socks and sandals any more. It was an unseasonably hot day, and most of the other teenage girls had bare legs. Bare flesh in church, though, was a definite no-no for the twins.

The hum of conversation behind them gradually rose in volume as more and more people arrived. And Sarah suddenly had a brilliant idea.

She got up and walked to the pulpit.

'Sarah!' Evie hissed.

Sarah ascended the stairs and stood with her fingers laced together.

A sudden hush.

Later, Evie said people probably thought she was going to make an announcement about Dad being indisposed and the service being cancelled. But she took a deep breath and began.

'Welcome to you all, on this glorious Easter Day!' she boomed. 'I'm afraid Dad is otherwise *engaged* at the moment, but I think we all know how his sermon would start.' She had to stop and press down the hysteria that was bubbling up. 'He'd start off by trying to make the God stuff "relevant" to our ordinary lives.' She made her voice as deep as it would go. 'If God was someone who lived in the village, what kind of neighbour do you think he would be?'

In the front pew, Evie was shaking her head frantically, but couldn't help the grin pulling at her mouth.

'Do you think he would be the kind of neighbour you could borrow a cup of sugar from?' Sarah continued, warming to her theme. 'Or who would water your plants while you were on holiday? Or do you think he'd be the man in the dodgy raincoat, shouting mad stuff in the street? *"Praise me, you fuckers, or you're all going to hell!"'*

Evie got to her feet at that point.

And at the back of the church, she saw Mum clutching the tin of Andrews Liver Salts, her mouth actually hanging open.

'What kind of a bighead,' Sarah continued rapidly, as Evie mounted the steps to the pulpit, 'thinks they're so great that everyone has to praise them all the time anyway? If he lived in the village, you'd cross the street to avoid him.'

Now Evie had a hold of her hand, pulling her away from the lectern.

Too late.

In the doorway to the corridor that led to the vestry, Dad was standing, his face even greyer than it had been before he'd locked himself in the toilet.

'If God was one of his parishioners,' she shouted, pulling away from Evie's hand, 'Dad would probably report him to the Parish Council!'

In the vestry, Dad had bellowed at her: 'What do you suppose they're all thinking, the people out there who've just been subjected to that *blasphemy* – and *here*, what is more! In St Stephen's! What do you suppose they're saying to one another about your mother and me, and how *utterly* we've failed with you, you *wicked, wicked* child?'

'Some of them were laughing,' Sarah had muttered.

As if that made it any better. As if that wasn't going to

incense him all the more, because, of course, the one thing guaranteed more than anything else to rile Dad was the idea that people might be laughing at him.

For a while, it had been one of the twins' catchphrases, trotted out when one of them had done something bad: *Some of them were laughing.*

Oh God. Literally, *oh God.*

On the other sofa, Eve was wiping her eyes, shaking with suppressed laughter. 'Dad's face!'

Sarah grinned. 'It was almost worth it.'

They looked at each other, their smiles dropping away. And suddenly, Sarah couldn't be in the same room.

'Have to pee,' she said, and bolted.

When she returned to the living room, padding noiselessly in her moccasins, she found Eve bent over Sarah's bag, which she'd left on the walnut table behind the middle sofa.

Eve held up her hands when she saw Sarah. 'I know, I know, it's –'

'– the ultimate violation,' Sarah finished weakly.

'I need a nail file, but I know, I know.'

'There isn't even a nail file in there. I'll get you one.'

When she'd fetched it from the bathroom, Eve stood over the hearth, filing the nail that Sarah was sure didn't need it. What had Eve been looking for in her bag? What might she have found?

Nothing, surely?

There was nothing incriminating in her bag now, but she went cold as she realised that, if Eve had searched it a few days ago, she'd have found the DNA test kit. Sarah had hidden it away now at the bottom of the Christmas box in the storeroom, but when it had been in her bag, had she left it, at any point, where Eve might have had an opportunity to search it?

She couldn't remember.

'Sorry, Vee-Bee, but I'm absolutely knackered. I need to hit the sack.' You could say that sort of thing to your sister.

'Okay, we're out of here.'

Walking by her side through the dim cloister, a pale moon washing the atrium with an other-worldly light, the wheels of Oliver's buggy turning on the flagstones the only sound apart from their own, muffled footsteps, Sarah shivered. There had been a surreal quality to the evening, as if she had stepped into a parallel universe – a midnight garden, a sinister, off-kilter, shadowed version of reality from which there was no way back, no portal she could step through and be back in the world where Eve was Evie, Vee-Bee, the beloved twin sister who had always been her better half.

When she opened the outside door, Eve turned to her.

'I love you, Rah-Bee,' she said, pulling Sarah into a tight hug.

But they never said they loved each other; they always scoffed at people who did, saying it was practically an admission that you didn't, a papering over of the cracks, if you had to spell it out to the person.

It really was as if Eve *wasn't* Evie.

Was this a test?

Sarah felt herself stiffen; had to consciously relax as she squeezed Eve back.

'I love you too, Vee-Bee.'

Eve squeezed tighter, almost too tight, and finally Sarah had to break away, laughing, whining in a high voice, '*Love you,*' in a parody of Naomi, a girl they'd known at uni, who used to sicken them all by whining 'Love you' down the phone to her boyfriend fifty times a day.

'I know, not cool,' Eve grinned, but it was definitely a forced grin. 'I'm sorry.' And, a barely heard whisper as she turned away, she repeated: 'I'm sorry.'

Sarah's stomach plummeted.

She knew what this was. It was proactive guilt, as they used to call it when Oliver would give them a placating smile before splashing his bathwater everywhere or throwing broccoli on the floor.

'Be careful,' Sarah managed to get out, her mouth sticky and dry. 'Have you a torch?'

'Yep,' said Eve, bending over Oliver. 'Thanks for tonight. See you soon.'

When she'd gone, when Sarah had locked the door behind her, she ran back through the cloister. Into the hall, through the kitchen to the living room.

She grabbed up her bag and upended it on the wooden floor. The contents spilled out, loose coins rolling away, receipts fluttering. Her purse, a pack of tissues, tampons, a pen, a mirror, a small tube of moisturiser, the tiny mother-of-pearl vintage penknife George had given her one Christmas, which he'd probably picked up for a couple of quid but which was actually quite useful...

She picked up her purse and opened it.

And there, not quite pushed down properly into the card slot, was the orange and white rectangle of the ticket for her return journey from Inverness to Golspie.

18

The next morning, Sarah woke from a nightmare in which she was carrying Oliver through the streets of Inverness, buildings towering up all around them. She had to find somewhere for them to stay, but every window was shuttered, and she knew, somehow, that behind one of them was Eve, waiting for them in the dark. Waiting for Sarah to make the wrong choice.

Because Sarah always made the wrong choice.

She sat on the edge of the bed, rubbing her face and trying to think. She was certain that Eve knew what Sarah was planning and was plotting a pre-emptive strike. A devastating pre-emptive strike. Hence the proactive guilt of last night.

But the twin sixth sense worked both ways.

She pulled off her nightshirt and stepped into the shower and, as the hot water ran over her sweaty hair, made herself contemplate what it was Eve could be planning. If plan A had been to gaslight Sarah, to make her believe that Oliver was 'James'... what was plan B?

It must be something bad.

She groped in front of her for the wall of the cubicle.

Flopped her head down, between her arms, water running now into her eyes, like tears, splashing off her nose, down her naked body.

What if plan B was to get her out of the way again, but this time permanently? Make it look like an accident... or suicide...

And then Eve would have Oliver forever.

Could it be? Could Eve possibly be contemplating anything so drastic?

Killing her own sister?

Her own *twin*?

She staggered from under the water, not even stopping to turn it off. She grabbed a towel and rubbed roughly at her hair, her skin. Pulled on underwear and a top and leggings before her skin was properly dry.

She had to get Oliver and go *now*. She had to take the money and –

But where would they go?

Where would they go?

The idea of being out there, alone, with Oliver, having to find a safe place for them both but not knowing where to go, having *nowhere* to go where they wouldn't be found, caught, brought back...

She staggered back into the en suite and turned off the shower.

She had to plan this properly. She had to plan where they would go, how they could hide from the police, the authorities in whose eyes she would be the kidnapper, the transgressor, the dangerous one.

Eve was unlikely to do anything today. She had only just found the train ticket. She wouldn't have had a chance to put plan B, whatever it was, into operation.

Or would she? Could Sarah take that risk?

Okay.

She had to calm down and think.

She lay down on the bed and shut her eyes.

What kind of a life would it be, for Oliver, on the run? What would happen when he was ready to start school? He would be a non-person. She would have to buy identities for them both, she supposed, from criminals. How would she do that?

But that was something to worry about down the line. Right now, she needed to find somewhere safe for them to hide. She needed to get Oliver and go.

Now.

Jumping up so fast it made her dizzy, she staggered through the house to the living room and her laptop. She could book somewhere, a holiday cottage, under a false name... But how would she pay for it? The police would be able to trace card payments, and the owner was unlikely to accept cash.

A hotel. It would have to be a hotel, at first, maybe in a city, somewhere they could be anonymous. She Googled 'hotel Glasgow'.

But could she manage it, being in a city, amongst all that hustle and bustle?

And an abducted child would be all over the news. The hotel staff would recognise them.

No.

They'd need somewhere they could hole up, somewhere out of the way. They could rent somewhere, but then there would be problems with identity checks and references. She'd have to somehow contact criminals who could supply false identities.

She Googled 'how to get false identity'.

This brought up lots of useless stuff which turned out to be fictional, and people stating the bloody obvious on forums, like 'Find your friendly neighbourhood con artist' and other people saying 'Don't do it' or 'It's easy'. Mostly the stuff was from the US and about fake identity cards, but she didn't need an identity card, she needed a proper, comprehensive fake identity that would pass any checks the landlord carried out.

Okay, so that was all going to take time she didn't have just now. Long-term, renting somewhere was obviously the way to go, but for now she just needed to disappear until the fuss had died down, until she and Oliver were off the front pages of the papers and had been buried in everyone's Facebook feeds.

Holiday cottages.

They were all empty at this time of year in Achnaclach and would be until Easter, a month away. It would presumably be the same all over the country. She needed to find a holiday cottage website that showed the booking calendar blocked out as 'unavailable' for the winter and early spring months. Then she could break in and stay there for a week or two until she got sorted out. Somewhere reasonably near, but not too near.

A few false starts later, she found a place called Woodend Cottage just outside the village of Boat of Garten, about eighty miles away, which seemed to fit the bill. It was a gorgeous little cottage, with original windows and doors and a big woodshed tacked on to one end, tucked away up a forest track but just half a mile from the village, which was on the 34X bus route. Oliver would love it there, with all the wildlife. They might even see ospreys! And maybe, after a few weeks of lying low, after she'd managed to buy a fake identity on the internet, she could get to know some of the locals and maybe find a job and somewhere to rent.

A job was maybe pushing it. But maybe someone would have a little cottage or a cabin they would rent out to her on a monthly basis.

Woodend Cottage, according to the website, was 'available to rent from 15 April to 31 October'. Perfect. It was the kind of place where they left a key under a flowerpot by the door. Failing that, she could break a window at the back. Board it up later with cardboard or something.

Okay. Decision made. And if Woodend Cottage wasn't suitable for some reason, she was sure there'd be other empty properties in that area that would be.

She closed the laptop. She would take it with them.

Right.

Think, think.

First and foremost, how to get Oliver?

She seemed to remember Eve saying something about a site visit today. She checked the calendar on her phone.

Yep, meeting today in Wick at 11:30.

So Oliver would presumably be with Margaret now. She could go and get him, book a taxi to take the two of them to Golspie, get the train to Inverness, another to Aviemore... But snatching Oliver should be the last thing she did, in case Margaret raised the alarm. She needed to get everything else ready, so all she had to do was jump in the taxi once she had him.

First, the money. She got the bag out of the wardrobe and stuffed the notes into a carrier and then into the bottom of a large rucksack. She added underwear, clothes and toiletries more or less at random. Oliver – what about clothes for Oliver?

She'd have to buy some. She could break the journey in Inverness and buy some essentials.

She went to the loo, and then she pulled her wet hair back into an Evie-esque ponytail. She slapped her cheeks to give herself an Evie glow, rather than fiddling with blusher that her hands were trembling too much to apply properly.

She slung the rucksack over one shoulder and hefted it through to the living room, where she pushed her bag and her laptop in on top.

All set.

She called A1 taxis and booked a taxi from the Roman House to Golspie railway station for half an hour's time, asking the driver to wait if she wasn't at the house when he arrived.

She took a precious few moments to rush round saying goodbye to the house before lugging the rucksack into the atrium and leaving it just inside the door. Then she shrugged into her big Barbour and left.

It had started to spit with rain. She put up her hood and fastened the coat, making sure both phones were in her pocket, along with the small bottle of water. The first few steps were an effort, but soon she was striding down the drive to the road, breathing in deep, calming lungfuls of the damp air, pungent with the smells of the earth and pine resin.

Over the brow of the hill the road dipped down, and for the first time she could see the chimneys of Eve's house, the grey slate roof, the Victorian dormer windows painted midnight blue. And beyond it, Margaret's smaller, lower roof.

Where Oliver was? Oh *please please* let him be there!

She was passing First House, as it was called – the first house you came to if you approached the village along the road. And now she was running into the heart of the village, as she had run that awful night of the storm, heart pounding.

The houses got closer together the nearer you got to the harbour, where the oldest houses were clustered. As she ducked off the road and up one of the pends between a dilapidated stone shed and a long, low cottage with a red door, she felt as if she was being watched, although she knew all these houses were empty. It was something to do with them being so crammed together, cheek-by-jowl, so there wasn't a window that didn't look straight into three or four others across a pend or a tiny yard.

Grannie used to tell them about how, when she was a child, they all used to be in and out of each other's houses all the time, so there was almost a sort of collective ownership. Now, each house seemed to be doing its best to close itself off, to deny the proximity of its neighbours.

Maybe it was the ghosts she felt watching her. The sad, wistful ghosts.

There was a sense almost of anger, or despair, the kind that came from happy memories when the happiness had gone. Was the village angry about its lost happiness? About what had been done to it, the obliteration of all it had once been, the community it had once housed?

As she shook off the fanciful notion, hurrying through a little cutting between pends, she couldn't help thinking about how happy they had all been, or seemed to be, she and Oliver and Evie. Evie had probably expected Sarah to struggle with a baby – hoped she would, perhaps, so she could justify to herself what she was doing. But after Oliver had been born, Sarah had never been happier. Or better. She'd even felt she might be able to take him out along the coastal path, but Evie had vetoed this. Evie had made sure that Sarah stayed hidden away, isolated, within the walls of the Roman House.

Now she was in the pend that ran up alongside Margaret's house to Eve's.

She knocked on Margaret's door, trying to regulate her breathing, to slow her heart rate, to plaster an Evie smile on her face.

'Oh, hi!' she beamed when the old woman opened the door. 'I'm back! Well, obviously. Thanks so much for minding him.'

Margaret frowned at her. 'Minding him?'

'James! Has he been okay?'

'James isn't here.' Margaret narrowed her eyes.

Had she sussed that this wild-eyed, wild-haired woman at her door wasn't Evie? Before she could slam the door on her like last time, Sarah pushed inside.

'What –?'

'Where is he?'

'Oh my goodness. You're *Sarah*.'

She quickly checked the downstairs rooms, then ran up the

steep little staircase to the attic rooms, but they were empty too, just empty rooms with boxes in them and, in one, a mattress on the floor.

He wasn't here. Oliver wasn't here. And now Margaret was going to tell Eve.

Oh God.

She made herself breathe. Made herself go back down the stairs and grimace at Margaret and apologise. 'I'm sorry, I thought Evie said she'd left him here.'

'Well, she hasn't.'

'Sorry.'

'Please get out of my house.' She was frightened, Sarah saw guiltily, looking at Sarah as if dreading what she was going to do next.

'Of course. I'm sorry. Just a – misunderstanding.'

In a daze, she retraced her steps, back through the narrow pends, back onto the road. She had to call Eve before Margaret could get to her. Oliver must be with Eve. Her sister must have wanted to keep him close, suspecting...

Suspecting what?

Well, it didn't matter what she suspected. What Sarah had to do now was call Eve and get her to come to the Roman House with Oliver. Then somehow overpower her; lock her in the storeroom. She'd have to cancel the taxi, tell them she would need one later but would let them know when.

She was sobbing by the time she'd got herself up the hill, her legs feeling unwieldy and heavy and at the same time as weak as water, hardly able to carry her weight. Was Margaret calling Eve now, to tell her that Sarah had barged into her house looking for James?

She staggered up the drive to the house, desperate to be back inside, to shut the door on the world.

She was so tired.

She had to get inside, calm down, and call Eve.

But as she rounded the corner of the house, she saw that there was a vehicle there.

Not the taxi. A police car. And there were two police officers, standing contemplating the Roman House, looking up at the windowless facade in evident bafflement. One of them was the policewoman who had hauled her off to Marnoch Brae to be sectioned in January.

Her first instinct was to turn and run before they saw her.

But what good would that do? How would that help Oliver? If they were here because Margaret had reported her for barging into her house, Sarah could explain that there had been a misunderstanding. Maybe she could make out that Margaret was confused.

And what if they were here with bad news about Eve and Oliver? What if they'd been in a car accident or something, and Oliver was in hospital?

'Hello,' she said, walking out across the gravel towards them, smoothing her hair where it had come out of its ponytail. 'Are you looking for me?'

19

When she opened her eyes, she knew she was in Marnoch Brae because she could remember, this time, every detail of the terrible events of the day before. She remembered arguing with the police as they'd arrested her for 'actual bodily harm and criminal damage'. She remembered insisting that she hadn't hurt Margaret and hadn't damaged anything. She remembered the feeling of dislocation when they'd told her that the alleged assault was of a man, Peter Drummond, and the damage had been to the Toasty Teacake café in Golspie. She remembered trying to tell them that she hadn't even been in Golspie that day. She remembered the awful journey to the police station, that bitch of a police-woman's contemptuous face as Sarah had tried to explain about Oliver and Eve, that this must be Eve setting her up. And, when they'd tried to put her in a cell, she remembered fighting them: kicking and punching and biting. The momentary satis-faction of sinking her teeth into that bitch's finger.

Which presumably was why she was back here. They thought she was having another psychotic episode.

But she didn't understand. Had Eve made a false report

against her? Who was this Peter Drummond that she was meant to have assaulted? The Toasty Teacake was owned by one of Eve's friends in the kayak club, she remembered, so presumably Eve had dragged her into the conspiracy.

She couldn't do this.

She couldn't fight any more.

She closed her eyes.

DR LAGHARI SAT SLIGHTLY FORWARD in the tub chair. 'You don't remember any of what happened in the café?'

'No,' said Sarah. *Because I didn't do it*, there was no point in adding.

'Okay.' He looked down at his notes. 'It seems you came into the place in a state of some agitation. The café owner, Kirsty Menzies, who is a friend of your sister Evie, greeted you in the mistaken belief that you *were* Evie. This seemed to enrage you. You snapped at her that you were Sarah. Then you... you engaged a couple in their sixties, Peter and Maggie Drummond, who were sitting having tea and scones, in conversation. Well, I say conversation.' He grimaced. 'You were haranguing them, telling Mr Drummond that he must provide you with a DNA sample so that you could prove that the child your sister had "stolen" was your own child Oliver, fathered by Mr Drummond. When Mr and Mrs Drummond tried to leave their table, you – I'm afraid you attacked them. They took refuge behind the counter with Ms Menzies, and at that point...'

'What?'

She could have sworn he was trying not to smile. She'd often wondered whether psychiatrists secretly had to struggle not to find their patients' antics amusing, and she suspected that it must be particularly hard for Dr Laghari, whose twinkly eyes suggested a well-developed sense of humour.

'At that point, you grabbed a pottery hedgehog from the

countertop, containing approximately fifteen pounds in tips, and threw it at Mr Drummond's head. Fortunately, it struck him only a glancing blow and there was no concussion. You shouted that you were going to get a court order to force him to provide a DNA sample. You then grabbed a buggy belonging to another customer – the child was thankfully not in it at the time – and used it to smash the glass cover of the cake display, raining glass down on Mr and Mrs Drummond and Ms Menzies. As Ms Menzies called the police, you ran off.'

Sarah let the silence go on and on, expanding to fill the room.

Eve had pretended to be Sarah. She must have looked at the search history on her laptop and seen all the stuff about DNA samples and court orders. She must have realised that Sarah had found a possible way to prove Oliver's real identity.

But after that stunt in the café, no court in the country was going to demand a DNA sample from Andy. There were now at least three witnesses to 'Sarah' accusing a different random man of being Oliver's father, and shouting madly at him about a court order.

'I see,' she said, at last.

'Oliver,' said Dr Laghari. 'Do you still think you have a child called Oliver?'

It was futile to try to explain. It was futile to say anything. Dr Laghari wouldn't believe her and nor would anyone else.

Sarah shook her head, but not in denial. She shook her head and she kept on shaking it, to say *I'm done, she wins, that's it, no more.*

No more.

No more.

It was over.

20

She had tried to call Eve, twice, the nurse sitting there beside her to monitor the call, but Eve wasn't picking up. She didn't know what she would say if she did get through. She just needed to know that Oliver was all right.

Mostly she stayed in her room, sitting in the wing chair by the window, staring at nothing. Thinking. Trying not to think.

There was no use in fighting any more. She knew it, but it was so hard.

So hard, to accept that she would never get Oliver back.

That Eve had won, as she always did.

Evie could always jump higher, run faster, think smarter. She always got better marks than Sarah, in every single subject at school. Not because of any innate superiority, but because Evie was so much more focused, so much more determined. And if there was ever an argument between them, even about something as trivial as which way to turn at the end of the drive when they were off out to play, nine times out of ten, Evie would win it.

She had even, latterly, begun to outwit their parents.

When they'd been tiny children, they had accepted the

punishment of being locked in their room reasonably stoically. They had known there was no point making a fuss – no matter how hungry or thirsty they were, no matter how much the bucket that was their improvised toilet began to stink, no matter how much they called and cried, no one was going to come and let them out. They could be in there for hours. Occasionally a whole day, or even two days if they'd done something particularly bad.

Then, the summer they were eleven, Evie had worked it out. She had worked out how to beat them.

Sarah shut her eyes, remembering that day.

It had been so hot.

The grass in the churchyard had been yellow with the heat, the ground baked hard like concrete after a long dry summer, dusty when you scuffed along. Sarah and Evie had crawled into the shade under one of the table graves, with the idea of lying there for a while in the cool as the other children they'd been playing with searched for them in vain. They'd raided the pantry earlier and their stomachs were full of stolen ice cream and profiteroles. They needed to relax for a while.

But instead of comfy grass, what they found under the grave's sheltering slab of stone was disturbed earth, a big hole where a fox or badger had been digging, the earth from deeper underground darker in colour, damper. And amongst it, a bone.

A small white bone, maybe a centimetre long, that Evie said was part of the dead person's finger. She used her sandal to kick earth over it. But as they crawled out again, Sarah burrowed her hand into the soil and found it, that smooth little bone, and put it in her pocket.

At home, she cleaned it in secret at the scullery sink where Mum did the flowers for church, scrubbing off the earth with a nailbrush. She knew exactly what she was going to do with it.

The way their family worked was that Dad was the only person who really mattered. So if there was only one of something nice left, Dad always got it. And Sarah knew that there was only enough of the profiteroles left for one more serving. She went to the fridge, and took out the bowl, and pushed the little bone deep inside one of the delicious choux pastry balls.

She had hoped, with the way he gulped his food, that he might swallow it whole at lunch, but he crunched on it and spat it back out onto his spoon.

'What the –? Deirdre!' Accusingly, he took the bone between finger and thumb and held it up so Mum could see. 'What on earth is *that*?'

Mum twittered that she had no idea.

And Sarah couldn't help it – she started to laugh. 'You almost ate a bit of mouldy dead person!' she crowed.

Dad stared at her. 'What?'

Evie kicked her under the table, but Sarah wanted him to know, she wanted him to know what he'd just had in his mouth. 'I found it in a grave,' she exaggerated. 'It's a bit of dead person's finger!'

His chair crashed over as he shot up from the table and ran out of the dining room, and even right across the hall they could hear him gagging in the bathroom, and Mum stood and grabbed Sarah by her hair and said, 'You wicked, *wicked girl*!' and pulled her out and up the stairs, and it was *really* sore and some of her hair came out, and Evie came behind, wailing, 'Let her *go*!'

But then Dad came, and picked up Evie, and barged ahead and threw her inside their room so she landed on the floor and knocked her head, and Mum pushed Sarah in after her and Dad shouted, '*Above all, taking the shield of faith, wherewith ye shall be able to quench all the fiery darts of the wicked!*'

And they heard the key turn in the lock.

Sarah spat on a T-shirt and cleaned the blood off Evie's forehead where the skin had been scraped on the floor when she fell.

All afternoon they lay on their beds, trying not to think about water. Outside it was a 'glorious summer's day', as Dad would have said. The leaves of the horse chestnut stretched out in the air, not moving at all, but there must have been a tiny breeze because it blew in the sweet, succulent smell of cut grass through the open window.

Juicy, juicy grass.

Evie started to play *When We're at Grannie's*.

'When we're at Grannie's, we can go to the castle and I'll be Mary Queen of Scots arriving for a visit, and you can be the Earl's new wife. You're only eighteen, but you have to get the place ready for me and make it all fancy.'

'We'll help Grannie make pancakes and you'll burn them.'

'I will not!'

'Then we'll have a game of Scrabble and Grannie will cheat!'

That autumn, *When We're at Grannie's* would stop abruptly, after Mum told them one day, quite casually as they walked with her to the shop, that Grannie had died. But that long hot afternoon, the thought of Grannie was a wonderful comfort. For a while.

At last, Sarah could keep it in no longer. 'I need a drink of water.'

'I know.' Evie sat up, and went to the door, and squatted. Peered into the keyhole. 'I can see the key.'

'That's no use, is it? It's on the other side!'

But Evie was galvanised. She tore a sheet of paper from a pad and pushed it carefully under the door, leaving about a quarter of it on their side. Then she got two more sheets and pushed them through too, one on either side of the first one.

By this time, Sarah was kneeling next to her.

'Get me a pencil or a pen,' Evie instructed, like a surgeon speaking to a theatre nurse. 'One that'll fit through the keyhole.'

Sarah fetched her pencil case, and the second pencil they tried fitted.

Evie pushed it into the keyhole, wiggling it about.

They both heard the key drop to the floor on the other side.

'Let me do it,' Evie said as Sarah made a grab for the middle sheet of paper. And slowly, carefully, she pulled the paper back inside the room, the key resting on top of it.

'Okay, okay!' Sarah jumped up and down in glee.

'Shhhh!'

Evie retrieved the two other sheets of paper and returned them to the pad before pushing the key into the lock and putting her ear to the door. When she was satisfied there was no sound from the passage outside, she slowly unlocked and opened the door.

They took off their sandals and tiptoed along the passage to the bathroom.

Nothing had ever tasted as good as the water gushing out of that tap. They drank until their stomachs were as tight as drums. Then they sneaked back to their room for the big Tupperware box in which they kept their beads and buttons and ribbons, and tipped out the contents, and took it back to the bathroom to fill to the brim with water.

They debated going downstairs in search of food, but concluded it was too risky.

They couldn't, of course, lock themselves back in, so they just left the key in the keyhole on the other side of the door. When Mum came to let them out next morning, they heard her try to turn the key – but of course it wouldn't budge. She gave a little 'Oh!' of surprise, but nothing was said. She must have thought she'd forgotten to lock it.

That first time, anyway.

The second time, when they'd been locked in their room after Sarah had spilt juice, Dad was summoned to investigate the Strange Case of the Unlocked Door, as Evie called it later.

He thundered at them, demanded to know what had happened to the door, and Evie stood demurely by Sarah's side, head slightly bowed.

But she was ready with a brilliant story.

When Dad had finished, she looked up at him from under her lashes and said that Lissa had let them out. She'd come looking for them and unlocked the door. And although the twins had refused to go with her, explaining that they were locked in as a punishment for Sarah spilling orange juice on the drawing room carpet, they had of course been unable to relock the door when Lissa had gone.

Mum and Dad didn't know they'd fallen out with Lissa.

That had been the end of that particular form of 'discipline', and Dad had told them they must explain to Lissa that it had been a game, that he hadn't really locked them in as a punishment. He'd always been terrified that his adoring parishioners would see through the disguise he put on at the door.

'WELL, SARAH,' said Dr Laghari, ushering her into the consulting room. 'There's good news!'

Sarah's heart bumped. Good news – could it be, was it possible that Eve had come clean? That her conscience had belatedly kicked in? That Sarah was about to be released, that Oliver was to be returned to her?

'What?' she breathed.

'The charges against you have been dropped.' Dr Laghari gestured to her usual tub chair and sat in his usual one opposite.

'Oh.' She'd forgotten all about the criminal charges.

'We've had written confirmation from the Crown Office and Procurator Fiscal Service that all charges have been dropped in view of the fact that it's clear that, as a consequence of your mental disorder, you lacked criminal responsibility – pursuing a conviction, given the minor nature of the offence, isn't seen to be in the public interest. The shattered glass of the cake display didn't cut anyone. And the man was only slightly injured by the, uh, flying hedgehog. Just a bit of a bump on the head.'

He was smiling at her.

'Okay,' was all she could summon. 'So can I go home?'

He sighed, and sat back, and shook his head. 'No, Sarah. You've been detained under Section Three of the Mental Health Act. That means you can be detained for six months, and that period can be extended if your doctors feel it's necessary for your own or others' safety.'

'But I'm not *dangerous*.'

'You were arrested for attacking people.'

'But you just said it was "minor".'

He raised his eyebrows. 'Yes, but it could have been rather more serious.'

Sarah sighed. No, she couldn't fight this.

How clever Eve was.

'Okay.'

THE BLINDS in the rec room were pulled across the windows to create a murky underwater gloom, relieved only by the flickering TV. Sarah sat slumped in her dressing gown at the end of the semicircle of chairs arranged around it. The only other person 'watching' was a slack-mouthed, doped-up woman with flakes of dried drool on her collar.

It was *Homes Under the Hammer*.

The nauseating, unjustifiably upbeat music blared as the estate agents clopped up the path in their heels to examine the property after the 'improvements' had been made – all original features ripped out to transform every room into a bland magnolia box. A slum landlord's dream. They'd even managed to shoehorn in four extra bedrooms by splitting the front room and the dining room in two, the partitions cutting each window in half.

'Enjoying that, are you, Sarah?' trilled Carol, 'accidentally' knocking Sarah's knees with the trolley she was pushing.

'Piss off,' Sarah managed.

Carol's fat face appeared in her vision. 'Oh dear. Looks like we might have to ask Dr Laghari to up your meds.'

Sarah closed her eyes. And she must have slept, because the next thing she knew was a scream from behind her, and a thump as someone hit the floor.

'She's fitting, she's fitting!'

Sarah didn't bother to look round as she heard racing feet, and one of the nice nurses saying, 'Okay m'dear, okay. We've got you.'

One of the other patients laughed.

Marianne strolled in front of the TV as if nothing was happening, and plomped herself down a couple of chairs along from Sarah. Sarah was half expecting her to produce the box of peppermint cremes, but instead she took a family-size bar of Dairy Milk from her pocket and peeled back the wrapper. She broke off a line of squares and popped the whole thing into her mouth, opening her eyes wide at Sarah to indicate pleasure.

'Want some?' Marianne mumbled through the mouthful, offering the bar.

'No thanks.'

Sarah had no appetite. It was a chore to get food into her stomach. If it hadn't been for Oliver, she might have been tempted to chuck it all up in the loo afterwards, like Julia used to.

'Oh my God, those kids want culling,' said Marianne.

It was *Bargain-Loving Brits in the Sun* now.

Sarah was becoming very familiar with daytime TV.

'Let's get them out on the water on an inflatable banana and oh dear, little Johnny's fallen off the end and no one's noticed.'

Marianne cackled. 'Next thing he's on the front page of the *Daily Express* and the family are crowdfunding for a search for the body. They're grieving all over social media for their "cheeky wee rascal" – translation, "He was a fucking nightmare and we're stoked he's finally contributing something to this family". They're offski with that money. Little Johnny's fish food and they don't give a fuck, off on another holiday to Lanzarote, let's get the remaining kids on a giant inflatable doughnut and see what happens.'

Sarah closed her eyes.

'Sure you wouldn't like some choc?'

'Yes. Thanks.' She stood. She'd go back to her room and sleep.

In the corridor, Carol was pushing the trolley in front of her. She seemed to sense that it was Sarah behind her, and stopped, smiling round at her. 'Well, Sarah! Having a good day? That was sad about Julia, wasn't it? Poor lassie was only twenty-three. But that was only ever going to end one way. I don't suppose you got to the funeral?'

Julia was *dead*?

Sarah didn't stop – she changed tack and sped up, giving Carol a wide berth.

'Such a shame. But once you've pressed the self-destruct button, you can't unpress it, eh, Sarah? Can't unpress it.'

Sarah kept walking. She wasn't allowed to shut the door of her room, but she pulled the blinds and crawled under the sheet and the waffle blanket, and turned her face to the pillow.

21

Carol banged down the bowl of porridge so the milk slopped over the side and onto the invalid table that had been positioned in front of the wing chair. Some of it trickled onto Sarah's lap.

'Oops.'

Sarah ignored the spilt milk and picked up her spoon.

'Aren't we forgetting something?' Carol tapped the miniature plastic beaker containing Sarah's morning dose of antipsychotics.

Sarah tipped the pills into her mouth and washed them down with some water.

'Open wide.'

Sarah opened her mouth.

'Good girl!' Carol placed a hand on Sarah's head. 'Very good.'

When she'd left the room, Sarah pushed the bowl away.

Ridiculously, she wanted Evie.

She wanted Evie to march in here and tell Carol what for. Stand there with her hands on her hips and tell *Sarah* what for. Tell her to eat the porridge because it was a great source of slow-release energy and nutrients. And then give her a hug.

When they'd given her a bag with a selection of her belongings in it – clothes and her purse and toiletries and her Kindle – brought in by Evie, she'd found herself being disappointed that Evie hadn't stayed, hadn't come to see her.

But Evie was the reason she was in here.

Evie – *Eve* had masqueraded as Sarah in order to get her arrested and sectioned. And this time, she wouldn't be getting out any time soon.

What were they doing today, Eve and Oliver?

Maybe they were walking along the cliff path, Oliver in his BabyBjörn, burbling away in Eve's ear, grabbing at her coat. But all the time, all the time he was with her, he'd know deep down that it was wrong. That Eve wasn't his Mummin.

Where's Mummin?

He couldn't say it. He couldn't ask Eve where his Mummin was. And Eve wouldn't mention her, she wouldn't go anywhere near the Roman House, she wouldn't do or say anything to bring Sarah's spectre between them. But no matter what Eve was telling herself, no matter how hard she tried to be his mother, no matter how much she wanted to be, she wasn't.

She wasn't.

The question would always be hovering between them, unspoken, wherever they were:

Where's Mummin?

SARAH KNOCKED on the door of Room 14. It wasn't quite shut, but it wasn't open far enough to see in, which Sarah was pretty sure was contravening the rules.

'Come in!'

Marianne danced across the room towards her in a neon-green T-shirt, yellow joggers and a yellow baseball cap.

'Hey there, Sarah!'

'Hi.'

'How's things? Nice to get a visitor! I'm bouncing off the walls here, honey, I don't mind telling you!' She bobbed on her toes as if to an inaudible beat. 'Hey hey *hey*!' She nodded her head in time, and then started waggling her hips. The waggle morphed into a shimmy, and then she was body-popping – at least, Sarah assumed that was what she was attempting – across the room.

'*I'm...* too *schizo* for my *shirt!*'

She pulled her T-shirt up over her head and flung it in the direction of a chair. She wasn't wearing a bra. Before Sarah had a chance to avert her gaze, she got a flash of pendulous boobs.

'Oh God no!' she blurted.

'Too schizo for my *shirt!*' From the corner of her eye, Sarah was aware of Marianne shimmying back in her direction. 'I'm... so... schizo it *hurts!*' And she yelped out a laugh, and pirouetted to the bed, where she flopped down on her back. 'I'm not, actually. I'm bipolar, but I'd highly recommend telling folk in here you're schizophrenic. Even the other schizos aren't so off their trolleys they don't know not to mess with a fellow sufferer, you know, who's as likely to commit a homicide as they are?'

'Okay...'

Marianne cackled, and flung her arms out on the bed. 'If you play it right, it's not so bad in here. Three square meals a day plus snacks, and waited on hand and foot. No bills, no bloody housework, no fucking kids on your case twenty-four seven. I've three boys at home, Sarah, over the age of thirty, and two of them are also bipolar. You try watching *Neighbours* with those two both in a manic phase – because they sync, you know? Like lassies with their periods? And I've no nice nursies to come and take the fuckers back to their rooms. A few weeks of that and getting yourself sectioned starts to look like a very attractive option. A very attractive option indeed.' She closed her eyes, as if she were topless sunbathing on a beach in the Bahamas.

And then she was up again, shimmying over to where her T-shirt had fallen on the floor, pulling it on. 'Hey, sorry about the gratuitous nudity there, Sarah. That's the great thing about being a loony-tune, though, is it not? You can get away with bloody anything!'

'I guess so.'

'What can I do you for? Want to give the tramadol/SSRI cocktail a whirl?'

'Maybe later. Just now, I need sedatives. I need to knock myself out.'

'Permanently?' As if she was asking if Sarah wanted chocolate or vanilla.

'No, of course not! I just need to zonk for a while.'

'Okay, no probs.' She opened the bedside cabinet and brought out the box of peppermint cremes. 'Diazepam do you? That's all I've got at the mo.'

'How many would I need, just to knock myself unconscious for a bit?'

'Ha! You're lucky I'm an honest injun, Sarah. I could tell you that you need twenty of these babies, when actually that's likely to put you in the morgue, you know?'

'Although I don't suppose it's in your interests to kill off the customers.'

'No indeed.' Marianne frowned, pushing the pills around in the bottom of the box. 'I'm sorry, Sarah, looks like some light-fingered bastard's been in here. I could have sworn I had half a dozen.' She corralled two white and blue capsules into a corner of the box. 'Can only offer you two.'

'Okay. Would that be enough?'

'Not to knock you out. I'd say you'd need three, minimum. Safer with four.'

'Right. Well, I'll take the two you have, anyway. How much do I owe you?'

'Twenty.'

'Twenty pounds for two pills?'

'They're capsules. They command a higher price than tablets, obviously, provided they're intact – active substance still a hundred per cent present and correct. Whereas put a tablet in your gob for thirty seconds, some of it's going to dissolve off.'

'But twenty pounds?'

'Take it or leave it.' Marianne's good humour was rapidly dissipating. 'It's a market economy in here. Supply and demand.'

Sarah took her purse from her robe pocket and pulled out two ten-pound notes.

When Carol came back to collect the porridge, she made a show of examining the bowl and tut-tutting. 'Oh dear. Someone hasn't eaten her breakfast.'

'If only we could say the same about you.' Sarah smiled sweetly. 'Let me guess: bacon and eggs, fried bread, beans, black pudding, white pudding... At least two helpings, because let's face it, it's not easy, consuming enough calories to keep that fat arse busting out of its size twenty-four uniform.'

Carol's face was a picture.

Sarah suddenly shoved the invalid table so the edge of it slammed into Carol's thighs and she staggered back. And now Sarah was up and out of the chair and Carol was yelling, 'Assistance, *assistance!*' and as Sarah closed her hands round the woman's fat neck, people were pouring into the room, someone was restraining her, and a doctor appeared – not Dr Laghari, one of the female ones – and gave her a shot in the arm.

When she came to, she confined herself to shouting and

sobbing that she wanted something to calm her down. And sure enough, after a 'chat' with the doctor, a white and blue capsule was produced in the inevitable miniature plastic beaker.

'Here you are, Sarah,' said nice nurse Nicola.

'Evie,' said Sarah. 'My name's *Evie*.'

Nicola's smile didn't waver. 'No, dear, that's your sister, isn't it?'

Sarah put the pill into her mouth and, as Marianne had instructed, pushed it with her tongue down between her gum and her cheek. The slug of water she swallowed left it *in situ*, and when Nicola asked her to open her mouth, there was 'nothing to see here', as Marianne had put it.

When Nicola had gone, Sarah got out of bed, opened her toilet bag and took out the little box of tampons she kept there. Opening it, she spat the capsule into the space vacated by one of the tampons she'd used.

'I NEED to get a message to my sister,' said Sarah when she next saw Dr Laghari. 'She's not taking my calls. Could someone contact her and tell her I need to see her? The sooner the better. We're partners in our architectural practice, Sister Archt, but that obviously can't continue. If I'm going to be in here for a while, I want to sign over the business to Evie. So she has full control.'

'I see.'

'It makes practical sense, and I think... Well, it would be a weight off my mind.'

'That seems sensible.'

'I feel... I know it's not good to be negative, but, realistically, I think it's pretty obvious I've been... spiralling. Deteriorating, mentally. I'm getting these weird thoughts, and I...' She took a breath. 'I'll tell you about those, but I just wanted to ask you if someone could contact her? Tell her I'll sign whatever I need to sign while I'm still, well – relatively compos mentis.'

'I'll give her a call myself, if you like.'

Sarah smiled weakly. 'Great. That would be great.'

22

Sarah sat, slack-mouthed, in the wing chair in her room, staring through her hair at nothing. In honour of her visitor, Nicola had helped her wash and dry her hair, and now it was falling loose around her face in the style she had always favoured – although it wasn't styled, as such. It was just falling in two curtains over her eyes.

She often sat here to vegetate, staring out of the window or dozing.

It was scary how little acting was required, now, to play the loony-tune. The performance was uncomfortably close to the reality of what she had become. Of what Eve had made her.

Nicola had positioned another chair, a low-backed one from the rec room, opposite Sarah's for her visitor. Who was late. Might she not turn up?

But no. She could hear Eve's chirpy tones in the corridor, chatting to Nicola.

'Well, Sarah, here we are, then!' Nicola bustled in. 'Here's your sister to see you!' As if it was the best treat ever.

Sarah didn't look round.

'Hi, Sarah!' Eve's voice was too high. Nervous.

'Hi,' Sarah mumbled.

'We ask visitors to leave the door open, okay, Evie?' said Nicola. 'Just come and see us at the desk or use the buzzer if you need anything.' Subtext: *if the loony-tune kicks off.*

'Right. Thank you!' Oh-so-cheery Evie.

When Nicola had gone, there was a silence.

'How are you doing, Rah-Bee?' Eve said, her voice tight.

Sarah looked up at her at last. 'Evie?' she said groggily.

Eve was wearing make-up, which was an unforeseen problem: inexpertly applied mascara, foundation and a touch of lipstick, presumably 'armour' for this difficult visit.

'Yes, it's Evie.' Eve put her bag on the bed and dropped into the chair opposite. She half-reached for one of Sarah's hands, slack on her lap, and then evidently thought better of it. 'How are you?'

'Evie?' she repeated. 'Why are you here?'

'You asked to see me, remember?' Eve had a rictus smile on her face. 'About the practice? I've brought the forms –' She obviously didn't believe Sarah was going to sign anything. She knew that was just a ruse to get her here. And yet she had come.

Why?

'But why... Why would you do this to me, Vee-Bee?' She shook her head and kept shaking it. 'Why would you? Why do you hate me so much?'

'Oh Rah-Bee, I don't hate you!' And now Eve did take Sarah's left hand in her right and squeeze it.

Sarah didn't squeeze back. She let her hand lie limp in Eve's.

'Oliver,' Sarah said dully. 'Why have you taken Oliver away from me?'

'I...' Eve let go her hand and stood and walked suddenly away.

'My little boy,' Sarah wailed.

'I'm sorry.'

'You're my *sister*. Why would you do this to me?'

When Eve turned to her, there were tears in her eyes. 'I'm so sorry.'

Sarah sighed, and slumped back in her chair. 'It's okay. I'm not going to fight you. You've won, Evie. You've won.'

'It's not a question of winning.' She was choked, now, with tears. 'I had to. I had to do it, Rah.'

'Should we have a cup of tea?' Sarah said, listlessly. 'They have herbal.'

'Oh.' Eve put a tissue to her face. 'Uh. Yes, okay.'

'Could you get it?'

Eve came back with two steaming mugs. Lemon and ginger, unless she was very much mistaken. Perfect for ministering to someone whose life you had ruined.

'Thanks,' said Sarah as Eve got coasters from the top of the bedside cabinet and set the mugs on the windowsill. 'They have biscuits too. In the tin in the rec room.'

'Okay. Shortbread, if they have it?'

Sarah nodded.

As soon as Eve was out of the door, Sarah took the twist of paper from her pocket, into which she'd emptied the contents of five diazepam capsules, and tipped it into Eve's hot tea. She used the plastic teaspoon she'd hidden in the pocket of her robe to stir it until the powder had dissolved.

When Eve returned, Sarah was slumped back in the chair.

'Here we go.' Eve set a plate with two pieces of shortbread by Sarah's mug.

'You not having any?'

Eve shook her head. 'I'm not hungry.'

'Neither am I.' She picked up her mug, and watched through her hair as Eve sat and did the same.

'That nurse seemed nice.'

'Yeah.'

Silence. Then: 'Is Carol still here?'

'Yeah.'

'But she – she isn't picking on you or anything, is she?'

'No.' She didn't want Eve getting all emotional about poor Rah-Bee's situation and not being able to drink her tea. Which was why the topics of Oliver and Eve's crimes were also off limits now. 'She's been fine. It's not so bad in here, I suppose.'

Eve nodded rapidly, as if desperate to believe that this was true. 'What about Julia? I don't suppose she's still here?'

'No. But I've sort of made another friend. Marianne.'

Eve took a big slurp of tea. 'That's good.'

'She knows the ropes. She's kind of a repeat offender. She has bipolar disorder.' And she began to speak about Marianne as Eve drank her lemon and ginger tea.

'It's good that you're settling in.'

Yeah, it's great. 'It's not so bad,' Sarah repeated.

After a silence, in which Sarah drank more of the sickly tea to encourage Eve to do the same, she said, 'I'll take a look at the documents now.'

'Okay.' Eve set down her mug and went to her bag.

Sarah raised herself slightly off her chair so she could peek into Eve's mug. She had drunk three-quarters of it. Would that be enough?

She took her time 'reading' through the documents while Eve spoke about how Sarah could use the financial settlement to extend the Roman House if she wanted, or maybe launch a new venture.

'I know how you hate all the red tape and the niggly stuff,' she chattered on. 'You could concentrate purely on the design side. I mean, obviously I would be eager to pay for your services, but you could branch out, design for other firms... After the award and everything, I'm sure you'd be snapped up.'

Sarah reached for her mug and took another sip of tea. Eve did the same.

'I'm sorry, my brain's turned to mush,' Sarah apologised. 'I'm going to have to read it through again.'

Eve nodded. At last, her eyes had a hooded look. 'No hurry.'

Five minutes later Eve was zonked in the chair, her head falling forward.

'Evie?' said Sarah, reaching out and touching her arm.

No reaction.

Folding the documents back into the envelope, Sarah shoved them back into Eve's bag and went to the door, pushing it almost but not completely shut. Then she threw off her robe and knelt in front of Eve.

It was surprisingly difficult to undress her. She was a dead weight, seeming to passively resist Sarah as she pulled off her fleece and long-sleeved T-shirt and unfastened her sensible white cotton-rich bra. Then Sarah hauled her over to the bed and flopped her onto it. Boots, and then the most difficult items – the jeans and pants.

She baulked at the pants, but it was important not to mess this up in any way. To be thorough. Sarah didn't wear pants under her pyjamas, so Eve mustn't either.

She shrugged out of the pyjamas and quickly dressed in Eve's clothes, reversing the pants and bra. The jeans were just a tiny bit tight at the waist – they had always been the same size, but Eve, of course, had never carried a baby to term.

That was the critical stage done. If anyone came in now, she could just say 'Sarah' had been sick on herself and 'Evie' had had to help her change.

But her hair!

She dragged the scrunchy off Eve's ponytail and pulled her own hair back into it.

And then she dressed Evie in the pyjamas and robe, forcing the floppy arms and legs into the appropriate holes. She had new respect for the nurses who had to dress and undress doped-up patients every day.

Okay.

'Let's get you back in your chair, Sarah, shall we?' she said in a chirpy Evie voice.

She hauled Eve off the bed and dumped her unceremoniously in the Parker Knoll. Her head bounced off the back of it and she groaned, but she didn't wake up.

'There we go!'

She used the mirror above the sink to redo her hair and slap colour into her cheeks. Now, the make-up issue. She wetted a tissue and leant over Eve, putting a hand on her forehead to push her head back. She scrubbed off the lipstick and put the telltale tissue into Eve's bag before getting another to remove what she could of the foundation and mascara.

She found a lipstick in Eve's bag and applied a little to her own mouth, smiling perkily into the mirror. That would have to do. She didn't really look like Eve. Her eyes were too dull. Her face too pale. She slapped her cheeks again.

Then she adjusted the collar of the fleece, picked up Eve's bag...

But the sedatives. They might come in handy again.

She got the remaining capsules from the tampon box and dropped them into an inner pocket of Eve's bag. Then she picked up the bag and opened the door.

A nurse, not Nicola, was helping another inmate walk down the corridor. Sarah gave her a bright smile and strode past, her heart bumping, expecting any second that the nurse would shout: 'Assistance!'

But she didn't.

Nicola was sitting behind the long curve of the nurses' desk, staring at a computer screen, but when Sarah approached, she looked up at once, all smiles. 'How's it going?'

Sarah swallowed, the smile stiff on her face. 'She's fallen

asleep.' The cheery smile was inappropriate in combination with what she was about to say. She turned it into a rueful grimace. 'We were in the middle of a conversation and she just nodded off. Is she okay? She seems very dopey.'

'Yes, it's the sedatives,' Nicola said, coming out from behind the desk. 'But we're hoping to taper the dose and bring her off them soon.' She touched Sarah's arm. 'It's nothing to worry about. I'll come and check on her if you like?'

Sarah didn't like, but she couldn't very well object.

Back in the room, she was relieved to see that Eve was still out of it. Nicola bent over her and touched her wrist. 'She's fine. Did you manage to have a nice chat?'

Sarah grimaced again. 'She seemed very confused. She kept calling me Sarah and insisting that she was Evie. Imitating my voice.'

Nicola also grimaced. 'She's been having a bad few days. Keeps contradicting us when we call her Sarah – insists that she's Evie.'

'We used to play a game when we were children, where we'd switch identities with each other.' Sarah smiled sadly. 'That must be where this is coming from. But why?'

Nicola shook her head. 'There's often no rhyme or reason to their delusions.'

Sarah nodded. 'Well. I don't suppose there's much point in me staying.'

'No. I'll tell her you said goodbye.'

'Yes. Please tell her it was lovely to see her and I'm glad she's making such good progress.'

Nicola nodded, the cheery mask slipping a bit.

Because, of course, 'Sarah' wasn't making good progress. And she was about to get a whole lot worse. The delusion that she was Evie was about to take over, big time.

'Thank you so much for looking after her so well,' 'Evie' gushed.

'Oh, you're welcome! She's one of our favourites, although we're not meant to have them!'

Sarah walked past the now empty desk and down the corridor to the double doors at the end of it. These doors were always locked, and there was a buzzer for visitors to press to be let out. She pressed it and waited, her heart bumping so hard she was sure she was going to pass out. It seemed to take an age for a nurse to appear –

And oh God, it was Carol!

Coming down the corridor with the rolling walk necessitated by her huge thighs. A stately procession of one.

'Thank you!' Sarah said brightly, smiling so hard it was making her cheeks sore.

Carol said nothing, just poked a fat finger at the keypad to key in the combination.

The doors clicked.

'Thank you so much!' beamed 'Evie', and pushed through the doors to the outer corridor.

She had to stop herself running down it. She walked, the soles of her boots on the shiny linoleum clipping along confidently. A visitor on her way to the exit. Nothing to see here. She smiled at the people she met coming the other way.

And all the while, she expected a shout behind her; running feet.

But no one came after her. No one stopped her. She found her way, after a few false turns, to the main lobby and smiled at the receptionist as she clipped past and out of the door and into the car park.

It was a beautiful day.

The sun was bright on the dry, pale grey tarmac under her feet, and the shrubs by the main door were just coming into new leaf. She could see Eve's car over by the far wall, but she took a detour to look at the daffodils and crocuses in the strip of grass down the centre of the car park and to take between finger and thumb one of the long, swelling buds on a little birch tree.

Spring.

It was spring, and everywhere life was returning, unfolding, opening out to the sun.

23

'Oh, hello, dear,' said Margaret, opening the door wide. 'How did it go? How is she?'

Sarah grimaced. 'Not good, I'm afraid.' She stepped inside. She could hear Oliver somewhere through the house, burbling away, but she wasn't about to barge past Margaret to get to him. She was Eve, and Eve would be calm and collected, if sad and a bit weary. Eve wouldn't be a bundle of nerves, Eve wasn't an agoraphobic who had just driven a car, incredibly badly, for the first time in eight years.

Sarah sighed. 'She's very confused.'

'Aye.' Margaret sucked in a breath. 'It's an awful thing, right enough.'

Oliver was in a tiny playpen in the kitchen, standing up and holding onto the bars. She wanted to run to him and grab him out of there. It was like they'd put him in prison!

'Hello, darling!' she cooed instead, and lifted him out and up into her arms.

But he struggled and started to whine, his feet kicking against her.

'Oh, now, now,' said Margaret. 'Now, now, now.'

Oliver stopped kicking and looked over at Margaret.

'Only good boys who don't kick their mummies get sweeties!' Margaret opened a drawer and took out a lollipop. 'Oh! What have we here?'

Ollie's eyes were riveted to it, to the translucent, bright red globe that emerged from the wrapper. Margaret handed it to him with a smile. He snatched it and stuck it straight in his mouth.

What was Eve thinking, letting the old biddy give him rubbish like that? Sarah shuddered to think of all the E-numbers that must be in it. The red colour was almost fluorescent. And the sugar, rotting his little teeth! But worst of all, lollipops were a terrible choking hazard.

Eve couldn't know. Surely? Risk-averse Eve would never have sanctioned this.

'Thank you!' she gushed. 'Thanks so much for taking him – you're a lifesaver!'

As soon as they were inside Eve's cottage, Sarah pulled on the stick.

'Open wide, Ollie.'

He looked at her.

'Oliver.' She tugged gently. 'It's not nice. Dirty.'

Oliver shook his head, his lips closed firmly on the stick.

'I'm sorry, darling, but you can't have it.'

As his mouth contorted in protest, Sarah took the opportunity to remove the lollipop.

He wailed. He kicked at her again.

'Stop that!' she snapped.

He stopped kicking, but carried on crying. She took him through to the kitchen, which was a surprisingly spacious room with a comfy old sofa in front of a little wood-burning stove. 'I think we can find something a lot nicer than a nasty lollipop.'

Setting him down on the sofa, she started opening cupboards. She found a bag of chocolate buttons and a banana, which she cut up and put on a plate with some of the buttons. Meanwhile, Oliver was grizzling to himself and kicking the sofa.

'Ooh, Ollie!' she smiled, taking the plate across. 'Look what *we've* got!'

He interrupted his grizzling to examine the offering.

A little hand reached out to a button.

She lit the stove, and they sat snuggled on the sofa, eating the treat and watching the flames. Soon, Ollie's head against her side became heavy, and he relaxed against her. She put her face to the top of his head and breathed him in, the quiff tickling her nose. He was soft and warm and smelt of digestive biscuits. 'Good enough to eat,' she whispered, hugging him close.

As she watched the flames, unbidden, a memory came.

The fire in the study.

Dad, telling them to set it and then go and get 'those ridiculous logs' and burn them.

The Baron and Belle!

Their daily walks round the village had 'come to his attention'. They hadn't meant it as a dig at Dad, to show him up, to embarrass him, but he had seen everything in relation to himself, so when he'd found out about the log dogs, he'd immediately assumed that this was yet another example of the twins' wickedness in trying to turn people against him, trying to suggest he was too mean to buy them proper toys.

Sarah had been distraught, but Evie, she suspected, had rather enjoyed the tragedy of it. She had whispered to Sarah as they had stood there, watching the flames lick around the Baron's smiling face... Belle's cute fat stomach...

'Belle was messing around and accidentally fell into the fire, and the Baron immediately flung himself after her because he didn't want to live without her!' Her eyes had shone with tears. 'Because she has him *in thrall*!'

They had gathered the cold ashes, when Mum and Dad were out, and scattered them on the brook, where the Baron and Belle had been happiest. Evie had said an elegy.

When a phone started ringing, for a moment she wondered where it was coming from, before she realised it must be Eve's mobile in her bag. Easing Oliver horizontal, she slipped out from under him and excavated in the bag until she found it.

It was Jagan Laghari.

Taking it into the hall: 'Hello, Dr Laghari?'

'Hello, is that Evie Booth?'

'Yes.'

'I'm just calling to ask how you felt today's visit went. We've been a little concerned about your sister – that she doesn't seem to be improving as we'd hoped.'

'Mm.' Sarah sighed. 'I was a bit shocked, to be honest, by how much worse she seemed. Worse than last time.'

He sighed too. 'Yes.'

'I'm afraid my visit – I don't think it helped.' She put a little tremble into Evie's voice. 'We used to play this game as children, where we'd pretend to be the other twin. But Sarah – she seems to actually be confused as to which of us she is! One minute she was calling me Evie, and the next Sarah.'

'Yes, the nurses did report that she was very confused... I've just seen her. She was very agitated. Insisting that she's Evie, not Sarah.' A pause. 'When you were growing up, do you think that sometimes perhaps she wished she were you? Or later, after she developed her mental health problems?'

Sarah swallowed. 'I don't know. Maybe.'

'I know you've always had to be the strong one. You've always looked out for her.'

She swallowed again. 'Yes.'

'That can't have been easy.'

She didn't know what to say.

'But,' he continued, 'it also can't have been easy for Sarah, having to watch from the sidelines, in the shadows, one might almost say, while you were out there enjoying life. She wouldn't be human if she didn't feel some envy. If she didn't sometimes wish you could swap places.'

'I suppose that's maybe true.'

'I think it might be a good idea not to visit again for a while, until we've tackled this new delusion.'

'Yes. Of course. Thank you, Dr Laghari, for all you're doing for her.'

'Not at all. It's my genuine pleasure.'

'She's not always – easy. I know it's not her fault, but still.'

'Sarah is a delight, Evie, I can assure you! She is a keen observer of the human condition!'

'Uh – well, yes, I guess so. But I'm just so worried about her! The episodes are obviously becoming more frequent, and that's not a good sign, is it?'

'I'm hopeful that we can address her problems while she's here.' A neat sidestep of the question.

'Oh, well, that's good. But... How long do you think she'll need to stay at Marnoch Brae this time?'

'Mmm, that's not something I can determine at this stage, but I'm afraid her stay this time may be more protracted.'

'So we could be talking months rather than weeks?'

'I'm afraid so. Let's wait and see, but I'm afraid so.'

As she ended the call, she allowed herself a soft little whoop of triumph.

Months.

There was a text message, she saw, from Lewis:

How did it go?

She fired off a reply:

As well as could be expected.

And almost immediately, he'd texted back:

I'll come over tonight, shall I, and you can tell me about it?

She grimaced.

Make it tomorrow? James grouchy.

She was too tired for close scrutiny. If anyone was going to rumble her, it would be Lewis. She was going to have to see him at some point, of course, and she was curious about what he was going to say. What he would give away.

Okay. See you then.

She carried Oliver upstairs to his cot. It was his own white cot, from the nursery at the Roman House – and above it was the bird mobile, the familiar brightly coloured silk birds bobbing gently in the air disturbed by her movements.

And there was his ride-on bus; his roll-and-ring ramp tower... All his toys, although she didn't see the shop she'd made. And there were new ones too. A wooden Noah's ark with sweet little wooden animals; an adorable cleaner's set with miniature mop and bucket and broom, and even a little dustpan and brush; picture dominoes, set out in a pattern in one corner of the room; a chunky train set...

And next to it, the wooden pull-along dog.

She stroked its head absently, remembering that summer's day by the brook with Evie, that perfect summer's day when they'd gorged themselves on biscuits smuggled from the vicarage pantry and the log dogs had frolicked in the water before they'd all collapsed on the grass to dry out in the sun.

Evie had set the Baron on his back so the cars could dry and not go rusty.

'*O what can ail thee, knight-at-arms, alone and palely loitering?*' she had intoned. '*The sedge has withered from the lake, and no birds sing.* I can't remember any of the rest except for *La Belle Dame Sans Merci hath thee in thrall!*'

And they'd both looked at Belle, soggy and battered and, it had to be admitted, unattractive, even for a log – and laughed their heads off.

Sarah sat down, suddenly, on the child's chair by the

window, next to which there was a low shelf containing a selection of books.

Oh Evie.

No.

No. She wasn't Evie, she was Eve; she was someone Sarah barely knew. She mustn't weaken. She must remember what Eve had done and what Sarah herself must now do because of it.

She was managing to play the role of Eve convincingly. Neither Margaret nor Dr Laghari had even suspected that she might be an imposter. Her plan had been to get Oliver and go, but what was the rush? Eve was going to be in Marnoch Brae for months – how was she going to prove that she was Eve, not Sarah?

She couldn't.

Sarah smiled, imagining what must have happened when Eve came to and realised where she was; that she was wearing Sarah's pyjamas and dressing gown. She must have gone mental when she'd realised what had happened, what Sarah had done –

All adding to the medical staff's concerns about her deterioration.

She chuckled, and wondered if Eve appreciated the irony – that Sarah had got the idea for the switcheroo from Eve's stunt in the café.

Might it be possible to live, for a while, as Eve?

Dr Laghari had been right – she *had* always envied Eve her easy life, her easy confidence, the way everything went right for her. And it had felt so good, when she'd impersonated Eve at the health centre... It had almost been as if she *was* Eve. It had almost been as if she'd sloughed off Sarah's problems. She hadn't felt even close to a panic attack, although in theory the situation had been very stressful. She had coped because she had been Eve, not Sarah.

Why shouldn't she have Eve's life for a while?

Eve owed her this.

It would give her a chance to plan everything properly and obtain new identities. Maybe she could even manage to buy fake passports for herself and Oliver on the dark web.

Leaving the room quietly, she crossed the landing to Eve's bedroom. Eve had never been much into the interiors side of creating a home, and the room was bland, whites and creams, with just a tweedy throw over the armchair by the window providing texture and colour. A couple of Victorian prints on the wall that had belonged to Grannie. Photos of Eve and Sarah on the bedside cabinets, and lots of Oliver.

And oh my God –

A photograph of Eve and George. Not their wedding photo. It was a casual selfie taken halfway up a mountain, their sweaty faces grinning at the lens, distorted and odd-looking.

When Sarah had lived here with Evie, before the Roman House, before Oliver, she was sure this photo hadn't been on display. Why would Evie want to look at a photo of that bastard?

But it was after she met George, perhaps, that Evie had begun to change. She and Sarah had been living happily together in their flat when he'd come along, worming his way in, despite Evie's initial misgivings. The flat had immediately felt different, with his man-smells everywhere, his stubble in the sink – because he never cleaned up after himself – and his mountains of meat in the freezer. He had loved a roast, and the smell of them had permeated everything, her hair, her clothes –

And he'd been so jealous of their twin bond, always trying to drive a wedge between them. It was the first time she'd ever felt betrayed by Evie, that day in the kitchen, when they were washing up together, when Evie had 'suggested' that Sarah might sometimes give her and George 'space' as a couple and spend time in her room. George had been behind that, of course, but Evie had gone along with it.

She'd sided with George against Sarah.

Sarah had given them 'space' the next evening, sitting in her room with a book she couldn't read for the tears that kept welling up, as if there was an infinite supply, as if she would never be able to stop crying. To make it worse, she could hear them laughing, through the wall. Laughing about *her*?

She'd felt unwelcome in her own home.

In the end she'd found the courage to challenge them; said they had their own room and if they wanted 'space' they could get it there, rather than making Sarah incarcerate herself in an even smaller space when she was already confined to the flat. George had *not* been happy, of course, but Evie had immediately backed down, tearfully apologising. But had Evie secretly resented her presence too?

Had Eve started to appear then – or had Evie *always* been Eve, underneath? Had Sarah never really known her at all?

And did it cut both ways?

Did Eve not really get what it was like to be Sarah?

Well, she was getting it now, because for the next few months she was going to have to live Sarah's life, whether she liked it or not.

She returned to the kitchen and made herself a cup of tea in Eve's favourite mug, a chunky blue one made at a local pottery. Then she called the Bank of Scotland to report Eve's visa debit card stolen and request a new card and pin number – she didn't know Evie's pin, so this was the only way she could think of to enable her to use the card. She had to answer some security questions about her mother's maiden name and the make of her first car, and then she was told a new card and pin would be sent out separately to her address.

She curled up on Eve's sofa and opened Eve's latest *Paddler* magazine. She had zero interest in the Freestyle World Cup or kayaking round the Channel Islands, but she should probably gen up a bit in case she had to interact with the people in the kayak club. There was no way they'd actually get her out in a kayak, but fortunately they didn't go out much in the winter, and she always had Oliver – no, *James* – as an excuse for crying off.

She could see why Eve liked this mug. It felt good and weighty in her hands, and the crude, thick sides kept the tea nice and hot. A Biscoff was all that was missing to complete the picture. She got one from the tin in the cupboard and took a small bite.

Crisp and satisfying and very faintly cinnamony. Very nice. Very nice indeed.

24

A s Oliver was carefully placing his picture domino next to Sarah's on the kitchen table, tongue slightly protruding in concentration, Eve's phone trilled.

Sarah took it from her pocket. It was Lulu Shaw, a client for whom Sarah and Eve had designed a 'bothy' to be built in her garden as somewhere for her autistic teenager to hang out for a bit of peace and quiet, away from the rest of the family. She'd better take this.

'Hello?'

'Hi, Evie! We've got a bit of a situation. You know you speci-fied reclaimed Welsh slates for the roof? The bastard is trying to fob us off with revolting new Spanish things. I've just been down there and they've already got about half of one side of the roof covered with them, and Willie Black is refusing to take them down; says he's doing us a favour and these are superior to what's on the spec.'

'Oh God.' This builder, Willie Black, was notorious for quoting low and then clawing back profit by cutting corners and sneaking in cheaper alternatives to what was on the spec. He got very little repeat business, but there always seemed to be a big enough pool of unsuspecting new clients who were unaware of his reputation until it was too late. 'Well, he's signed a contract to the effect that he'll supply what's on the spec, so it doesn't matter what he says. Reclaimed Welsh slates are on the spec, so that's what he has to supply. Would you like me to give him a call?'

'Well... I was hoping you could do a site visit. I've lost all confidence in him, to be honest. I'm sure he's probably trying it on with other materials, but I don't have the knowledge to be able to challenge him. Would you be able to come over? The sooner the better?'

Sarah grimaced. 'Um, I'm rather busy at the moment, Lulu, with other projects.'

'Just a quick check would be all that you'd need to do. A quick check of the materials he's using against the spec.'

The Shaws lived a good ten miles away, which would necessitate a twenty-mile round trip. But Sarah would have to get used to driving Eve's car, and a country drive was probably a good way to ease herself in.

'I could do that. Would eleven tomorrow morning be good for you?'

'That would be perfect! Thanks a million!'

'No probs!' She gave a bright Evie inflection to the words, realising that she'd been a bit un-Evie in this conversation. She was going to have to watch that. 'See you tomorrow!'

But during lunch – Oliver's favourite mashed potato, cheese and peas – a text came in from Chrissie, one of Eve's friends from the baby and toddler group:

Really looking forward to lunch tomorrow after the group and a catch-up! Haven't see you for yonks! Still fine to take James for the afternoon. ☺

Sarah looked across the table at Oliver, who had managed

to get a huge tottering load of mashed potato onto his spoon and was carefully lifting it to his mouth. She reached over with her own fork and pushed some of it back onto his plate. 'Not so much at once, Ollie.'

'Yus!' he objected, picking up the fallen potato with his fingers and cramming it back onto the spoon, at which, of course, the rest fell off.

'Oh, the bad potato!' she smiled, in an attempt to avert the tantrum she could tell was imminent.

Too late.

He flung down his spoon and tipped his plate onto the floor, mouth opening wide in a face that was suddenly bright red. She let him scream it out for a while, and then she took a wet cloth and wiped the mucus and tears off his face, talking calmly and cheerfully, and offering him a drink of milk.

As he glugged it, she cleared up the mess and heated up some more potato, cheese and peas in the microwave, making sure it wasn't too hot before she gave it to him.

'Mm, I like this cheese, don't you?' she said, taking a forkful of her own, now cold, lunch from her plate.

He spooned a reasonably sized amount of food into his mouth, and Sarah looked back at the text message.

She didn't want to leave him with this Chrissie person, even for a few hours. She wanted to be with him all day every day, from now on, until he was... oh, maybe thirty. And damn, the baby and toddler group clashed with her site meeting.

She was tempted not to go to the group or to this lunch thing, but if she was going to live as Eve, she was going to have to do Eve things. She fired off a reply to Chrissie:

Perfect! You're a star! Can't wait to see you and hear all your news!!! xx

Eve was big on exclamation marks.

Then she called Lulu back and rearranged the site visit for three tomorrow afternoon. That would actually work out quite well, as she could leave Oliver with Chrissie while she was at Lulu's.

Oliver, she realised, had stopped eating. He was staring across the table at her, his little face full of concern.

'It's okay, darling, just boring work stuff!' she said brightly.

It broke her heart, that look of uncertainty. He must be so unsettled by all this, by everything Eve had put him through – being suddenly separated from Sarah and being called 'James', and living here instead of at the Roman House, and then Eve disappearing...

'Everything's fine,' she assured him, going round the table to take him on her knee. 'Everything's going to be fine from now on. No one's ever going to take you away from me again. That's a promise.'

SHE'D JUST PUT Oliver to bed at seven when there was a tap at the door.

Lewis stood on the step, smiling, a bottle of wine dangling from one hand.

'Hi!'

'Hi.' She smiled back, pulling the door wide.

He stepped inside, set the bottle down on the hall table, and pushed the door to behind him. 'Don't worry – I did the old commando crawl under Margaret's windows!' And he took her face in his hands.

She made herself keep smiling.

Slowly, he brought his mouth down on hers.

Oh God. Oh *God*! How could Eve...

Yuck, he was trying to get his tongue into her mouth!

She didn't know what to do with her hands. Instinctively, she had put them up to push him away, but he had surprised her with the tongue thing before she could make contact, and now her hands were frozen in mid-air between them.

She opened her mouth to accommodate the tongue – which tasted unpleasantly of garlic – and set her hands on his shoulders.

This explained a lot.

They were obviously keeping the relationship under wraps in case anyone thought to investigate the twins' medical records and what might have been going on there, and realised that Eve and Lewis had been in cahoots.

But oh God! She wasn't sure she could do this! Yes, he was an attractive man and everything, but...

Eeuuw!

He was *Lewis*!

He pulled back from the kiss. Thank God. He frowned at her. 'You okay?'

She made herself wrap her arms around him – nice hard-muscled back, she had to admit – and press her face into his shoulder. 'Yesterday was awful,' she whispered. 'Sarah...'

He squeezed her. Rubbed her back.

'I can imagine. But you got through it.'

She relaxed against him. 'Only just.' And then she stepped away, with a sudden, Evie-ish *I'm pulling myself together now* smile. 'I'm sorry, I know it has to be done, but... Anyway! Distract me! Entertain me! Tell me about your day! I want to hear confidential stuff about patients that you're not meant to disclose!'

He laughed. 'Maybe I can think of a better way to distract you.'

Oh God.

'Hmm. I'm sure you can!' she laughed. 'But first, I need a drink! Ha ha! Sorry, I don't mean it like that –'

Yes she did.

She snatched up the wine and practically ran ahead of him

into the kitchen, pulling open the cutlery drawer and grabbing the corkscrew.

SHE FOUND a second bottle of wine in a cupboard and they polished off most of that too, in Sarah's case, on an empty stomach. She'd been hoping to incapacitate him, but no such luck. He pulled her down onto the sofa and played with the zip on her fleece for a while, like a chimp who'd found something shiny. She shrugged the fleece off.

Big mistake, as he seemed to take this as an invitation to move things along and began snuffling under her T-shirt. *Ugh ugh ughhhh!* She braced herself for breast action, but – oh God, he was *licking her armpit!*

Was this normal?

She supposed she'd better do something to him, not least to take her mind off what was happening in her armpit. But he was so tall that she couldn't reach further down his body than his belly button.

She undid his shirt and poked a finger into it.

Ugh.

He groaned. She gave a little gasp of what she hoped sounded like pleasure. Maybe this would be all he wanted to do? Maybe he was too drunk for anything more?

But no, he was suddenly standing, pulling off his clothes, and it was horribly obvious that he wasn't too drunk at all. He took a condom from his jeans pocket and she averted her gaze, feeling her face redden. *No!* This was awful! She didn't even want to *see* that, much less –

It was only sex. She could do this. Gaze still averted, she sat up and began taking off her own clothes.

He was a doctor. She should think of this as a gynaecological procedure.

When she was naked herself, she lay down and tried not to

tense up. She looked past him at the picture of a stormy sea hanging on the wall next to the window, like a patient in a clinic trying to distract herself.

Now then, here we go, she imagined him saying, penis wielded like a surgical instrument. *Please just try to relax.*

This wasn't going to work.

'Sorry, just have to...' She jumped up and scooted from the room.

Oh God.

She locked herself in the loo; had a pee, and then just sat there.

She mustn't think of him as Lewis. Who was he like on TV that she fancied? That contestant on *The Great Pottery Throw Down* she'd had a thing about – Josh – he was quite like Lewis. Same build and hair.

She remembered watching Josh's hands caress the clay, the way he'd manhandled that massive sculpture of Gaia, the earth goddess, when he'd had trouble with the breasts and hips. The camera had lingered on him for ages, and Sarah had played that sequence back quite a few times. Okay so Gaia's proportions had been all wrong and Josh had been eliminated that week, but still. That had been a great moment, the combination of his angst, all sweaty and tortured-artist, and the way his hands...

Back in the kitchen, Lewis was sitting on the sofa. He seemed to have been putting in the time leafing through Eve's *Paddler.*

She took an indirect route across the room, tacking like a sailing boat, pretending she wanted to look at something on the table, and then on the mantelpiece, so as to expose as little as possible of her naked body to his gaze.

When she eventually reached the sofa, she sat down next to him. 'Sorry about that.'

He threw the magazine to the floor, and they carried on

where they'd left off.

She ran her hands over his shoulders, his back. 'Can you sort of... massage me? Like you're sculpting me from clay?'

'Uh...'

'Like this?'

She wouldn't say it was great, but she successfully conjured Josh, and it wasn't terrible. Afterwards, he obviously wanted her to lie there with him, their bodies entangled in front of the stove, but she couldn't do that. She got up, pulling her fleece on, pretending she'd heard Oliver.

'Back in a tick.'

But he came with her, lacing his fingers through hers as she stood looking down at Oliver in his cot. Tears came to her eyes as she looked at him, so innocent and perfect, little knowing what his mother had just had to do.

Lewis pulled her closer. 'He's a happy little chappie,' he whispered, his garlic-breath on her face.

She smiled, and pulled him from the room.

AFTER THEY'D SHOWERED – separately – and dressed, they returned to the kitchen.

'Are you hungry?' she asked him.

'No, thanks, I ate earlier.'

'I might make an omelette. Sure I can't tempt you?'

He gave her a leer that was presumably meant to be comical. 'Always.'

How could Eve bear it?

Maybe he would expect to stay the night. She'd have to let him share her bed. She wasn't sure she could sleep with him lying right next to her. She'd have to make an excuse, make up a reason why he couldn't stay.

But oh God – he was going to expect her to service his

needs on a regular basis! She'd have to develop some sort of medical condition...

No she couldn't, because he was a *fucking doctor*. He'd know she was faking it.

What was she going to do?

'Oh Evie,' he said, putting an arm round her and gently removing the frying pan from her hand. 'You sit. I'll make.'

So she sat at the table in a daze while he cracked eggs and hunted down the pepper.

He thought she was upset about her sister.

'She was so pathetic,' she said on cue. 'She's really... spiralling down.'

He didn't turn round. 'So what was the real reason for summoning you? Presumably she wanted to confront you?'

'I don't know if *confront* is the word. She wanted to know why. Why I'd done it.' She didn't have to fake the tears that came.

'So did she admit that she knows that James is Oliver?'

Admit? As if Sarah was the one in the wrong.

'Yes. It was horrible. I didn't know what to say.'

'Did she say how she found out?'

'No. But I don't think she ever really believed it. She's his *mother*, Lewis. How could I ever have thought this was going to work? She'd have to be really off her trolley to accept that her *own child* isn't hers.'

He was looking at her oddly. 'Well, that was only ever the best-case scenario.'

Was it?

He sighed, in a *not this again* long-suffering way. 'There's no guarantee that a higher dosage would have produced a more severe or longer lasting delusional state,' he said slowly, as if rehashing an old argument. 'It's not a simple dose-response relationship.'

He was talking about the psychotic episode that Sarah had

assumed had been triggered by Oliver's disappearance. But...
he was saying it had actually been caused by a drug? That he
and Eve had deliberately given her something to make her
delusional and psychotic?

Of course.

It didn't make any sense the other way round, the way she'd
assumed it had happened. It didn't make sense that Oliver's
disappearance had conveniently triggered her delusional
episode, because they *couldn't have known* that would happen. If
they'd taken Oliver and got her sectioned when she was
completely compos mentis, there was a huge risk that the
doctors at Marnoch Brae would have taken her story that she
had a child called Oliver more seriously.

They'd needed her to be genuinely delusional, and the only
way they'd been able to guarantee that had been to trigger the
episode themselves.

What had they given her?

She swallowed. 'I suppose a higher dose could have been
dangerous.'

'Well, yes, with any drug, generally speaking, the lower the
dose, the safer it is.'

'Is there such a thing as a safe dose?'

He looked round at her again, head slightly tilted, as if they
were discussing an abstract medical question. 'Antidepressants
are usually safe at low doses.'

Antidepressants.

Of course. Antidepressants had accidentally triggered her
very first delusional episode, when she'd conceived Oliver. It
had been explained to her at the time that she'd probably experienced the rare side effect of psychosis because her existing
mental health issues had made her more susceptible to it than
the average patient.

And Lewis, as her GP, knew all about her bad reaction. And
so he'd conspired with Eve to give her antidepressants. Laced

her food or drink with them.

He slid the omelette onto a plate and set it down in front of her. She didn't even look at it. As he set his hands on her shoulders, she pulled away from him.

'She's really shaken you up, hasn't she?'

She stood, but he came after her, pulling her into a hug – and she couldn't do this, she couldn't pretend she felt anything but revulsion for him. She pushed him away, so hard that he staggered back against the table.

'I'm sorry,' she managed. 'It's just... It's been a terrible day. She's – she's my sister, my *twin*.'

'I know.' He grimaced at her. 'But we're doing the right thing, Evie. You have to hold onto that.'

'Really?' she blurted. '*Really?*'

'You have to hold onto the fact that Sarah's in no fit state to look after a child.'

So that was how Eve had sold it to him.

The bitch.

The absolute bitch.

She took a long breath. 'She was doing pretty well until we fed her antidepressants and kicked all this off! She was doing pretty well for *eighteen months!*'

Eighteen months. Why had Eve waited so long? Why not put the plan into operation right after Oliver's birth? Why give Sarah all that time to bond with him, so when they did take him, she was so much less likely to accept their lies?

'We should have taken him immediately after he was born,' she said, and waited.

He shook his head.

'What?' she challenged him.

'Don't start blaming yourself. Why do you always blame yourself? You were acting with the best intentions. How were you to know she wouldn't have another episode? Statistically, she was right up there in the high-risk group for postpartum psychosis.' He shook his head. 'You acted with the best intentions in waiting for nature to take its course, and when it didn't, you acted with the best intentions in giving her as small a dose as was feasible. Stop beating yourself up.'

She couldn't believe what she was hearing! 'How can I pat myself on the back for... for having a plan A of waiting until my sister had a psychotic episode before *stealing her child*? For being *reluctant* to go to plan B – *precipitating* one – but *doing it anyway*! *God*, Lewis!'

'It all worked out for everyone, didn't it, initially at least? We got our best-case scenario – she accepted that Oliver was James and was let out of Marnoch Brae, back into the bosom of her family.'

'And if she hadn't... if she hadn't accepted it... You'd have been happy for her to stay locked away forever?' A shiver ran through her. That, of course, had been the non-best-case scenario: Sarah refusing to accept that Oliver was James, assessed as being a danger to him, and kept in Marnoch Brae indefinitely.

'If she'd been kept in there long enough, doped to the eyeballs for a few months – years, even – she'd probably have been pretty much a zombie by the time she was released. People generally get out of these places more damaged than when they went in. There was a high chance she wouldn't know what year it was, let alone whether a child she hasn't seen for yonks is hers or not.'

'And you're hoping that happens now, now that she's back in there? You're hoping it breaks her?'

'Evie. You know this is right for James. She's mentally unstable. She's a danger to him.' It sounded like he was trying to convince himself as much as Eve.

'And what if they let her out, and it *hasn't* broken her?' Sarah said tightly. 'She's going to come after us. She's going to come after Oliver.'

For a long moment, he said nothing, and she waited, her heart hammering in her chest. *What were they going to do?*

'God, Evie, it's a bit late to be having second thoughts now!' he finally flared up.

She took a step back. Did he mean second thoughts about the whole thing? Or second thoughts about whatever they were planning to do when Sarah got out of Marnoch Brae?

What *were* they planning to do?

'We could give him back.'

He gaped at her, as if she had suddenly grown two heads.

Big mistake. Eve would never back down, never give Oliver back, never let Sarah win. And Lewis surely knew that.

She sighed. 'Sorry, momentary wobble. But... Maybe we don't have to do anything. I mean, she's got no money now.' She hadn't been up to the Roman House yet, but it was a safe bet that they'd found and appropriated the money in the rucksack she'd left by the door. 'What can she do?'

'She'll snatch him. Of course she will, money or no money. Doing nothing isn't an option and you know it.'

'Yeah, sorry. I know.'

He nodded, but with narrowed eyes, as if wondering when Evie had had the personality transplant. Sarah was going to have to be more careful. And she couldn't push to find out what it was they were planning to do to her next. She had to bide her time. He was bound to bring the subject up himself, eventually.

She had gone cold, right across her shoulders and up her neck. Whatever it was they were planning, Sarah was unlikely to survive it in any meaningful sense. How could they let her just go back to her old life? Because Lewis was dead right – she would never willingly let Eve keep Oliver.

'I'm sorry I dragged you into this in the first place,' she said.

He shook his head, and stepped towards her, and tucked a stray strand of hair behind her ear. 'No dragging required.'

'I know you put your career on the line. Not just falsifying your own notes, but logging in as Fiona Cameron – If they found out you did that...'

He frowned. 'But I didn't.'

'B-but her notes,' she stuttered.

'Her notes were all Fiona's own work.'

Which meant... Of course! Eve had masqueraded as Sarah in those video consultations. She'd convince Fiona Cameron that she was poor delusional Sarah.

'I thought you tweaked them?' she improvised.

He looked nonplussed. 'No. Why would I need to do that?'

Oh-oh. 'I must have misunderstood something you said. Sorry, my head's all over the place. That's the problem with a guilty conscience, I guess.' She attempted a sigh. 'I should never have involved you in this.'

'Look, it's fine. I'm a big boy, and I take full responsibility for my actions. I knew you were right about Sarah, about her not being able to cope. And even if I hadn't...' He gazed into her eyes. 'I'd do anything for you. You know that.'

She couldn't hold his gaze.

'Evie –'

'I know,' she made herself say. 'And I do appreciate everything you've done. I really do.'

'Would you like me to stay?'

She sighed. 'In a way, yes, but I think I need some time to myself. But – thank you. I don't know what I'd do without you.'

She wouldn't have been able to steal Oliver, for a start.

He was leaning in for a kiss. She ducked past him and picked up the plate with the cold omelette on it. She opened the cupboard under the sink and slid it into the compost bin.

'I'll maybe see you tomorrow?' he said.

'Oh, I don't know – I've got a full-on day of babies and toddlers, a girls' lunch and a site meeting. I think Oliver and I will just zonk after that.'

'James.'

She turned with a rueful smile. 'James. My brain's turned to mush! I'm sorry, I'm terrible company at the moment.'

He came close and pulled up the zip of her fleece, arranging the collar snugly under her chin. 'No. Never. You could never be that. *I'm* sorry, for pushing too hard. I just... When we're apart – I don't know, it's as if I go into some sort of suspended animation and I only come back to life when I'm with you.'

Pathetic. He was just *pathetic*.

'I feel exactly the same way,' she said slowly, and watched his face transform.

25

'All right then!' Sarah said brightly, watching Oliver in the rear-view mirror. 'Here we go!'

She stalled the engine at the first attempt. At the second, the car leapt forward and she had to turn the wheel at lightning speed to avoid the wall of the cottage on the corner. But then they were moving smoothly off, as her feet seemed to remember what to do with the accelerator and clutch.

It was another bright sunny day, and the colours of everything seemed to zing – the red of the postbox by the old village hall was like something in a kids' picture book; the sea was a million points of silver dancing on a turquoise blue that was positively Mediterranean; the brown of the ploughed fields was rich and chocolatey; the grass a vivid, almost unnatural green.

But when she got to the junction with the main road, the sun was in her eyes, and what with that and having to do a hill start, she was distracted, and then Oliver made a sudden noise, and before she knew it, she was pulling out right in front of a car she hadn't seen, and the bastard sounded his horn at her, loud and long.

'Oh piss off!' she yelled. Then: 'Sorry, Oliver.'

She was a sweaty mess by the time they got to the church hall in Golspie where the baby and toddler group was held.

'Okay. Okay, it's fine,' she whispered to herself as she stood on the pavement, looking at the terribly parked car. It wasn't even straight, its nose sticking way out into the road. She would take Oliver in and then come back out and find another space, one with more room to manoeuvre.

She was Evie. She could do this.

It was strange how she couldn't think of herself as Eve. She wasn't Eve, she was Evie. The old Evie.

'Come on then, darling.' She smiled at Oliver in his car seat.

He seemed to have picked up on her tension and started grizzling as she carried him inside, her heart rate going through the roof as she realised just how many people there were in here. It was a huge space, which didn't help, the loud chatter and laughter and kids' screams bouncing off the hard surfaces, assailing her.

'Hi Evie!' screamed a tall blonde woman in skinny jeans, coming right up to her and subjecting both her and Oliver to a hug.

Oliver wriggled in her arms in an effort to get away, and Sarah knew just how he felt.

Could she make an excuse and go? No. If she was going to be Evie, she had to do whatever Evie did.

But she didn't even know who this woman was. Was this Chrissie, who was taking Oliver this afternoon? Sarah plastered a smile to her face as the woman bent to talk to a small girl dressed in denim dungarees over a yellow T-shirt. Was that her child, or someone else's?

'I love your outfit!' Sarah told the girl. 'You're a little Minion, aren't you?'

The girl frowned in incomprehension. She was singularly unattractive, with heavy-framed glasses and pale blonde hair that seemed to be receding from a freakishly high, bumpy fore-head. She really did look exactly like a Minion.

But that maybe wasn't something Sarah should have said out loud. The mother was frowning. The girl really *did* look like a Minion, though. The stupid woman should have realised the effect dressing her in those clothes was going to have.

Sarah found herself desperately swallowing hysterical gulps of laughter, which she had to disguise as a coughing fit. 'Glass... of water,' she got out, hurrying off with Oliver on her hip to the door at the far end of the hall. But it was locked.

She wheeled away, hoping no one had seen her. Kitchen. Where was the fucking kitchen? Oliver was crying properly now, kicking his feet against her.

'Shh, shh, it's okay,' she said, jiggling him. 'Let's see if there are any biscuits.'

Not even the prospect of a biscuit worked. By the time she had located the kitchen, he had worked himself up into a tantrum, twisting in her arms, his face red. This could be her out. She could say he wasn't well –

'*Hiya James!*' A plump woman in an unfortunate choice of leggings and a sparkly top made a clownishly cheerful face at him. 'How excited are *we* today? Because you know what it is today – it's *bunny hops!*'

The change was miraculous. Oliver stopped in mid-wail, his mouth open, a tantrum-drool hanging off it.

'Bunny bunny hops!' the woman crooned, doing a little jump herself, her hands flopping in front of her breasts ridicu-lously, her teeth protruding over her bottom lip.

Oliver wriggled to be let down. Sarah wiped his face and set him on his feet and he put his own little hands up against his chest, pushed out his little teeth and did a sort of stamping skip after the woman. Adorable! And then suddenly, from nowhere, all these people appeared, all these mums and small children, a baby howling, a whole army of toddlers being hopping bunnies, most of them screeching in delight, a cacophony of fingernail-on-blackboard high-pitched noise that rang and echoed back on itself round the high-ceilinged kitchen, and it was like a nightmare, a nightmare she had to stay in because she couldn't leave Oliver, and she couldn't whisk him away when he was having such fun.

The plump woman hopped out of the door into the main hall, and all the kids followed like she was the Pied Piper.

'Good hopping, James!' the woman screamed.

Why did everything have to be so *loud*?

She went to the sink and ran water into a glass, gulping it down, wondering if maybe Oliver would be okay for a while if she legged it, before telling herself again that she was *Evie* and she could *do* this.

She hurried after the kids, smiling a bright perky Evie smile.

THE WOMAN with the Minion was called Iris, and it seemed that she, Chrissie and Eve were the best of friends. When the group finished, the three of them got their kids into their buggies, and they all trooped along to the café a few streets away, where Chrissie had booked a table for lunch.

Sarah concentrated on settling Oliver in a high chair while chaos reigned around them. She saw the poor waitress exchange a look with another customer as one of the kids suddenly screamed at a volume that didn't seem possible for such a small child.

'It was great today, wasn't it?' Chrissie yelled, retrieving her baby's sippy cup from the floor and giving it back to him.

Her other child, a boy a little older than Oliver called Mikey, was pounding a plastic superhero on the table and shouting, and Oliver was watching this bad behaviour in shocked fascination. Iris was wiping ketchup off the Minion's fingers and clothes and the back of the chair.

It was a wonder they were allowed in the café, but she supposed most places had to be child-friendly these days or they'd be hammered by one-star reviews on TripAdvisor. Ollie, she was proud to note, was sitting nicely and gnawing determinedly on a carrot stick.

Still, it was a relief to be out of the hell that was the church hall, presided over by the devil incarnate, aka Alice the bunny-hopper. Everything had to be loud and upbeat, literally. Everything seemed to involve noise and manic activity. When she and Evie were small, they'd gone to the church playgroup, but Sarah didn't remember all that noise and collective chaos. They used to play quietly, surely, at least some of the time? And each child had their choice of individual activity – you could choose to look at a picture book or play on a seesaw with your twin, or join in with a few other children splashing pails and other receptacles into basins of water.

How could Oliver stand it?

But he had seemed to enjoy it. That was the amazing thing.

'Yes, it was particularly lively!' Sarah yelled back.

She had a horrendous headache, but at least her heart rate had slowed and she had stopped sweating. She still wanted to snatch Oliver up and run, but she was no longer seriously thinking about it.

She was going to get through this. She had to leave at 2:30 at the latest, anyway, for the site visit to Lulu Shaw's bothy.

She stroked her palms with her thumbs.

It was fine now. It was *fine*.

'Hey, everything all right here?' the cheery waitress enquired.

Translation: *Shut that kid the fuck up!*

'Perfect!' yelled Chrissie. 'Thank you!'

Finally, Sarah could bear it no longer. She leant across the table, snatched the plastic figure out of Mikey's hand, and said, 'No toys for noisy boys!'

Sudden silence.

Mikey was staring at her, literally dumbfounded.

Chrissie was staring at her.

Iris was staring at her.

The Minion was staring at her.

'Got to think about the other customers,' she said weakly, attempting a smile, setting the plastic figure down on the table within Mikey's reach. 'I think that elderly couple by the wall were about to have a meltdown of their own!' She attempted a little laugh.

'Mikey wasn't having a *meltdown*, Evie,' Chrissie said tightly, taking the plastic figure and returning it to Mummy's Little Darling. 'He was just playing.'

But surely control-freak Eve might well have done the same thing? She had always been correcting Oliver, even before he became 'James'. Maybe she dialled it down when she was with her friends, though.

Mikey sullenly snatched the figure from his mother. His face had gone red and, to her horror, Sarah realised he was about to start crying.

'Sorry.' She grimaced as Chrissie pulled Mikey onto her knee and wrapped her arms around him. 'I've got a splitting headache.'

This was the right thing to say. Splitting headaches, she supposed, must be a common problem around Mikey.

Chrissie looked sympathetic. 'Sorry, you should have said.'

'Drink your water,' Iris suggested. 'Hydration, that's what you need.'

Sarah took a long slug from her glass.

'Oh, I was going to ask you,' Chrissie said. 'Have you decided yet about the twenty-sixth?'

Oh God. 'Um... No, not yet.'

'So what are your thoughts, venue-wise?'

'Oh. Well. I think I'll leave that up to you.'

Cue puzzled looks.

'I'm talking about the kayak club get-together?' said Chrissie.

Damn. Presumably neither of them was in the kayak club. Eve must have been trying to decide where they should meet, and Chrissie and Iris had been brainstorming with her.

'Oh, right, sorry.'

'What did you think I meant?'

She shook her head. 'I don't know – sorry, I'm all over the place. I – I was visiting Sarah at Marnoch Brae a couple of days ago, and it was pretty horrendous. She's in a bad way. I haven't been sleeping, and...' What would Evie say? 'I can't help feeling it's my fault!'

'Oh God, Evie, I didn't realise she'd gone back in!' Iris reached across the table and gripped her arm, and Chrissie made horrified sympathetic noises. 'What happened? Why didn't you call me?'

Sarah just shook her head.

'Oh, you poor thing! Group hug!'

They shuffled awkwardly into a space between the tables big enough for the three of them to hug. Oliver didn't like this at all, objecting, 'Mummin!'

She took him on her lap as she haltingly explained to the others that Sarah had had another 'episode' in the Toasty Teacake. 'Kirsty blew it way out of proportion – she called the police, and Sarah was charged before she was sectioned.' She sighed. 'Okay so there was a bit of damage done, something was smashed, but calling the police was an overreaction. A lot of people find mental illness frightening, though.'

The other two women nodded solemnly, although she could see them thinking yes, it was pretty damn frightening, and for good reason.

. . .

FINALLY, she'd found Lulu Shaw's place. She was ten minutes late as she turned off the road onto a sweeping drive. She knew from photographs and Eve's descriptions that the Shaws lived in a lovely Georgian house with extensive grounds. The drive was lined with mature lime trees, daffodils making splashes of yellow under them.

She tried not to think about Oliver. Should she really have left him with Chrissie and the awful Mikey? But Eve wouldn't have made the arrangement if there had been any actual danger. Mikey wasn't even two years old, for goodness' sake. How dangerous could such a young child be?

'Evie, Evie, Evie,' she said brightly, fixing on a perky smile.

Lulu seemed very glad to see her, taking her arm and thanking her profusely for coming at such short notice.

'It's so good of you,' she gushed. 'Look, do you mind if we go straight down there, and maybe have coffee and cake after? I wouldn't put it past that bastard to knock off for the day about now.' She kicked off her pumps and pulled on Hunter wellies in the porch.

The bothy was set in a little dell at the end of the lawn furthest from the house, across a rustic wooden bridge spanning a rushing stream. It was rather magical, with lots of ferns and moss and that green damp smell that reminded her of the river at home in the Cotswolds.

No no no, don't think about that.

Sarah breathed deeply.

'There's the bugger,' Lulu muttered.

There were two men at the site – a young lad up on the roof, and an older, bulky man, presumably Willie Black, with an incongruously feminine face – rosy cheeks and long eyelashes, and a sort of simper to his mouth when he smiled, which he did a lot.

'Okay,' said Sarah. No point messing about. 'I can see from here that you're not following the spec as regards the slates. Those will all have to come off.' She flicked through the spec to the relevant section. 'Reclaimed Welsh slate, eight by fourteen.'

'Oh, now, Evie.' The man sidestepped closer to her. 'You don't want to be using those! These here, see...' He stooped to one of the crates of slates. 'Top quality. They'll last two, three times as long as that rubbish.'

'I doubt it.' Sarah edged away from him, her chest starting to tighten. 'And that's not the point.'

'They look terrible,' Lulu agreed. 'They're so uniform they almost look like plastic.'

'Ladies, ladies, ladies.'

A phone trilled, and Lulu looked down at the screen in her hand. 'My daughter – I'm going to have to take this. Sorry.' And she walked away.

Don't leave me with him! Sarah wanted to yell after her.

'How long have you been an architect, then, Evie?' Willie asked as she walked inside the building, noting that the windows propped up ready to be installed were cheap imitation sash and case ones rather than the real things as detailed in the spec. And he'd started cement pointing the inside instead of using lime.

'Nine years.' She – *Evie* – marched back outside, looking up at the roof. Those slates really did look awful, and even the lime pointing hadn't been done properly. It was cracking because they hadn't covered it with hessian to let it dry out slowly.

He patted her arm. 'Guess how long I've been in the building game.'

'I've no idea.' She put distance between them.

'Thirty-eight years. *Thirty-eight years*, man and boy. And I can tell you, I can tell you this from thirty-eight years of experience, Evie – reclaimed slates are shite.' He sidled closer to her again, pointing up at the roof and putting a hand on her shoulder. 'How about that for precision? Looks great, that, Evie, eh?'

She was frozen. She couldn't concentrate on what he was saying, what he was pointing at; her eyes were darting about, she couldn't even focus on the roof, on the slates, and suddenly his voice was loud in her ear, as if it were surround-sound, as if it were echoing back at her from the mossy banks hemming in the little dell, and the banks themselves seemed to be moving –

And then the words were pouring out of her mouth.

'I've never seen such a – a sickening combination of incompetence and – *downright dishonesty!* You can't do a decent job of work, so you have to squeeze a profit by under-quoting and swindling people, cutting corners and substituting inferior materials and hoping they won't notice. Pocketing the difference in price. Maybe you're raking it in, maybe you're doing great business, but *you* – are – *morally bankrupt!*' She gulped in a breath. 'And a fucking sleazeball into the bargain!'

The young lad on the roof was gaping down at her with barely concealed delight. Lulu Shaw was also staring over.

She heaved in breath after breath, but she couldn't squeeze the words out at any more than a hoarse whisper: 'You – are – *despicable.*'

She backed away, the spec clutched in her hands like a defensive weapon. She caught hold of a branch and held on for dear life as everything seemed to move around her.

'Evie, are you okay?' Lulu came towards her with a worried expression on her long, ugly face.

Sarah gulped in air. 'That bastard... needs sacking! And he's... a sleazy creep!'

'Hey.' The builder had his hands up, as if to indicate where they were and that they were nowhere near any of Sarah's body parts. 'That's libellous.'

'Slanderous,' Lulu snapped, 'if it wasn't true, which it is! What the fuck have you done?'

'Nothing! I never touched her!'

Sarah managed to straighten. 'You want to learn – some respect for women! Just because – I don't have a penis – doesn't mean – I can't see through – your pathetic little scam!'

'Hey!'

She staggered away from them both, back to the bridge.

'Evie.' Lulu was coming after her.

'The slates – and the windows,' she managed. 'The pointing. All wrong... I'll send you – an email.'

'Are you okay?'

She shook her head. 'No. Sorry. I – had a call about my sister. Sarah. Urgent message... Hospital... Have to go...'

'Oh, I hope it's not serious. Are you going to be okay to drive?'

'Yes... Fine. Sorry!' And she ran, back up the lawn, the breath ripping in her throat. *Oh God oh God oh God!* She'd blown it! Maybe Lulu would call someone, social services, the police, with her concerns about Evie Booth's mental state, and everyone would realise that the Evie in Marnoch Brae was telling the truth, that *this* Evie was *Sarah* –

She dived into the car and sat, her head thrown back against the rest, panting in air. There were familiar grey splodges in front of her eyes.

But she couldn't stay here. Lulu was coming after her across the lawn.

She started the engine and stalled it, and stalled it again. Sobbing, she revved down on the accelerator – 'You bastard!' she yelled at the car – and shot off down the drive. The bastard car was beeping at her because she didn't have her seatbelt on but she ignored it, she didn't even stop at the junction with the public road, she kept on going, tears now blurring her vision.

She got back to Eve's cottage, somehow, but in the process managed to swipe a parked car, shattering a headlight. She pulled up at the end of the pend and slammed the car door and ran to the cottage, before remembering:

Oliver was *at Chrissie's*, and she didn't know the fucking address!

Eve would know where Chrissie lived. She couldn't call her and ask for the address.

What was she going to do?

Sobbing, she let herself into the house and then realised she had to go back to that fucking car for Eve's bag, with her phone in it. It was one of the hardest things she'd ever done, leaving the cottage again, walking down the pend to that car.

Back inside, she took the phone in her hand and switched it on.

Thank God, there was a message from Chrissie:

How are you feeling? Want me to drop him back?

Sobbing with gratitude, she replied:

That would be fantastic. Thank you soooo much!! You are amazing!!!

But she couldn't let Chrissie see her like this.

She took a quick shower and brushed her hair back into its ponytail. She dressed carefully in nice navy jeans, a fitted sweater and chestnut leather ankle boots. She applied make-up in an attempt to disguise her reddened eyes.

And then she remembered. She was supposed to be unwell!

And that was the door! Chrissie was here!

Running back upstairs, she scrubbed off the make-up, kicked off the boots and wrapped herself in Eve's white towelling robe.

'Aw, how are you?' Chrissie wheeled Oliver inside in his buggy and pulled Sarah into a hug.

'I've been better. Thanks so much for bringing him back. You're an angel.'

'What happened to your car?'

'Hmm?'

'Did someone go into you?'

That fucking car. 'Yes, nightmare – happened while we were at lunch. Someone must have gone into it and just driven off. They didn't leave their details.'

'Oh, some people!' She was looking rather uncomfortably searchingly at Sarah. 'Are you going to be okay with him? I can take him overnight if –'

'No!' she snapped. 'What, so I'm an incompetent parent now?'

Chrissie stared at her.

'Sorry, sorry, I'm... It's all this stuff with Sarah. I'll be fine. Thanks so much, Chrissie, you're a lifesaver!'

When she'd gone, she lifted Oliver from his buggy and just held him, sobbing into his back, and he let her do it for a while before starting to struggle. She set him down in the kitchen, and he immediately went to the table and reached up for Dubby, his yellow dumper truck, and started sucking it.

'Are you hungry, Ollie?'

His eyes over the truck were huge.

'Ready for your supper?'

She had just put the pasta on to boil when Eve's phone started ringing. She was so tempted to ignore it, but she couldn't. It might be Lewis, and if she didn't answer, he might call round. She couldn't see anyone else. She just couldn't.

Sure enough – fucking Lewis.

'Hi!' she chirped.

'Sarah called me,' he said with no preamble.

She had to grab a chair from the table and sit. '*What?*'

'At least, a nurse called me, saying Sarah wanted to speak to me. Of course I said I didn't think that was a good idea. What the hell is she calling me for?'

Oh God.

'Who knows? She probably just wanted to have a go at you.'

When she'd ended the call, she just sat there, holding the phone. Eve was bound to try calling him again. What if he agreed to talk to her next time? It would be simple enough for Eve to convince him of her identity. They were lovers, after all – there were any number of things Eve could tell him that only she would know.

Why hadn't she thought of this?

Stupid! So *stupid*!

Oliver pressed himself against her legs and held Dubby up to her. And she remembered how he used to do this when he thought she was sad – offer his most prized possession as comfort.

'Oh, my darling.' She took Dubby and kissed the damp yellow plastic; then she bent and kissed Ollie's little cherub mouth. 'You are just the sweetest!' And she pulled him onto her lap, and the three of them, Sarah and Ollie and Dubby, pushed the forks and spoons and plates into position on the table.

26

Hood up, Sarah strode out along the coastal path, hoping she'd done the right thing. She'd called Lewis early, claiming that the forecast was for the rain to clear by lunchtime, and suggesting a picnic at the castle. He, of course, had readily agreed. She hadn't wanted to leave Oliver with Margaret and so had stirred a quarter of a capsule of diazepam into his porridge. She'd left him out for the count in his cot.

He would be fine.

It was a tiny dose.

The sleety shower she had to walk through to get to the castle meant there was no one else on the coastal path, no one to see her. But she kept her hood up the whole way just in case, ducking her head and looking down at the path and her feet, counting her steps, periodically touching the phone in each pocket. She had dressed in Eve's anonymous black walking trousers and black jacket.

Unster Castle was at its most atmospheric on a day like this, looming out of the greyness, blurred by the sleet so if you squinted your eyes, you could almost pretend it wasn't a ruin at all but an intact building, full of people and life, and you were a lady of the 16th Century, approaching on horseback with your retinue, looking forward to drying off in front of a roaring fire.

She had come deliberately early.

Lewis would be driving from Golspie in his lunch hour. He'd park in the car park a couple of fields away and walk down the path, past the doocot. She couldn't see anyone on the path. Hopefully, on a day like this, there was no one in the castle either.

She hurried through all the rooms, most of them open to the sky, but some of the cellars still with their vaulted ceilings, dank and dark, so she had to walk in a little way, let her eyes adjust to the gloom, before satisfying herself that the space was empty.

The eastern range had a doorway that led nowhere, to just a grassy, rocky piece of ground that sheared off sharply to a dizzying drop to the rocky shore below – or so you'd think. There was a narrow ledge about four feet below the top of the cliff, which wasn't publicised because they didn't want people scrambling down onto it, but Lewis had boasted to Eve and Sarah about it once, describing how he'd climbed down to take a look. If you stood on the ledge and turned to face the cliff, he'd told them, you'd see a little niche cut into the rock, in which, the theory went, the castle's inhabitants used to hide valuables in case of attack.

The doorway in the eastern range was blocked by a metal grille, but it was obviously possible to get out there if you hoisted yourself through one of the windows.

She went back to the ruined gatehouse, from which there was a view of the path to the car park, and waited. Eventually she saw a figure moving along it: a tall figure in navy waterproofs.

Lewis.

Dr Lewis Gibson. Widely liked and respected local GP, and little-known evil monster.

She ducked back through the gatehouse and across the old courtyard, into the east range. She hoisted herself up through the window and, moving carefully on the slick grass, made her way across the clifftop. There was a very faint path to where the ledge was.

She sat on her bottom and, gripping tight to a clump of heather, lowered herself the few feet to the ledge. Then she waited again, looking out at the invisible horizon, at the sheets of sleety rain falling on the grey expanse of the sea, her back wedged against the cliff.

'Evie?' a faint call soon came from the castle.

'Here! Lewis!' She made her voice strained, going for panicked-but-trying-to-disguise-it, shamefaced, trying-to-see-the-funny-side. 'I'm out here!'

'Where?'

'On the ledge!'

And now, louder: 'For God's sake! What are you doing?'

'I'm stuck!' She craned her head round.

He was swinging himself up and over the windowsill.

'Okay, just hang in there! I'm coming to get you! Don't try to move! What the hell are you doing there?'

Such a hypocrite.

'I was bored!'

'God, Evie!' Now he was peering down at her. 'Take my hand.'

'I can't. I can't let go.'

'Okay. I'll come down.'

He deserved this. For what he'd done, he deserved it.

As he slid over the edge of the cliff on his bottom, waterproofs making a strange *zizzing* noise on the wet rocks, she moved quickly, decisively, pushing herself between him and the cliff and shoving sharply at his back, between the shoulder blades, above and directly in line with his centre of gravity. It was a simple case of helping him on his way, of using his own momentum.

He carried on over the ledge.

She dropped to her knees and clutched the rock, peeping over the edge to watch his body bounce off the cliff on its way down, flipping over and over on itself – his long legs cartwheeling, incongruously comical – until it could fall no further, its progress halted abruptly by the rocks that stretched out into the sea.

On TV, it was the limbs of fallen bodies that the special effects people seemed to concentrate on, making them stick out at unnatural angles. But in real life it seemed it was the head that took the most punishment – or perhaps it was just the way he had fallen. His head had cracked like an egg, splatting its contents over what seemed an unfeasibly wide area, already attracting the attention of a crow that had landed on a nearby rock.

27

'Oh, hi, Chrissie.'

'Hi, Evie. Just wondered how you're doing. Are you coming to the group today?'

Sarah sat up in bed. 'Uh, no. Ol – James has a bug and I think I'm getting it too. Immune system all over the place, I expect.'

'Oh, poor you! You *are* having a time of it!'

Tell me about it.

'Do you need any bits from the shops?'

'No! No, thanks, Chrissie, we're all stocked up.'

'What a shocker about poor Doc Lewis. I know we used to laugh about him, about the way he used to follow you around with his tongue hanging out like a lovesick St Bernard. Oh God, I shouldn't have said that. He was a lovely man.'

'He was. It's so sad.'

'I guess he was always a bit of a risk-taker, but it's odd, isn't it?'

'I don't suppose we'll ever know what happened.' She swung her feet over the edge of the bed and stood, making her head spin.

She hadn't slept properly for days.

The horror of it hadn't hit her at the time. Not that Lewis's death, in itself, had been horrific. To be honest, it had been deeply satisfying. It was still deeply satisfying, to replay the sight of him tumbling down the cliff, before he hit bottom. She liked to think that, in the few seconds it had taken him to fall, he had been absolutely devastated that his beloved Evie could have done this to him. She hoped he hadn't twigged that she was Sarah, not Evie. A few seconds, surely, wasn't enough time for him to do so.

No, she had no regrets at all.

But the sight of his head exploding on the rocks had brought back What Happened to Mum and Dad. The nightmares.

Wanting Evie.

Bizarrely, wanting Evie so much she had considered a visit to Marnoch Brae.

Chrissie sighed. 'I don't suppose we will. His poor parents. They must have been so proud of him...'

When she'd ended the call, Sarah padded across the landing to Oliver's room.

He was still asleep, his silky hair mussed around his head like a halo.

He'd had a disturbed night too, not settling, but he didn't have a temperature or anything. He was probably just picking up on her agitation. He had always been a sensitive child, anticipating her panic attacks, even as a tiny baby, by squalling and squirming in her arms, grabbing at her clothes and hair, as if by fastening himself to her, he could stop it happening.

And sometimes he had.

She'd never been so together as she had been after Oliver's birth. The knowledge that this little boy was depending on her had given her strength, she supposed, to fight her demons.

She sat down on the floor next to his cot.

The phone suddenly sprang back to life, and Oliver startled.

'Okay, darling, it's okay.' She set a hand on his head, and he relaxed back into sleep as she took the call. 'Hello?' she whispered.

'Hello? Hello? Evie Booth?'

'Yes.' She scooted away from the cot and out of the room. 'Sorry, I had to whisper, my baby's sleeping.'

'I'm sorry to disturb you – this is Gareth Jones at the Inchcraig Dental Practice.'

'Oh yes, hi.' Eve's dentist. 'Sorry, did I miss an appointment?'

'No no, nothing like that. I'm just calling to let you know that there's been a request for us to provide your dental records to a third party. I require your consent to release them.'

'A third party?'

'Nothing to worry about. It's just Sophie Stuart, the dentist who treats the patients at Marnoch Brae and a couple of cottage hospitals in the area. I understand your sister Sarah is currently a resident at Marnoch Brae? It seems she complained of toothache, and Sophie examined her – turned out to be just a sensitivity rather than a cavity, it appears – but the thing is, the records supplied by your sister's dentist don't correspond to her mouth.'

Oh God.

Clever Eve.

Clever, clever Eve.

'I understand that the two of you are twins. Sophie's wondering if there's been some confusion, given that you have the same surname and date of birth. She wants to check your dental records in case there's been a mix-up and the records we're holding for you are actually Sarah's, and vice versa.'

That was the cover story Sophie was peddling, probably for reasons of confidentiality, but this wasn't about possible confusion. Eve must have convinced them, given the mismatch, to compare her mouth with *Evie's* dental records. To check out her story that she was Evie, not Sarah Booth. That there'd been a switch.

It was over.

She walked into Eve's bedroom and stared at a photograph of them both as teenagers in their school uniforms, holding hands and smiling at the camera.

She had thought she would have more time, more time to enjoy a little bit of Eve's life. Had it been too much to ask? A few weeks, a few months...

But no.

Eve wouldn't let her have even that.

'I see. That seems – pretty unlikely? I mean, why would *you* have Sarah's records? She has a completely different dentist. In Golspie.'

'It's very unlikely, I agree – just a box-ticking exercise. I'll email you the form now, which you have to complete to consent to the release of the records – I think we have your email address on file. If you could fill it in and let me have it back by email later today or tomorrow, that would be great.'

'Yes, of course,' she managed, and ended the call.

She could hardly have refused – how suspicious would that look?

She didn't have much time.

First, she called Eve's bank and, after she'd answered the security questions, they told her that the current balance in her savings account was £52 344. So Eve must have put Sarah's cash, the cash she'd found in the rucksack at the Roman House, into her own account. The twins, spookily, always had about the same amount of savings. Eve must have had £27 000 already in her account.

She arranged to visit the branch tomorrow and withdraw

all but a hundred pounds. Then she tidied her hair, checked that Oliver was still asleep, and slipped out of the house.

MARGARET'S KITCHEN looked like it hadn't had a make-over since the 1950s. Very retro chic, with lemon-yellow units that looked a lot sturdier and better made than your average modern kitchen. And she had an old dresser with colourful crockery on it, and a rag rug in front of the Rayburn.

'He's asleep,' she assured Margaret when she asked about James. 'Zonked out.'

'Mm.' A look of disapproval.

'I'll only be a minute,' she snapped. 'He's perfectly safe in his cot.' She took a breath. 'Sorry. I'm a bit stressed.'

'Not surprising, dear.' Margaret set a cup of tea down on the table in front of Sarah. 'A terrible shock. Just terrible.' Tears filmed her pale blue eyes.

Oh. She was talking about Lewis. Sarah made her face suitably solemn.

'I know you weren't officially an item – I suppose he had to be beyond reproach, in his position – but I've got eyes in my head.'

Oh God. 'He didn't want people to know,' she whispered, looking down at her tea. 'It was something we argued about a lot. It was almost as if he was ashamed of me.'

'Oh now, I'm sure that wasn't the case. I know you young people are jumping in and out of each other's beds all the time, but we can be an old-fashioned lot around here.' This said with some pride, as she offered Sarah a digestive biscuit.

Sarah shook her head. 'Margaret – I seem always to be asking you for favours, but I really feel I need to get away for a while, you know?'

Margaret nodded.

'I've been thinking about taking James away for his first ever holiday. To France.'

'Oh?' Margaret perked up at this cheerful news.

'I was wondering if you could look after the house while we're away? Water the plants...'

'Of course I will, dear.'

'Oh, that's great! Thank you!'

'Which part of France are you thinking of?'

'Normandy. I'm actually about to book it now, and then we'll be off in a couple of days! I know it's impulsive, but... I was going to stay for Lewis's funeral, but his mother doesn't like me, so I thought I'd better not go.'

'Well. A bit of a holiday will do you a world of good.'

'I hope so.'

When they'd finished their tea, Sarah said, 'I'd better get back,' but she drifted across the kitchen to the corkboard next to the window, where postcards were pinned alongside information about the holiday cottages that Margaret looked after. She seemed to make a tidy sum for checking them periodically and overseeing any repairs that might be needed, in addition to supervising cleaners and tradesmen. She was the keyholder for those that didn't operate a key safe system, but Sarah had no idea where the keys were kept.

On the corkboard, though, under the colour-coded calendar that showed occupancy for each house, was a list of combinations for the key safes. She pretended to be examining a postcard of an Austrian mountain scene while looking down the list.

Creel Cottage.

It was one of the few cottages that, like Lewis's, faced the sea, although at a distance – it was set back against the grassy brae, looking down one of the wider pends and with a view, according to Eve, across the whole village from the upstairs skylights. Eve had been in the house once with Margaret after a storm, when they'd checked all the cottages for water ingress. It was on its own, detached. And Sarah knew that the owners only occupied it for two weeks every August. And that they had small children. There would hopefully be a cot and a playpen.

Combination 3467. Easy to remember – a sequence, but with 5 missed out in the middle.

Perfect.

IT WAS a risk for a number of reasons, driving to Tesco, but it was one she had to take. She had intended leaving Oliver with Margaret, but she'd forgotten to ask if that would be okay, and when she knocked on the door again, there was no answer and Margaret's car was gone.

So she had a choice between leaving Oliver alone in the house and strapping him into the car seat and hoping she could get to and from the supermarket without having an accident.

She didn't want to sedate him again, so she left him in his playpen with no toys or blankets. Nothing that could possibly present a hazard.

'I know, I'm sorry, you're going to be really bored, but look, I'll put on *Peppa Pig*. You can have a *Peppa Pig* binge!'

Oliver wasn't fooled. His lips started to tremble. She didn't look back as she quickly left the room. Left the house.

He would be perfectly safe.

She'd taped up the broken headlight, so at least it looked as if she was aware and on the case, and she parked at the end of the car park furthest from the store. She had managed to get here without killing herself, at least, but her hands were sweating on the wheel and she felt shaky and weak. The prospect of actually entering the supermarket, negotiating the aisles with all those people, all those random people doing random things...

Maybe she'd feel better if she had some food inside her.

So, as a sort of dipping of her toe in the water, she marched into the store with a basket on her arm, which she filled with two small bottles of orange juice, a cheese and pickle sandwich and a tube of fruit pastilles. She could put one of the bottles of juice and the tube in her bag in case she needed emergency hydration and/or a sugar rush while she did the big shop.

At the self-service point, she froze. The screen was a confused mess of images and text. What was she meant to do?

Heart pumping, she made herself slow down. Compartmentalise. That was another of Dr Laghari's coping mechanisms. She examined the screen slowly, from top to bottom, and realised it was asking her to place her bag in the bagging area.

She didn't have a bag.

'Everything okay there?' a young woman in uniform asked.

'I don't have a bag,' Sarah said, pathetically.

'Would you like to buy a bag for life?'

'Yes! Yes, I would. I'll take five, please. Oh, and... my *au pair* usually does the shopping. I'm afraid I don't...' She gestured helplessly at the screen. 'Could you...?'

The young woman's smile didn't waver, but Sarah got a definite whiff of contempt in her 'Sure thing. I'll just get the bags for you. Be right back!'

She opened the end of the tube of fruit pastilles and popped one in her mouth, the fortifying sugar going straight into her bloodstream. That was better. Marginally. She ate another.

The machine, though, didn't like the fact that the tube wasn't full – it was 'an unexpected item in the bagging area', apparently, and the young woman had to scan her ID into it and press buttons.

Sarah scuttled back to the car with her booty and sank into the seat, swigging juice and tearing open the sandwich. She wouldn't attempt the self-service again. She'd do two separate shops with a trolley, so she didn't attract attention with the ridiculous amount of tinned food and dry goods she needed to purchase, not to mention nappies.

First, though, she'd check her list again. It would be a disaster to forget something vital.

28

Using Eve's visa debit card, Sarah booked seats on the train to London for tomorrow and on a coach from London to Le Havre for the day after, and three weeks in a gite in the Normandy countryside. She put printouts of the details and the confirmatory emails into a folder, which she placed on a chair in the kitchen, pushed under the table, as if she'd forgotten it was there.

Right.

She needed to feed Oliver, and then she had to drive to Eve's bank and pick up the money. But the thought of getting back in that car...

In the end, she called A1 Taxis and asked if Jimmy could take her to the Bank of Scotland in Golspie, wait for her to carry out a transaction, and bring her home again.

Jimmy was his usual ebullient self. This time she had decided to take Oliver with her, and Jimmy didn't move off his arse as she struggled to fit the car seat into position. But they still arrived at the bank with ten minutes to spare before her appointment, which meant that Sarah and Oliver had to hang about in the waiting area.

Not good. While Ollie examined the box of toys, Sarah had to just sit there with her thoughts. What if they didn't let her withdraw the money? What if she had a panic attack and had to leave before she could get it? That was one of Dr Laghari's coping strategies – tell yourself you could just leave the stressful situation if necessary. But she couldn't. She needed that money.

She tried to read the leaflets.

She played with Oliver, pushing a wooden train across the carpet.

The ten minutes passed, then another five, and still she wasn't summoned. She closed her eyes, doing the breathing thing.

And when she opened them again, Oliver was gone.

She leapt to her feet.

'Oliver!'

Thank God, there he was, trotting to the door.

The door to the street!

She swooped on him and gathered him up and said, 'Never *ever* do that again, Oliver!' and she was sobbing, shaking, and one of the bank staff, a young guy who looked about twelve, sidled over and asked if everything was all right, and she snapped at him: 'No it *isn't*! My appointment was at 10:30 and it's now *10:40*!'

Another staff member, an older woman, came over, smiling fixedly, and said, 'Ms Booth? Would you like to come through?'

In the airless little office, she sat with Ollie on her lap while the woman said, 'Fifty-two thousand pounds is a lot of money!' She was looking at her computer screen. 'I see your visa debit card was recently stolen.'

Sarah babbled that she was withdrawing the money because her partner had stolen the card and withdrawn some money from her current account, and she was worried he might somehow access her savings account too.

'He has a gambling addiction,' she improvised.

The woman grimaced. 'There are alternative arrangements that could be made. He might find the cash, mightn't he? Isn't that a risk?'

'I have somewhere safe to put it. Please, I just want my money. It is *my* money, isn't it!'

'Yes, of course. I'll just fetch it from the safe.'

WHEN IT WAS DARK, Sarah returned to the Roman House for the first time since getting out of Marnoch Brae. She wore her big Barbour, hood up against the drizzle, a phone in each pocket.

The atrium smelt of the earth and wet stone.

She wished she could stay! She wished she could come back here with Oliver and stay forever!

But she couldn't.

Because of Eve.

She found the rucksack in the storeroom – somehow she'd known that Eve would have put it back there – and filled it with her own clothes. It would be so good to have her own underwear, and her own dresses and nice jeans and pretty silk fabrics instead of Eve's wardrobe, which mainly consisted of garments from outdoorsy shops, and high street jeans and trainers. She added the little alarm clock from her bedside cabinet and essential toiletries.

On her way back through the living room to the kitchen, she paused at the wall of photos, averting her eyes from the one of Eve.

She reached out and took Grannie and Grandpa off the wall.

'She's a strange one, your mother,' Grannie had once said.

The twins had never felt as if they'd inherited anything at all from their parents – they liked to speculate that maybe they were adopted, although they had never found any evidence of this. But maybe they had inherited something. She didn't want to think about what Grannie would have said about the Lewis thing.

When Sarah had done something naughty, Grannie would get this grim, unhappy look. In the photo, she was smiling so cheerily. Maybe Grannie wouldn't want Sarah to have this version of herself, eternally smiling on her, when the grim look was what was required.

She put the photo back on the wall.

They started it, she wanted to say.

Two wrongs don't make a right, Grannie would have come back at her.

'I don't care about *wrong,*' Sarah said aloud. 'All I care about is Oliver.'

IT TOOK two hours to transfer all the stuff from Eve's place to Creel Cottage, although it was only a short walk away. In the dark, navigating the narrow pends and cut-throughs, she felt as if the ghosts were looking at her from every window, from around every corner. If she turned quickly, would she see one of them behind her? Grannie's ghost, even, dogging her footsteps, shaking her head?

Encumbered as she was with the heavy rucksack on her back and a large shopper in either hand, she couldn't move quickly, although she tried, the breath sobbing in her throat.

In Creel Cottage, she just tipped the contents of the bags and the rucksack onto the floor of the little hall, apart from stuff for the freezer and fridge, which she'd switched on during her first trip – all that stuff had to be stowed away. It was important that neither of them got food poisoning, as medical attention would be out of the question.

The cottage smelt musty and strange. Unwelcoming. As if it didn't want them there.

There was the usual arrangement of a kitchen, sitting room and bathroom downstairs, plus a little bedroom. Upstairs, two attic rooms. She was relieved to find a cot in one of them and, disassembled in a cupboard, a playpen.

Finally, it was her last trip. She dumped the rucksack and shoppers and hurried back to Eve's cottage. Oliver, thank goodness, had slept through it all.

She felt awful. Light-headed and drained of energy. Exhausted. She tumbled into bed, but her brain was whirring at a hundred miles an hour. She couldn't sleep, lying in a sweaty heap of bedclothes, turning over and over, through all the hours till dawn.

'WE'RE GOING ON AN ADVENTURE!' she told Oliver at breakfast, stirring milk into his porridge. 'We're going to a new cottage! It's going to be really fun!'

Oliver's little cherub mouth was sticking out in a pout, and he had Dubby clutched to his fleece. He wasn't buying it. Poor Oliver! There'd been so much disruption in his short life. So much upset and confusion. An adventure must be the last thing he wanted.

'We'll still be here, in the village,' she said, putting the bowl in front of him. 'We'll just be moving a little way. Nothing will change, really. Me and you will carry on just the same. It'll be nice and cosy and safe.'

He glowered at her.

'Oh now, Ollie, let's not have Mr Grumpy-Pants! I don't think Dubby likes it when Mr Grumpy-Pants is in town, does he?'

Oliver squinted down at Dubby.

'Now, eat up your porridge before it gets cold, if you want to grow into a big boy.'

'Ah Mikey.'

Oh God.

'Yes, like Mikey. Come on now. Here's your spoon. Put Dubby down on the table.'

He shook his head.

'Oliver.'

'Ah Mikey!'

He was saying he wanted to see Mikey?

She took a calming breath. 'Mikey,' she said slowly, 'is a nasty piece of work with no manners. You don't really want to see Mikey. He's a bad boy. Bad Mikey.'

Oliver looked up at her uncertainly.

'Oh for God's sake, Oliver, eat your bloody porridge!' She grabbed Dubby away from him and closed his hand round the handle of the spoon. 'Or do I have to feed you like a baby? If you want Dubby back, eat your porridge!'

His lips trembled, but he dipped the spoon into the porridge.

'Oh darling, I'm sorry!' She caught him up in her arms, pressing him to her, not caring about the porridge getting smeared across her top. 'Mummin's sorry! Mummin loves you so much!' She pulled the spoon from him and pressed Dubby back into his hand. 'Here he is, look, here's Dubby.'

She did, in the end, feed him like a tiny baby, holding him on her knee. And then she changed both their tops and got the case on wheels from the cupboard, filled with the last of the things they'd need, such as a good tin opener – she and Eve had the same model – and their toiletries.

'We're off to France!' she said jauntily, holding out her hand to him. 'Let's get you into the buggy!'

When Margaret opened the door, Sarah apologised for

calling round so early, but she just wanted to say goodbye – they were off to France. The taxi was waiting.

'Oh, lovely!' Margaret beamed, bending to Oliver's eye level. 'That's going to be exciting, isn't it, James? You both have a wonderful time. And don't worry about the house. I'll take good care of it.'

'Thank you. Thank you so much for all you've done for us,' Sarah gushed. 'I'm sure France is going to be lovely, but we'll miss you!'

Margaret was looking at her strangely.

Good.

When Eve asked her about what had happened, Margaret was going to be able to tell her that Sarah had spoken about France as if she was moving there permanently.

'Well, I'll miss you too,' Margaret said eventually.

The case on its wheels rattled down the pend, the sound bouncing around the walls of the empty houses. It wasn't easy, pulling the case and pushing the buggy one-handed. Onto the road that curved between the end houses and the harbour, past Evie's car, round the corner, out of sight of Margaret's house... Up the next pend and into the cut-through, and then they were at Creel Cottage, and she was pushing open the door.

Shutting and locking it behind them.

'It'll soon feel like home,' she assured Oliver, lifting him over the piles of stuff in the hall. 'Mummin just has to sort this stuff out and we'll soon be shipshape and Bristol fashion, won't we?'

It did feel so much nicer here, actually, in the daylight. The place was 'tastefully' decorated in soft white and stone and seasidey blues and greens. There was a lot of wood, pine antique chests and tables, and comfy linen-covered sofas.

Yes, it was going to be fine here.

She could hunker down and start to recover, she hoped, from having to be Eve, which had actually been a nightmare.

She needed to recuperate, build up her stores of resilience. And then, when she was strong again, they could go. Make their escape.

But not, of course, to France.

One last thing. While Oliver padded around the downstairs, checking everything out, she opened her laptop and entered the Wi-Fi password she'd found on a laminated sheet in a kitchen drawer. Then she filled in the data release form and emailed it to Eve's dentist with an apology for the delay.

She liked to imagine Eve's expression as Sophie the dentist and Dr Laghari frowned over the records, as they shook their heads in amazement.

Her expression of triumph.

Because Sarah wanted her to think she'd won.

29

She knew it had been the right decision. Creel Cottage was lovely. The owners had created a real home away from home, with everything you could possibly need. In the tiny back yard there was even an old wooden shed coated in Archangel tar that was full of logs, and another with storage boxes containing enough washing-up liquid, washing powder and dishwasher tablets to last a decade.

The only thing was that Oliver seemed to be missing going outside – he'd go to the back door and reach up to the handle, looking back at her hopefully. She'd taken him out into the little yard, but only when it was dark, because she'd realised that it might be possible for someone on the coastal path to look down into the yard and see them.

He needed sunshine for vitamin D. Maybe they would have to risk being out in the yard in the daytime. She could keep a close eye on the path, and they could duck behind the shed if she saw someone appearing.

There was an amazing collection of DVDs, and Sarah was working her way through all the episodes of *Frasier*. Ollie was enjoying box sets of vintage children's TV, particularly

Dastardly and Muttley in *Wacky Races*. He and Dubby liked to join in.

As she buttered toast and heated soup for their lunch, she let herself wonder whether it might be possible to stay here a while. Could she somehow stop the owners from coming this summer? Could she phone them up pretending to be Margaret, and say the house had been flooded? She could say she had a new phone number, and that they should call her on that from now on. Offer to arrange for tradesmen to come in and repair the damage?

Oliver had developed a taste for tomato soup. Which was just as well – she'd discovered boxes of the stuff in the shed.

'Muzzy,' he warned her as she tested the temperature of the soup.

'Oh yes, good point. It will be messy.' She got his bib from the drawer.

And stopped. She could hear something. Faintly...

Yes. Sirens.

Coming closer.

'Okay, darling, you'll get your soup in a minute.'

She ran upstairs and got up on a chair to peep out of the skylight in Oliver's room, craning to see as far up the village as possible. Soon there were police cars whizzing down the road, lights flashing. Two... three cars!

They came to a halt at the harbour, at the end of the pend leading to Margaret and Eve's houses, and she could hear, through the thin, single-glazed old skylight, radios crackling and the voices of the police officers. Three of them ran up the pend, out of her sight because the pend was so narrow and the houses to this side of it blocked her view. Two others went round into the next pend, at the backs of the houses.

And as she waited, another car drew up.

Dr Laghari!

He opened the driver's door, but a policewoman went over

and bent to speak to him, and he closed the door again. The passenger door, meanwhile, had shot open, and then Eve was running round the car, running into the pend, with the policewoman shouting, and then running, after her.

Sarah smiled.

They wouldn't need to bash the door down because Margaret had a key. She imagined Margaret's shock at discovering that the woman she'd drunk coffee with at her kitchen table just two days ago wasn't Eve, but her mad sister Sarah! And the police would be finding the folder right about now.

Some of the police officers came running back down the pend. There was a hurried confab, and then three of them hopped into a car and drove off. Dr Laghari got out of his car and strode out of sight up the pend.

And now here was Eve, and the policeman beside her was carrying the folder! They were having what looked like an animated discussion. Eve was wearing badly fitting maroon joggers and a cheap-looking pink and orange jumper, no doubt provided by Marnoch Brae. She was red in the face. Sarah could imagine how that conversation was going – Eve was insisting on going to France with them, and they were saying that just wasn't possible.

She turned to Dr Laghari, who shrugged.

And now they were all driving off!

It had worked.

She laughed aloud as she imagined Eve turning up at the gite in Normandy, demanding to know where Sarah and 'James' were; running about the place frantically looking for James, just as Sarah had run about the village here on that stormy night when Oliver had disappeared.

The sounds of the engines faded away, leaving the village to its silence.

All those police officers... The folder with its 'evidence' of Sarah's intentions... Suddenly she was back in the vicarage, standing in Dad's study, staring stupidly as Evie printed something out and shoved it in one of Dad's thick creamy envelopes. Sarah hadn't even asked what it was. She hadn't had room in her head for anything but the meadow, and their parents lying there... Their heads...

And so it had been a genuine shock, later, when the policeman had produced the 'suicide note'. Maybe that was why Evie hadn't told her anything about it – so that Sarah's reaction would be convincing.

Another image – Evie again, Evie at the bottom of the garden behind the greenhouse, scrunching up newspaper and throwing it in a pile onto the area of packed earth where Jacob the handyman always had his bonfires. Adding twigs and branches... And finally, when the flames were at their height, the clothes from the bin bag. The fabric had resisted the fire, at first, where the blood spatters were thickest, but had soon started to smoulder and turn brown.

SHE HAD CUT up a Pink Lady apple to share with Oliver, and had turned to the sink to wash the juice off her hands, when she was conscious of a flash of pink and orange out of the window, down at the bottom of the pend. Freezing, she watched as Eve went past on the road with Margaret –

But no, they weren't going past! They were turning up the pend!

She dropped to her knees.

'Mummiiiin!' came Oliver's happy cry, burbling as he trotted towards her.

'Hush, darling, hush!' She caught him to her.

Scooting along on her knees, she guided Oliver out of the room and then picked him up, hurrying up the narrow stairs to the skylight. Peeking out, she saw Eve and Margaret standing at the door of a cottage on the right of the pend. Eve put a key in the lock and turned it.

'Sarah!' she shouted.

Margaret had a tissue up to her face, and now she wailed: 'Don't go in! We have to call the police!'

Eve looked round at her with an expression that seemed neutral, but which Sarah knew was impatient. She came back down off the doorstep and put an arm around Margaret. She said something Sarah couldn't hear, and led her away, into the cut-through that led to the next pend. Back towards her house.

Heart pounding, Sarah smiled at Oliver and tried desperately to think.

They thought she and Oliver were in that cottage?

But why?

Eve was back.

Back at the house across the pend. She disappeared inside, leaving the door open behind her.

Sarah waited at the skylight in Oliver's room, hardly daring to breathe. She'd given Oliver another quarter capsule of diazepam, and he was snuffling quietly in his cot. He hadn't had a bad reaction to the last lot, so she was sure it was okay. Whatever was about to happen, it was definitely best that he slept through it.

And now here was Eve again: shutting and locking the door behind her and walking up the pend. She stopped at the next house and tapped in a combination on the key safe next to the door. She opened it, withdrew the keys, and unlocked the door. She didn't go in immediately. She stood on the step, seeming to gather herself.

She called, again: 'Sarah?'

And then she stepped inside.

She was systematically checking all the holiday houses.

Of course she was. Sarah should have anticipated that her twin would know what she'd done. Eve was never going to buy it, that Sarah had gone off to France. The long journey would have been bad enough. The trains, the connections, all those people, all that confusion and noise. And then France, where she didn't even speak the language. Having to hire a car and drive in strange places, on the wrong side of the road. And then the gite, a completely unknown quantity, a strange place belonging to strange people...

No way.

Eve would know that Sarah could never do that. She would have rumbled the ruse straight away. And maybe then she had questioned Margaret.

'But did you actually *see* her get into the taxi? Did you even see the taxi itself?'

'Well, now you come to mention it...'

Oh God.

She had been an idiot to think she could ever outsmart Eve. Of course Eve was going to see through her pathetic little plan. Of course Eve was always going to be one step ahead. Always going to come out on top. Always going to get what she wanted.

And she wanted Oliver.

Sarah went to his cot and put a trembling hand on his back.

Maybe she could snatch him up and run, with just the bag of money, out of the village, up to the Roman House. Call A1 Taxis and tell them to send Jimmy right away.

But then what?

Eve would probably call every local taxi firm, or get the police to, and they'd find out that Jimmy had taken her to the station. What if there wasn't another train for hours?

They could get a bus. But either way, they'd be traced easily. They would be caught. And then what?

Sarah and Oliver were never going to be safe from Eve.

She stared out at the open door of the house into which Eve

had disappeared. Sarah imagined her searching it, calmly, systematically, relentlessly. Looking under beds and into cupboards. Checking the stove to see if it had recently been lit.

She left Oliver's room on shaking legs and walked carefully down the steep stairs, hanging on to the handrail. In the kitchen, she stopped and breathed, before forcing herself across the room to the worktop by the sink. Here there was a wooden knife block holding a selection of Wusthof knives – three knives of different lengths and widths and with different sorts of blades – but the one she wanted was long, smooth, narrow and sharp.

30

Weirdly, she felt almost calm. It was as if she had been waiting for this moment to arrive all her life, dreading it, doing everything possible to avoid it, but now it was here, she was ready. It was as if everything she had been through had been designed to prepare her for what she must do now.

She opened the kitchen door fully and stood behind it.

She could hear the ticking of the clock on the wall.

Outside, seagulls, crying like babies.

The knife in her hand felt right, shaped to fit her palm and thumb. She would wait until Eve had walked through into the room, her back to Sarah, before striking. That jumper she was wearing – would the blade go through it? Sarah could lift it up first, perhaps, before pushing the knife into her stomach.

Or the neck might be a better target. With Eve's hair pulled into a ponytail, it was exposed. Accessible.

She found herself watching the minute hand on the kitchen clock, watching it journey round the circle of numbers, but she couldn't have said how much time had passed when she heard a click and a swoosh from down the hall, and the seagulls' cries were suddenly too loud, as if they were actually inside the house. The front door had been opened.

And now footsteps. Slow footsteps on the sanded wooden floorboards.

And then nothing.

Straining her ears, she heard a faint creak. Eve was in the sitting room.

Okay.

Breathe.

Now the footsteps in the hall were back, this time coming closer, and then it all seemed to happen between one beat of her heart and the next.

Footsteps in the doorway.

Eve, walking away from her into the room, bringing with her the smell of the soap they used in Marnoch Brae, but under it the scent of her, of Evie, of her twin, as familiar as her own since, she supposed, the womb.

Eve must have sensed she was there, because as Sarah sprang, she was already turning to face her, eyes wide, hands held out in front of her, defensively, but Sarah had the momentum and as she barrelled into her they both fell to the floor, Sarah on top, knife lifted high for the strike.

All their childhood games came rushing back – wrestling on the grass in the churchyard, laughing so much they were both weak and helpless; tumbling in the snow, each trying to put an icy snowball down the other's back; the chasing games through the woods, jinking and dodging, the one always knowing, somehow, which way the other would turn, generally ending in a rugby tackle onto a cushion of dead leaves.

There were no words. Evie didn't beg. She didn't need to.

They had never needed words.

For a long time Sarah sat astride her, the breath sore in her lungs, the knife held aloft, while Evie just lay there looking up at Sarah, and Sarah looked down at Evie.

Finally, Sarah lowered the knife.

Not like this. She couldn't do it like this.

She stood, and went to the door, and closed it.

'Sit,' she said.

Eve pushed herself up off the floor.

Oh God, how stupid was she? The knife block! Eve was now between Sarah and the rest of the knives!

But Eve walked to the table and pulled out a chair and sat. She dropped her head to her hands, briefly, before sitting erect in that oh-so-familiar Evie way, back straight, facing whatever she had to head-on.

Sarah remained standing.

'Where's Oliver?' said Eve, at last.

'Oh, it's *Oliver* now, is it? Not James?'

Eve just shook her head.

'He's upstairs. He's sleeping.'

'Can I see him?'

Sarah didn't bother to answer that. Instead, she said, 'I need to know why. Why you did it.'

'You know why.'

'Of course I don't!' She could feel the tears, prickling at the back of her throat. 'No matter how much you might have wanted a child, I can't believe you would *steal Oliver from me!* You were planning it *even before he was born!* Why? Just tell me why.' And, through the choking in her throat: 'I would have shared him with you. I *was* sharing him with you.'

'I know,' Eve got out.

For a long moment, silence. Just the ticking of the clock and the wailing of the seagulls wheeling over the empty harbour.

'What happened to Lewis?' Eve said at last.

Sarah smiled. 'Like you care. Come on, Evie. I did you a

favour. You're not going to try to tell *me* you were in love with him? That you weren't shitting yourself at the prospect of having to actually marry the guy just to keep him quiet? Because you couldn't risk breaking up with him, could you? Because how might he react to that? He might go into self-destruct mode, go to the police and make a full confession. You'd both have gone to *fucking prison* and I'd have got Oliver back!'

Another long silence. Then: 'You were never going to cope,' Eve said. 'With a child.'

'You're saying I've been a bad mother to him? *Really?*'

'No. You've been a better mother to him than I could have dared hope. Which is why...'

'... you left it so long?'

Eve nodded.

'Before spiking my food or my drink with antidepressants and triggering a psychotic episode? So if I'd neglected him or – or left him unattended in the bath or something, you'd have done it sooner?'

'I was waiting... for nature to take its course.'

'Oh yes, so considerate! You were waiting for me to have another episode *naturally* so you could steal him and convince yourself you were doing the right thing for Oliver. Convince *me* he was a delusion.'

'I wasn't *stealing* him, I was –'

'So how do you explain the fact that you were planning to take him away from me *right after I got pregnant*?' She was yelling now.

'Just look at *how* you got pregnant!' Eve yelled right back. 'You were never going to cope, Rah-Bee!'

'*I was coping!*' The words rang round the room. 'But you wouldn't even give me a chance. You decided I didn't deserve to have a child and you did, so you took him.'

'I didn't *want to do it!* When I saw how you had bonded with him... Yes, I kept putting it off, waiting... telling myself I was waiting for you to have another episode *naturally*, as you put it, but really it was because I couldn't bring myself to do it to you. I was hoping that maybe I wouldn't have to.'

'So what changed? What made you decide to try to trigger an episode?'

Eve sighed. 'Oliver.'

'It's Oliver's fault now?'

Silence.

'What about Oliver?'

But she really didn't want to hear the answer.

'I think you know.'

'Of course I don't *know*.'

'He's not far off the terrible twos now, is he? Do you remember, that day in the living room, when you told him he needed his nappy changed and he had a tantrum, he snatched a vase of flowers off the table and dropped it on the floor, and you picked him up, and he hit your face, and you – you –'

Sarah shook her head. 'No.'

She wouldn't think about it. She wouldn't.

'You called him a fucking little bastard.' The words sobbed in Evie's throat. 'And there was such – such *venom* in your voice –'

Sarah shook her head.

'I know you would never hurt him. Not physically. But –'

'No.'

'That was when I knew I'd been right all along. I'd been right, to – to arrange to manage things in the only way I could think of that wouldn't absolutely devastate you. Yes, I could go to social services, to the police, and tell them... everything. I could have had him taken away from you that way. But I couldn't. I couldn't hurt you like that, Rah-Bee. I thought – I hoped this could work. You could still be a part of his life. You'd be his auntie. But I...'

'... would have control.'

Eve nodded.

'Because you didn't think I could be a good mother.'

'It was fine when he was a baby. When he was completely passive, completely amenable. But he's started to speak. To have a mind of his own. And if you can't handle the terrible twos, how are you going to handle any of it? He's going to challenge you. He's going to say things and do things that you don't like. That's what kids do. He's going to be a *fucking little bastard* and you're not going to be able to cope with that. What about when he's a stroppy teenager? What's going to happen then?'

'How dare you?' Sarah could hardly get the words out, she was so angry. 'How dare you sit there and pass judgement on my ability to cope with my *own child*?'

'But someone has to. Someone has to, Rah-Bee, because you sure as hell won't.'

The anger coursing through her – she had to use it. She could do this. *She could do it now.* She grabbed at Eve, pulled on her hair, yanked at the ponytail to bring her head back, to expose her throat while she slashed with the knife.

The knife wouldn't come down.

Evie had her hands out, she was groping at Sarah, right hand to left hand, but Sarah could have brought the knife down to slash her neck.

She could have done it.

Instead, she hauled Evie to her feet, the point of the knife held to the base of her throat. Evie was sobbing, chest heaving, and Sarah was sobbing too, and it was like it used to be when they were children, holding onto each other for comfort –

'Get in here,' Sarah choked.

She pulled open the pantry door and pushed Evie inside

and slammed the door, she slammed the door on her and locked it and threw the knife across the room.

Oliver.

She had the keys to Evie's car, and a bag with £52 000 in it.

She had to get Oliver and go.

Now.

31

'Off we go,' said Sarah brightly, strapping a sleepy Oliver into his car seat and opening the boot to throw in the holdall with some clothes and nappies in it, and the bag of money. They could buy food on the way.

'Dubby,' muttered Oliver, still dopey from the diazepam, but not dopey enough that he hadn't realised Dubby was missing.

She slammed the boot. 'No time, darling.'

A sudden clonking sound had her twisting round, adrenaline pumping, but it was just a boat in the harbour, knocking against its mooring.

'Dubby.'

'Okay! Okay, I'll get Dubby.'

Where the hell was he? She searched Ollie's room and the sitting room and the kitchen, ignoring Eve's muffled shouts from behind the pantry door. Eventually she found him in the bathroom, where she'd left him on a towel on the windowsill to dry out after submersion in the bathwater.

She snatched up her toilet bag and took a detour upstairs for more clothes, which she shoved into another holdall. She really didn't want to have to shop for stuff any more than she could help. Perhaps she should pack some more of Oliver's toys. The dominoes, for a start. These, some cars and his favourite picture books went into a side pocket of the holdall.

Oliver was asleep again when she got back to the car, but he drowsily accepted Dubby.

'Right then. Let's go.'

She stalled, of course, on the first attempt.

On the second attempt, the car bucked forward, and she gunned the accelerator to stop it stalling again, but when she looked up from the gear stick, there was Evie, Evie was standing in the road and the car was shooting forward into her –

And everything slowed down.

The key in the lock.

Of course – the old trick with the key in the lock.

There would have been plenty of paper in the pantry, packets of flour and sugar, for Evie to push under the door –

At the last moment, Sarah managed to wrench the wheel round, but she was still pressing down on the accelerator and the engine roared, the car shot across the road and the world tipped, the road had disappeared and the harbour walls were rising up above her head –

Bang!

She jerked forward and her seatbelt yanked her back.

Oliver wailed.

'It's all right, it's all right, darling!'

Oh God, they were in the water!

There was water all round the car and they were still going, the front of the car pulling them down and then the light was gone, the sky and the harbour were gone and there was only murk, a greeny-brown murk swilling all around the car as it bumped to a stop on the sea floor.

She tugged at her door handle and pushed at the door but

it was like pushing against a rock. There must be a rock or something keeping it shut. She couldn't open it even a crack.

'*Mummmmminnnnn!*' wailed Oliver.

'Okay darling, it's okay!'

She undid her belt and clawed her way into the back seat next to him. 'Silly Mummin, we've gone for a swim in the car! Keep still, darling.' She couldn't get the straps undone. Her hands were shaking too much and he was squirming around, trying to grab her.

Finally the straps came free and she lifted him, lifted him over the gear stick and into the front passenger seat. She tried that door but couldn't open it either. The car must be wedged between rocks.

They'd have to get out of a window.

She scrambled into the driver's seat and pressed the button for the electric window on the passenger side.

It whirred down.

Immediately, water started pouring into the car. They'd have to be quick. They'd have to get out before the car filled up –

The window whined and stopped.

Frantically, she pressed the button again.

Dead.

The circuit must have shorted.

Oliver was wailing as water cascaded down from the window above him, splashing over him, and he put out his arms to her, but she pushed him away, she slapped at the window controls, but nothing happened.

She shuffled across to the passenger seat, lifting a soaking Oliver onto her lap. Was the window open enough to be able to push him through it? Would he rise to the surface? Or would he immediately drown?

Already the water was up to her waist.

Movement, outside the window.

A face, grotesquely distorted and white, staring in at her.

She screamed.

And then she saw it was Evie, hair streaming behind her like a mermaid, blue eyes wide. Her hands reached in through the opening at the top of the window.

Without thinking, without hesitating, Sarah lifted Oliver and tried to push him through, push him, spluttering, against the force of the water, but he was too big. He was too big.

Oliver wailed.

Evie's hands tore at his jacket.

Sarah's helped her. She was having to hold him up now, out of the water, which was filling the car faster than she could have believed possible.

Jacket off, jumper off, and now as she pushed and Evie pulled he was through, he was through and out! And Evie had him, her hand over his mouth and nose, arms around him, and her legs scissored, powering her up away from the car, bubbles tracking their progress to the surface.

Safe.

He was safe.

The water was up to her neck now – cold, so cold. She was shaking, shivering uncontrollably, but it would be all right. Oliver was safe, and now Evie would come back for her and Evie would know what to do to get her out.

Maybe, between them, they could force the window down.

Evie always saved her.

But the water was rising so fast!

She knelt on the seat, pushing herself up out of the water as far as she could. She needed to get out now. She grabbed at the edge of the window and tried to push it down. Tried to kick it.

She needed to get out *now*!

Soon the car would fill up!

Soon there would be no air to breathe!

Where was Evie?

As the water rose up almost to the roof, sloshing from one side of the car to the other so she had to push her face up as far as she could to stop it sloshing into her nose and mouth, as she cried for Evie, she was back, somehow, back in that long-ago meadow where the skylark sang and the willows dipped low over the river and she stood and screamed, she screamed for Evie, and suddenly Evie was there.

Standing next to her in the long grass and the wild flowers but not moving, not saying anything, just staring at what had until five minutes ago been Mum and Dad.

Six minutes ago, they had been very much alive.

When she had asked if they were enjoying their constitutional, Dad had shouted at her:

'*What are you doing with that?*'

Sarah had looked down at the shotgun in her hands. The shotgun with which Jacob the handyman blasted away at rabbits and never hit them. The shotgun that wasn't kept under lock and key but in the old dusty cupboard in the shed with the door you had to jam shut with a piece of paper. Right next to the cartridges.

'Sarah,' Mum had said, in the false, singsong voice she used when she wanted something or there were other people around. 'Put that down.'

Sarah had grinned, not really meaning to fire it but bringing it to her shoulder and aiming right at Dad's head, just to freak them out. 'Prepare to meet thy maker.'

'*Sarah!*'

'Actually, scrub that. Prepare to meet the other guy.'

And then:

Why not?

The idea had sprung, fully formed, into her head, like it really might have been put there by divine intervention. *Mum first, if you're going to make it look like a murder-suicide pact.*

She'd swung the barrels round and pulled the trigger –

Boom! – and that had been Mum's head gone. She'd only fired the gun a couple of times before, at the oak tree by the stream, years ago, when she was still at school. But she could hardly miss at that range. Mum's body had sort of flipped backwards and blood and gore and stuff had flown everywhere, onto Dad, onto Sarah, onto the grass and the flowers.

As Dad had stood there staring down at Mum in shock, Sarah had walked right up to him – it had to be close range – and given him the other barrel.

Boom!

And then the next five minutes had been taken up with just standing there staring numbly, and shouting for Evie. And then the two of them had stood and stared.

'Rah-Bee,' Evie had said, eventually. 'What –'

'I'm sorry. I just –'

'Okay. Okay.' Evie had been thinking fast. She'd picked up the shotgun and pulled her T-shirt off and used it to wipe it down. Then, holding it in the T-shirt, she'd knelt by Dad and closed his hand over it in a few places, the places you would hold a gun, and then she'd dropped it next to him in the long grass, into a pool of blood.

'Come on. We have to go. Rah-Bee. *Sarah!* We have to *go!*'

Back at the house, Evie had made Sarah strip off all her clothes on the lawn and had bundled them into a binbag. Then she'd taken off all her own clothes too and pushed them in on top. She'd guided Sarah upstairs to the shower and the two of them had stood under it while Evie washed Sarah's hair and body all over, and her own, and then she'd emptied the drain trap and turned the shower back on to flush out any remaining bits of Mum and Dad.

They'd dried their hair and dressed in clean clothes and Evie had made them both drink a cup of hot, sugary tea. And all this time, no words had been spoken.

Evie had burnt the clothes on a bonfire, and Sarah had just

stood and watched her, not helping, not gathering sticks or throwing them onto the flames. It was better if Evie did it, because Evie would do it right.

And she had.

Every scrap of material had been burnt to ash. She had even disposed of the ash on the compost heap, strewing dead leaves over the site of the fire, before turning to Sarah and saying, 'Right. Now you have to go and find them. We've been a bit worried because they've been out longer than usual on their walk. You've got to find them.'

Sarah had shaken her head. 'No. I can't. Why can't *you*?'

'Because *look at you*, Rah-Bee! You're obviously traumatised, and the best way we can explain that is if you found their bodies.'

'I could be traumatised by the fact that they're dead.'

Evie had shaken her head. 'This is best. Trust me. It's best this way.'

It's best this way.

Evie always knew best.

'Vee-Bee,' Sarah said into the now-tiny pocket of air.

Evie would be back for her. Evie had saved Oliver and she would save Sarah.

'Vee-*Bee!*' She hardly had time, now, to gulp in air before the water sloshed over her and she had to hold her breath until it sloshed away again. Something hit her face, something small and hard, bobbing on the surface of the water.

She grabbed at it. Smooth plastic and rubbery wheels.

Dubby.

EPILOGUE

He didn't, thank God, associate the harbour with what had happened under the water there. To a two-year-old, Evie supposed it must have seemed like another world in those murky depths, a strange and terrifying place that was nothing to do with his everyday life.

Like a bad dream.

Now, on a sunny July day, he toddled along happily at her side, pausing frequently to squat, bottom in the air, to investigate something on the ground: a beetle, a dandelion, a sweet wrapper. Or just to stand and stare, in awed wonder, at the 'big boys and girls' who ran about in colourful T-shirts and shorts or in black rubbery wetsuits that made their arms and legs look so comically skinny.

On the bench outside one of the holiday homes, three generations were sitting in the sun – grandmother, mother and daughter. Evie had chatted to Senga, the grandmother, a couple of days ago and learnt that they lived in Glasgow, but that the family had been coming to this area in the summer for decades, since the days when the locals would move out of their houses for the summer season to camp in sheds adapted for the purpose, renting the house to holidaymakers from Glasgow or Aberdeen.

'My grandparents used to live in my cottage,' Evie had told her. 'I wonder if you remember them? Robert and Jeannie Mowat.'

Senga had smiled. 'In number seventeen? Oh yes, I remember Jeannie – what a lovely lady she was. What a baker!' And she'd told Evie that the kids used to be always 'chapping her door' for a homemade biscuit or slice of lemon cake. Evie vaguely remembered all the children in the kitchen, and Grannie slicing cake for them. Some of those kids had maybe been Senga's.

The memory of that lemon cake had come back so vividly that Evie's mouth had actually watered, and that evening she'd searched out the recipe and attempted to make it herself. It had turned out not too badly – James had finished a whole slice and been looking for more – and she had taken Senga what was left of the cake the next morning.

'*Hello*, James, my wee man!' Senga crooned now, beaming at him and Evie, and Lydia, the little girl, hopped off the bench and danced over to take James's hand. She was maybe seven or eight, a picture-perfect little thing with plaits, wearing a simple white cotton dress, her bare legs brown and sturdy. She was a sunny child, always smiling and chatty. She was chatting now to James, asking him if he wanted to make a daisy chain.

They were so nice, the Glaswegian families, with the indiscriminate open friendliness for which the city was justifiably famous. All the holidaymakers seemed to be from either Glasgow or England, but Evie supposed there must be other, less obtrusive people from other places too.

The village came alive in the summer and became a proper little community again, most of the families returning year after year at the same time so they knew their fellow-holiday-makers as neighbours rather than just faces on the beach.

As James sat on the grass, frowning at the daisy Lydia had, rather optimistically, given him to slit and thread, Evie sat on the bench with Senga and her daughter Louise and watched him. He was happier. She was sure of it. In the weeks and months after Sarah's death he would have terrible tantrums, screaming fits, and would not be comforted – or not, at least, by Evie. She always had the feeling he was pushing her away because it was Sarah he wanted, Sarah he was waiting for. He knew – he had always known – that Evie was not his Mummin.

But she thought they had turned a corner. He smiled more, and came to her for cuddles and fun. He had always been a sensible, pragmatic little thing and seemed to have accepted that nothing he had tried had brought Mummin back, so he might as well make the best of it.

He had never once called Evie 'Mummin'. He didn't call her anything, just made a sort of 'Uhh' noise when he wanted her. She was hoping that that might morph, eventually, into 'Mum'.

'Terrible about that young doctor!' Louise said.

'Yes,' said Evie, glancing past her to the For Sale sign in the garden of Lewis's house. An 'Under Offer' sticker had already been slapped over it. Cottages in Achnaclach never stayed on the market long.

'He'll be missed, I'm sure,' said Senga tactfully, before changing the subject to crabs and lobsters, and Evie wondered what Margaret might have said. She and Senga were thick as thieves.

She wasn't sure how she felt about Lewis. She supposed she missed him, in a way, but it had been such a strain. The relationship they'd had would never have happened, in the normal course of events. The few dates she'd been on with him had confirmed her instincts that he wasn't for her – too intense, too needy, which was odd given that he seemed so confident and alpha.

And then had come Sarah's pregnancy.

And Evie had needed him as much as he'd seemed to need her. She'd agreed to another date. Let herself be seduced, with the help of a lot of wine. And the sex had been fine – that hadn't been an issue. It was just the way he clung to her, following her about like a puppy from room to room. It had been relatively easy to persuade him to go along with her solution to the Sarah-and-baby problem.

She hadn't ever confided in him fully, of course. She hadn't told him just why giving Sarah control of a helpless little human being was so dangerous.

She couldn't tell him, or anyone, about What Happened to Mum and Dad.

Evie still couldn't think about that dreadful day without experiencing a physical response, all the blood seeming to drain from her body, leaving her light-headed and faint. She leant back on the bench and focused on James, letting Senga and Louise's chatter wash over her.

But it was back, that smell in her nostrils, the smell of the blood- and brain-spattered garments she'd had to burn that day in the vicarage garden. It had been so overwhelming, the need to protect her sister, that she couldn't remember making an active decision to cover up what Sarah had done. And Sarah had obeyed her in a sort of daze, standing watching in the shadows as Evie had destroyed the evidence of their parents' murder.

What other choice had she had? If she'd told anyone what her sister had done, Sarah would have gone to jail, or at the very least to a secure psychiatric unit a hundred times worse than Marnoch Brae. Sarah couldn't have coped with that.

Oh Rah-Bee!

I'm sorry I'm sorry I'm sorry!

She had intended to go back. She had intended to dive back down and get Rah-Bee, but Oliver – James – had needed her. When she'd got him out of the water and up onto the quay he had stopped breathing. She had had to do chest compressions to push the water out of his lungs, and then hold him as he coughed it up.

She couldn't have left him. Not for anyone. Not even for her beloved Rah-Bee.

Who would have understood.

Sarah had, it seemed, tried to push down the window to get out that way – there had been deep red gouges on her fingers. It would have been possible for her to open a door once the car had filled right up with water and the pressure had equalised, but for some reason she hadn't done so. Evie thought she knew what must have happened – Sarah had tried both doors when the car was first submerged, and neither had opened, so she'd assumed there were obstructions of some sort. Poor Rah-Bee probably didn't know about the pressure differential thing.

There had been so much Sarah hadn't known about the world because in many ways she hadn't been part of it. She hadn't had any friends or colleagues or family apart from Evie. She never went out. She wasn't interested in social media. She'd had her house and her garden and her work and her twin.

And then Oliver.

And suddenly Evie couldn't be here. She couldn't look at the harbour any more.

She stood, she said something to Senga and Louise, she swooped on James and lifted him into a cuddle. He protested, but she carried him off, back to the cottage, where she changed him and then got out the buggy, packing a quick picnic into Tupperware, filling one water bottle with apple juice and another with water, cramming ice into their narrow necks.

They walked up the road to the beach, to the long expanse of sand stretching out to meet the cliffs on the other side of the bay. There were surfers, and people playing rounders, and lots of dogs and kids running about, much to James's delight.

She left the buggy by the surfers' hut and hefted the beach bag and the rug, and she and James made their way across the short, wiry grass to the dunes where there was shelter from the sun.

After the picnic, James fell asleep on her lap, his little body so weighty and reassuring and warm. From here, it was just possible to see the tops of the pine trees around the Roman House. It had sold, even more quickly than Lewis's house, and for way over the asking price. It was, of course, a lovely house. A unique, award-winning design, as the sales particulars had boasted. It had been snapped up by a couple from Kent who had known of Sister Archt's work. The woman, like Sarah, suffered from agoraphobia. They had cried, according to the estate agent; at their first sight of the atrium they'd both burst into happy tears.

Which was wrong on so many levels.

The house had been a huge mistake. It had let Sarah retreat completely from the world, and be happy doing so. Evie now realised that the whole ethos of their architectural practice had been wrong, and George had been right. You didn't help people by allowing them to ignore their problems. That poor couple were going to shut themselves away in the Roman House just like Sarah had done.

Perhaps she should have bulldozed it, but she wasn't quite altruistic enough for that. James came first. With the proceeds of the sale and the money recovered from the holdall found in the car, they had a good financial cushion. She was undecided, still, about what to do, whether to stay in Achnaclach or move away. She had a hankering for the landscape of her childhood – their childhood, hers and Rah-Bee's. For meadows and woods and squat limestone churches. Trysting trees and village greens. Twee little shops. The smells of green living things drifting in at an open window. Church bells and evensong and velvet summer nights.

The world was old, there; your own little life just a blink in time.

All those ancient bridleways, the grassy mounds of the Saxon barrows, the flint workings dating back into prehistory.

She had always felt its magic.

It was a magic that came not from anything supernatural, from a god or a devil, but from the connections that reached out to you from the past, the feeling that nothing could happen to you that hadn't happened to someone there before. Someone lying at peace in a shaded churchyard, their grave perhaps still tended, as she and Sarah used to tend little Eliza's, dead two hundred years but once as warm and real as James was now, sleeping on her lap.

Perhaps they would go back there, she and James. Keep Grannie's cottage for holidays. The best of both worlds.

Oh Rah-Bee.

If only Rah-Bee could have come with them.

She kept thinking *I must tell Rah-Bee* or *When Sarah...* – until she remembered. Sarah would never do anything again. Evie would never speak to her again.

And she needed to so badly. She needed to try to explain.

I'm dead because of you, Sarah would yell at her.

And all Evie could say was that she was sorry. That she would give anything to go back, to go back to the moment that Sarah had handed her the pregnancy test and a terrible thought had popped into Evie's head, as if they had swapped places.

I'm sorry.

All the rest of her life, it would be her litany.

George had wanted to attend the funeral. She'd been back in touch with him recently. But she had told him no. Having George there would have felt like another betrayal of her twin, another kick in the teeth. She knew George wanted to rekindle their relationship, but that wasn't going to happen. Every moment, every second they were together would summon Sarah's disapproving ghost, glowering malevolently.

She had tried to remember, over the past weeks and months, when exactly she had realised that there was something terribly wrong with the sister who was her other half, her mirror image, her sweet, funny, outrageous, generous, beloved twin Sarah. But she didn't think there had been just one revelatory moment. She had always known that Sarah wasn't right. That she lacked the 'brake' that stopped people doing awful things.

When a thought popped into your head and you knew it was bad, you didn't say it out loud, but Sarah did, unless Evie stopped her. If someone laughed at your picture of a horse that looked more like a bear, you might want to bash that person with the tin of paints, but you didn't, unless you were Sarah. If your dad told you God was always watching you, you might want to tell him God was a fucking pervert...

Wicked.

The word that had been constantly on their parents' lips, whether spoken aloud or not.

The twins were *wicked*. Evie had been lumped along with Sarah because she never spoke up to defend herself, she never pointed the finger, she never apportioned the blame where it belonged. Because Vee-Bee loved Rah-Bee more than anyone or anything in the world. And Rah-Bee loved Vee-Bee. Evie was the one person Sarah never hurt, because that would only have been hurting herself.

Evie had been her brake.

The control freak, as Sarah had called her.

Her sister's keeper.

One of her earliest memories was of the two of them at the church playgroup. A little boy had been running round and round and had accidentally bashed into Sarah. Sarah had been holding a toy spade at the time, and Evie had seen what she was about to do a split second before she did it. She'd grabbed the spade. Sarah had held on, but so had Evie. And then, slowly, Sarah had let go. Evie had taken Sarah's left hand in her right one and they'd just stood there together.

'Aren't you sweet!' one of the women had gushed at the sight of the two little twins standing so nicely, hand in hand.

It had got so much worse after Grannie had died – Grannie, who had loved them and been kind and who had known, she suspected, what Evie was trying to do and taken some of the load, some of the burden of that never-ending duty to her sister. After Grannie had died, there had been no one else to love them but themselves. No one else to take care of Sarah.

Sarah hadn't been an evil person. When she did something terrible, she always, or nearly always, felt bad afterwards. After What Happened to Mum and Dad, she'd been so filled with horror at herself that she'd descended into what the Victorians would have called madness. She had retreated from the world because, Evie sometimes felt, she couldn't trust herself in it.

When Sarah had become pregnant, Evie had known that she had to act to safeguard the child. She had to. She'd had no choice. Well, yes, she'd had a choice – she could have gone to the police and told them what Sarah had done.

That she'd murdered Mum and Dad.

That she'd tried to murder George.

Evie hadn't been there when it had happened, but apparently they had been arguing on the landing just outside the flat, and Sarah had run at him and shoved him backwards down the stairs. She had claimed she didn't mean to, that she'd been trying to push her way past him, but George had said that was nonsense.

And it had been the final straw.

'I know it's a cliché,' he had said, lying beside her in bed that night, his arm in a plaster cast, a dressing on the head wound that had required five stitches. 'But you have to decide. It's her or me, Evie. I can't do this any more.'

No contest. Sarah had needed her.

And, truth be told, Evie had simply loved her sister more. That was the thing about having a twin: you had no option but to love them more, more than all the other people in the world, because the bond you had shared from the womb was stronger than any other.

Any other but one.

Evie lowered her chin to James's head and hugged him close.

Was she kidding herself? Had Sarah been right? Had Evie wanted a child at all costs, and telling herself that Sarah couldn't cope had just been an excuse, a justification? It was true that Sarah had coped with Oliver so much better than Evie had dared hope. On the whole, she had been a good mother.

On the whole...

But she had tried so hard! She had loved him so much! Had Evie really the right to take that away from her?

Yes.

Yes I did, Rah-Bee.

But it should never have come to that. And Evie was to blame. In acting as Sarah's brake, she had prevented her from developing one herself. Why should Sarah learn to control her impulses, when she had Evie to do that for her? Evie the control freak, Evie the killjoy, Evie the one who made everything right.

James stirred, coming awake all at once, reaching out a hand towards the beach bag. 'Need juice,' he told her.

'Do you *need* it or do you just want it?'

'Need it.'

'Hmm. I think you've had enough for now.' Four ounces a day was the recommended daily amount, and he'd probably had more than that already. 'Let's have some water instead.'

He pushed himself up off her lap and plonked down onto the rug by the beach bag, reaching in for the bottle of juice, pulling it out as if surprised to find it there. For a while he contemplated it, little fingers grasping the top, attempting to open it, before he turned, the sun in his eyes, and squinted up at her, his mouth slightly open in the smile he already knew melted her heart.

She grinned back at him. 'Oh, give it here, then.'

She opened the bottle and gave it to him with a straw, and, as he drank, he looked at her over the bottle with those blue eyes, Sarah's eyes, Evie's eyes, and a fragment of a poem came into her head – Edwin Muir, she thought:

How could it be? There was the stifling grove
Yet here was light; what wonder led us to it?

'Is that nice?' she said.

FROM JANE

Thank you for reading *The Child Who Never Was* – I really hope you enjoyed it. This is a book that I hugely enjoyed writing, not least thanks to Brian Lynch at Inkubator Books, who spent many hours knocking the plot into shape so that I didn't have to do my usual floundering around in a morass of half-baked ideas. Many thanks are due to Brian and his colleague Garret Ryan for all their work on this book – and for making talking about murder such fun! I'm also very grateful to Jodi Compton for her thoughtful editing and suggestions and to Pauline Nolet for her thorough and precise proofreading.

As ever, I must thank writers Lesley McLaren and Lucy Lawrie for all their encouragement and help – I couldn't imagine doing this without you – and my family for putting up with my writing obsessions and always pretending to be interested.

In the early stages of thinking about this book, I had a wonderful day in Aberdeen with Helen Ure at the crime-writing festival Granite Noir, eating cake and discussing the disturbed minds of my characters. My idea of a perfect day, if not yours, Helen – thank you for putting yourself through it!

Finally, reviews are so important to us authors. I would be very grateful if you could spend a moment to write an honest review (no matter how short). They really do help get the word out.

Leave a Review

Best wishes,

Jane

www.janerenshaw.co.uk

ALSO BY JANE RENSHAW

WATCH OVER ME

(A Psychological Thriller)

Published by Inkubator Books
www.inkubatorbooks.com

Made in the USA
Monee, IL
12 October 2020